SMALL TOWN MURDER

"It kept going. That car, it didn't stop." Earlene crept closer, wringing her hands, juggling her purse and tote bag. "It hit that woman and kept going."

"A hit-and-run?" I asked.

"That's Iris Duncan," Sarah said, punching numbers on her cell phone.

"Who's Iris?" I asked.

"Hideaway Grover's new librarian," Sarah told me.

I stared at them both. I'd come here for the peace and quiet, the tranquility of a small town—only to find somebody had been callously *run down*?

I left Los Angeles for *this*?

Books by Dorothy Howell

Hayley Randolph Mysteries

HANDBAGS AND HOMICIDES
PURSES AND POISON
SHOULDER BAGS AND SHOOTINGS
CLUTCHES AND CURSES
TOTE BAGS AND TOE TAGS
EVENING BAGS AND EXECUTIONS
BEACH BAGS AND BURGLARIES
SWAG BAGS AND SWINDLERS
POCKETBOOKS AND PISTOLS

Sewing Studio Mysteries

SEAMS LIKE MURDER
HANGING BY A THREAD

Published by Kensington Publishing Corp.

DOROTHY HOWELL

Seams Like Murder

A SEWING STUDIO MYSTERY

Kensington Publishing Corp.
www.kensingtonbooks.com

KENSINGTON BOOKS are published by

Kensington Publishing Corp.
119 West 40th Street
New York, NY 10018

All Kensington titles, imprints, and distributed lines are available at special quantity discounts for bulk purchases for sales promotion, premiums, fund-raising, educational, or institutional use.

Special book excerpts or customized printings can also be created to fit specific needs. For details, write or phone the office of the Kensington Sales Manager: Attn.: Sales Department. Kensington Publishing Corp., 119 West 40th Street, New York, NY 10018. Phone: 1-800-221-2647.

The K and Teapot logo is a trademark of Kensington Publishing Corp.

First Hardcover Edition: October 2022

First Mass Market Printing: September 2023
ISBN: 978-1-4967-4040-3

ISBN: 978-1-4967-4041-0 (ebook)

10 9 8 7 6 5 4 3 2 1

Printed in the United States of America

With much love to Stacy, Judy, Brian, and Seth

ACKNOWLEDGMENTS

Many thanks to my editor John Scognamiglio for the faith he's shown in my books and for all the amazing opportunities he's given me.

I owe much of my writing success to my agent Evan Marshall whose patience, guidance, and knowledge have been invaluable.

A huge thank-you to the team at Kensington for their work bringing this book to fruition.

A special thanks to Stacy Howell, Judith Branstetter, Brian Branstetter, Seth Branstetter, and Martha Cooper for their ongoing, unfailing love and support.

Many thanks to June Cerza Kolf who rekindled my love of sewing.

Heartfelt thanks to Laura Levine, author of the awesome Jaine Austen series, for her kind words, encouragement, and especially her good advice. I wish I'd taken it sooner.

I'm very grateful to Michael D. Toman and Paulette Claus for generously sharing their expertise, and to William F. Wu, Ph.D. for his friendship and advice.

And, of course, my thanks to all the readers who've recommended my books to friends and family, emailed, messaged, written reviews, and stayed in touch.

CHAPTER 1

"Abbey? Abbey Chandler? Is that really you?"

The woman who'd stopped in front of me, mouth open, eyes bulging, shouting my name, had recognized me. Darn it. My escape into anonymity wasn't off to such a hot start.

"I can't believe it's you!"

And I couldn't believe I'd been recognized so quickly—my first hour back in Hideaway Grove—by, of all people, Brooke something-or-other, whom I couldn't really place but who left me with the feeling that I'd never liked her.

We were standing on Main Street on a warm spring morning amid storefronts painted inviting creamy pastels and festooned with flowering plants. Young moms watched their kids play in the village green, and older folks ambled toward early-bird lunch specials. A handful of tourists strolled along the sidewalk taking in the specialty shops, antique stores, and art galleries the town was known for.

"You're back!" Brooke exclaimed.

Brooke was a year or so older than me—I'm twenty-four—with a carefully styled blond pony-tail, full-on makeup, dressed in yoga togs. I was a little taller, with dark hair that I hadn't combed since maybe sometime late yesterday, the remains of the makeup my tears hadn't washed off, and I wore jeans and a T-shirt I'd pulled out of my dirty laundry hamper shortly before sunrise.

"So . . ." Brooke's gaze flicked from my head to my toes, and she stretched her smile wider until it froze in place. "What are you doing here?"

I was hiding out. Not because I was the star witness in a high-profile government investigation, protected by federal marshals. I wasn't on the run from a drug cartel. I hadn't embezzled millions from my employer, or murdered someone. I was hiding out from . . . well, everything.

So I certainly couldn't talk about it—especially to Brooke, whose last name I'd probably remember eventually, along with the reason I'd never liked her.

"I'm visiting my aunt," I said.

"Oh, yes, of course! Your aunt Sarah. Sarah's Sweets."

Brooke nodded down the street to the bakery my aunt owned. Sarah's Sweets turned out delicious cookies, cakes, cupcakes, and other goodies, all beautifully decorated. Her business had been a mainstay in Hideaway Grove for decades.

"You used to live with her during the summers," Brooke said, "when your parents were off seeing the world and didn't want you with them."

Now I remembered why I didn't like Brooke.

My parents were tenured university professors

whose idea of a fun summer was digging through ruins in a remote jungle, or investigating obscure museum archives in settlements accessible only by camel train. They didn't want me with them—any more than I wanted to be there.

"Well, good seeing you," I announced. It wasn't, of course, but this was an easy out for me. I walked away.

"We'll have to get together!" Brooke called.

I pretended I didn't hear her.

I paused outside Sarah's Sweets. The building was painted buttery yellow. Beside the entrance were low flower beds bursting with color. The bell over the door chimed as I walked inside and the delicious scents hit me, bringing on a wave of emotion I hadn't expected. Memories swamped me, causing tears to pop into my eyes. I blinked them away and saw my aunt Sarah standing behind the glass display case, sliding a tray of fresh baked brownies into place alongside rows of sugar cookies.

I hadn't seen her in years, but she matched up perfectly with my memories of the summers I'd spent in Hideaway Grove. Tall, like most of our family, her hair still dark—she always said she'd never go gray—trim and fit, looking far from the "senior" label she'd likely acquire next fall when she turned sixty. She wore jeans, an on-trend shirt, and shoes I'd love to own, all topped with a crisp white apron.

"Welcome! I'll be right with—" She looked up and saw me. "Abbey!"

Sarah dashed around the display case, her arms spread wide, and captured me in a firm hug. "You made it. I'm so glad you're here."

She pulled me tight against her. Wonderful memories bloomed in my head once more.

Sarah, even though she'd never had children of her own, hugged me like my mother never did, nurtured me like my mother never did, loved me like my mother never did. Sarah was my anchor. I hadn't realized how adrift I'd been without her until a few days ago.

She stepped back and rested her hands on my shoulders, her welcoming smile still glowing.

"You look beautiful," she said.

"I look awful," I said, and blinked away tears again.

"You look beautiful to me," she declared.

I couldn't help smiling.

"You've got to have one of these brownies. They're fresh from the oven. I'll get you some milk," Sarah said, and rounded the display case again. "Come on back. Sit down and we'll catch up."

I followed her, taking in the shop. It was painted mint green, with accents of pale pink and yellow. Four tiny white tables with yellow padded chairs sat by the front windows. Shelves held specialty cakes for weddings, birthdays, anniversaries, all beautifully handcrafted. Another shelf had a rainbow of sprinkles in glass jars. There were charming gifts for sale—cookbooks, mugs, birthday candles, plates and napkins, cake stands, cookie cutters, and measuring spoons. A large, refrigerated case held orders for pickup; another featured cakes ready to be personalized for walk-in customers.

I gestured to the double pocket doors across the room, closed tight. On the other side of the doors was a large space that Sarah had used for storage. I used to play in there during my summer visits; the sunlight beaming through the windows had made the big, cluttered room seem warm and cozy.

"I thought you were opening this up for a dining area," I said, remembering an email she'd sent me several months ago, and feeling bad that I hadn't asked her about it since.

"It's on hold," Sarah said, placing a brownie on a plate.

"For how long?"

"Indefinitely. Gretchen—you remember her, she worked in the needlepoint shop before it closed—she wanted to use part of the space for a gift shop and souvenir sales. You know how tourists love shopping, especially for Hideaway Grove's owls."

Aside from the specialty shops, art galleries, and antique stores, we were known for owls. The town's founder had been a bird watcher and was particularly fond of owls, so likenesses of them had been incorporated into light posts, park benches, even a jungle gym in the village green.

"Gretchen planned to sell gift items, and I intended to serve goodies to our customers," Sarah went on. "I knew I could increase business and expand my menu a bit if folks had a comfortable place to sit, visit a little, and eat. And, of course, tourists would flock to the gifts and souvenirs."

"Sounds like you two would make a great team," I said, joining her behind the counter and sliding onto the tall wooden stool I'd sat on as a child.

"We had it all planned out. We even got started, cleaning up the space, doing some repairs." Sarah poured a glass of milk. "Gretchen was going to make new curtains for the windows—no small task, with windows that big, but she's a whiz with that expensive sewing machine of hers."

Sarah passed me the brownie and I bit into it. Still warm from the oven, the delicious flavor bloomed in my mouth. I nearly moaned aloud.

"Then her daughter over in Fresno was diagnosed with cancer, and her so young and with those three children," Sarah said, and placed the frosty glass of milk on the counter beside me. "Gretchen had to move there to help out."

My eyes started to water from the chocolate melting in my mouth, but I managed to ask, "How's her daughter?"

"Receiving treatment, but it's a difficult thing. We're all praying and hoping for the best."

"You didn't want to continue the renovations without her?" I asked.

"Bad timing," Sarah said. "The air-conditioning unit went out and had to be replaced, then the roof needed major repairs."

I understood Sarah's caution. She hadn't kept her business thriving all these years by being reckless with her finances.

I finished the brownie, licked my fingers, and downed the milk, suddenly feeling like I was a child again—which was kind of nice.

Sarah looked at me with a familiar expression on her face, the one that assured me she was listening, wouldn't be mad no matter what I said, and would help me figure out any situation, if I wanted her to.

"You want to tell me what's going on?" she asked softly.

I hardly knew where to start but I finally said, "Everything is a mess. A complete mess. Everything."

"Everything?"

I slid off the stool and circled the big butcher-block work island in the center of the kitchen; surrounding it were ovens, appliances, cupboards, and a walk-in fridge.

"I know what you're thinking," I said, and rinsed my glass and plate at the sink. "Everything couldn't possibly be wrong. Not everything. But it is. There was so much happening, so much chaos, so much—everything."

"You've lived in Los Angeles for a while now, six months, isn't it? Your emails sounded like you were doing well," Sarah said. "What changed?"

I put my cup and plate in the dishwasher and shook my head. "It was—everything, somehow. All I could think was that I had to get away, come here, where things are quiet, and slower, and easier."

I'd made the decision to leave, to come to Sarah's, while I'd been walking the floor last night, unable to sleep, trying to determine what, exactly, my life had turned into and where, exactly, it had all gone so wrong. I'd finally realized I was never going to figure it out, not there, not in the middle of everything, so I'd packed a bag and headed north. Thankfully, Sarah had answered my phone call and told me to keep driving, she'd love to have me visit.

"You did the right thing coming here," Sarah said. "Sounds as if what you need is some peace and quiet."

I sighed. "That sounds delightful."

"But what about your job?" Sarah asked. "Were they okay giving you some time off?"

I glanced away. "It wasn't a problem."

"You probably want to go to the house and get some rest," she said.

Sarah's house was just around the corner on Hummingbird Lane. I'd left my car there and walked over.

"I could use a shower," I said.

"Go on. The extra key is under the—"

"—yellow flowerpot beside the back door," I said.

"Make yourself at home. We'll figure out how to handle things when I get there. Sound good?"

It sounded better than good. It sounded perfect.

"Maybe get a nap," Sarah said, as she headed for the trash bins beside the back door.

"Taking out the trash used to be my job," I remembered.

We each grabbed a plastic bag out of the bins—even the trash smelled delicious—and headed for the rear exit, which led to the alley out back. Just as I pushed the door open, I heard a loud noise and a woman scream.

Sarah and I shared a troubled glance, and I flung the door open.

The alley was narrow, barely wide enough to accommodate the Dumpsters and the delivery trucks that served the businesses facing Main Street. Something flashed atop the high retaining wall that separated the alley from the neighborhood behind it, then disappeared.

"My goodness, what is going on?" Sarah exclaimed, pointing.

A woman stood farther down the alley, off to our right, screaming. In one hand she held her purse, in the other was a tote bag, and she was flinging them in the air and jumping around. I figured her for about Sarah's age, short dark hair, dressed in a coral pantsuit.

"That's Earlene," Sarah said. "What's gotten into her now?"

We dropped the trash bags and headed toward her, then realized she was pointing at something lying near the building.

"It hit her!" Earlene screamed. "That car! It hit her!"

Fear swept through me as I went closer and realized that a woman was lying on the ground. She wore a cardigan twin set, elastic-waist pants, and flats. Her handbag was a few yards away, open, its contents strewn across the alley. Nearby was her cell phone. Her body lay still, her head smashed against the side of the building, the rest of her twisted at unnatural angles. Blood flowed everywhere.

"It didn't stop! It kept going!" Earlene yelled, pointing to where the alley turned between the buildings and intersected with Main Street.

Sarah placed a hand on my arm, then leaned forward and gasped.

"Oh my goodness, that's Iris, Iris Duncan," she whispered. "I'll call nine-one-one, get some help here."

I didn't stop her, of course, but from the look of the poor woman, I knew there was nothing paramedics could do to help.

"It kept going. That car, it didn't stop." Earlene

crept closer, wringing her hands, juggling her purse and tote bag. "It hit that woman and kept going."

"A hit-and-run?" I asked.

"That's Iris Duncan," Sarah said, punching numbers on her cell phone.

Earlene gasped. "Iris? It can't be Iris!"

"Who's Iris?" I asked.

"Hideaway Grove's new librarian," Sarah told me.

I stared at them both. I'd come here for the peace and quiet, the tranquility of a small town— only to find somebody had been callously *run down?* And that somebody was the librarian? The *librarian?*

I left Los Angeles for *this?*

CHAPTER 2

Most of the Hideaway Grove Sheriff's Department rolled out to the accident scene—which meant about six men. No helicopters circled overhead, no crowds of onlookers intruded, no reporters angled for photos.

I definitely wasn't in L.A. anymore.

Sarah, Earlene, and I had stayed in the alley, though with our backs turned to Iris, until the paramedics showed up, followed by the sheriff and deputies. Sarah and I went into the bakery. Earlene had to stay and answer questions.

Right away Sarah had fired up her big coffee maker, then ventured out back just long enough to let everyone know it was available. She'd come back inside and reported that yellow crime-scene tape had been strung, the alley had been blocked off at each end, and merchants in the businesses facing Main Street had been instructed not to open their back doors.

"The paramedics couldn't do anything for Iris," Sarah said.

She picked up a sponge and began wiping down the work island. I grabbed another sponge and started cleaning the already spotless island with her.

"Was Iris a friend of yours?" I asked.

"Everybody knows everybody in Hideaway Grove," Sarah said. "Iris was a newcomer, moved here a few months ago. But she had fit right in. Everybody liked her. She was doing great things at the library. She let some of our groups use the meeting room without charging, and Mrs. Nance, the previous librarian in charge, was a real stickler about that sort of thing. Iris started a children's reading group and scheduled an arts and crafts program, and so many other new ideas to get readers into the library."

"She had kids?" I asked, and felt queasy thinking there might be some motherless children in town right now.

"Oh, no. Iris was single, in her mid-forties, so not likely to ever have children," Sarah said. "She never dated, and believe me, if she'd stepped out with a gentleman caller, everybody in Hideaway Grove would have talked about it."

No texting, emailing, Facebooking, or phoning needed, not in a small town.

"Somebody hit her and didn't stop—didn't even slow down, just kept going," I said, the ugly thought creating a yucky feeling in my belly. "Who would do that?"

"It was an accident," Sarah said. "It had to be. The driver didn't see her, or maybe didn't even realize he'd hit a person. Texting, probably."

I thought for a moment, mentally going back to the seconds when I'd opened the door to go into the alley. I'd heard noise, a sound that didn't make sense, along with Earlene's screams. I played them over in my mind a few times. Something—several things, maybe, like an odd flash of color—didn't seem right, but I couldn't figure out what they were.

"Do you think Earlene recognized the car or the driver?" I asked.

"She would have told us, if she had."

Earlene had been terribly upset, understandably so. With her attention likely focused on Iris, I wondered if she'd even noticed the driver or the details of the car that hit her.

"Security cameras in the alley?" I asked.

"No need for them. Well, until now." Sarah shook her head. "I hope whoever did this will come to his senses and turn himself in."

The bell over the front door chimed and three women hurried inside. All of them looked to be about Sarah's age and were dressed in comfortable, sensible clothes. All of them looked worried.

"Is it true?" one of the women called. "Somebody was killed in the alley?"

Sarah leaned closer to me and lowered her voice. "Shop owners along Main Street."

"Oh, goodness, it can't be true," another woman said. "Not now. Word of this kind of incident could ruin everything."

"I wish Ed were here to speak with them," Sarah whispered, then explained when she saw my raised eyebrows. "Ed Grumman, the sheriff. Out back, with . . . Iris."

"Should I go get him?" I offered, though I wasn't all that anxious to go into the alley again.

"No, I don't want to disturb him." Sarah frowned for a few seconds. "I'll handle things here. You go on home, Abbey. Get some rest. I'll be along as soon as I can."

I opened my mouth to protest but Sarah shook her head and told me again to go. I didn't want to leave her, but I was nearly exhausted from the long drive and so little sleep last night and, really, there was nothing I could do.

The other shop owners didn't even notice as I slipped past them and out the front door.

Aunt Sarah's house—more a cottage, really—was just down the block and around the corner on Hummingbird Lane. The small one-story was painted blue, trimmed in white, and boasted a front yard alive with shrubs and flowers, all of it surrounded by a picket fence. A narrow driveway ran alongside the house to a detached garage. The other houses in the neighborhood looked much the same, almost like a storybook land come to life.

I grabbed my suitcase and laptop out of the trunk of my car which I'd parked at the curb, opened the gate, and followed the flagstone path to the back of the house. The yard still had the birdbath, flowers, and benches I remembered from my summers here as a child. I found the extra key under the yellow flowerpot beside the door and let myself in.

Memories flooded back as I walked through the mudroom into the small kitchen that sparkled with white cabinets and countertops. I circled through the dining and living rooms—updated but still

boasting floral prints—and turned down the hallway to the bedrooms.

The smaller room—the one I still thought of as
mine, even now when I hadn't been here in years—
was neat and tidy, just as I remembered. The walls
were painted pink and the furniture was white; a
shelving unit still held some of my books and toys.
Plantation shutters opened to a view of a wall of
morning glories that separated Sarah's side yard
from the neighbor.

The house was silent, peaceful. A wave of calm
wafted through me. Los Angeles and *everything*
seemed a long way off.

I dropped my laptop and suitcase on the bed,
dug out toiletries and clean clothes, and headed
for the bathroom. With the shower running at the
perfect temperature, I undressed and stepped in.
A much-welcomed wave of ease washed over me
along with the water as I scrubbed myself, sham-
pooed my hair—and that's where the peace and
quiet ended. My cell phone, which I'd left on the
sink, buzzed and the doorbell rang.

I was tempted to ignore both, then saw Sarah's
name displayed on my caller ID screen. The doorbell stopped ringing, only to be replaced by what
sounded like a fist pounding on the front door.

With no clue what was going on, I rinsed my
hair and jumped out of the shower. I hit the green
button on my phone but Sarah had already hung
up. I tried calling her as I toweled myself dry and
pulled on the underwear, capris, and T-shirt I'd
brought into the bathroom with me. Her voicemail picked up as I hurried down the hallway finger-
combing my wet hair.

The pounding on the front door was louder and more urgent now, and it flew into my head that maybe something had happened to Sarah, or the bakery, or Earlene, or maybe one of those women who'd come into the shop. My anxiety spun up.

I yanked the door open. A man stood on the porch, tall, broad-shouldered, with a touch of gray showing beneath the brim of a large hat. The hat matched the gray uniform he had on. The uniform sported a Hideaway Grove insignia; a star was pinned to his chest along with a name tag that read GRUMMAN.

The sheriff. The man I'd halfnoticed in the alley behind Sarah's Sweets who was heading up Iris Duncan's hit-and-run accident.

Why was he here? And why was he frowning?

I stared up at him. I couldn't make sense of it, not with my imagination running wild, conjuring up every crazy possibility of what horror could have befallen Sarah in the short time I'd been away.

"Abbey Chandler?" he demanded.

I managed to nod. "Did something happen to Sarah? Is she okay?"

"Your aunt's all right," he told me, none too pleasantly.

While I was relieved to hear the news, I still couldn't quite understand what was happening.

"Then why are you here?" I asked.

Sheriff Grumman eased closer. "I came to find out why you ran away from my crime scene."

Now I understood even less.

"Crime scene? Do you mean Iris? It was an accident—"

"Can I see some ID?" he asked.

"I didn't run away—"

"ID?" he asked.

This, at least, was something I could make sense of.

I went to my bedroom, grabbed my wallet out of my handbag, and returned to the front door. Sheriff Grumman still stood on the porch, still looked intense. I pulled out my driver's license. He took it and studied it for so long that I started to wonder if there was some sort of secret code embedded in it that I wasn't aware of—and should be concerned about.

"You live in Los Angeles?" he asked.

"Like it says," I told him, and gestured to my license.

"When did you arrive in town?"

The drive here had been long, I'd been tired, and I'd had *everything* on my mind, so I hadn't been watching the clock.

"About an hour ago, I guess," I said.

"You must have left before dawn," the sheriff said. "Rush trip?"

"I was anxious to get here," I said, thinking a simple response would be best.

He nodded thoughtfully. "Rush trip on a weekday. What about your job? Did you have vacation scheduled?"

Again, I went with something less complicated than getting into the real reason I'd come to Hideaway Grove, and said, "No, but it wasn't a problem getting time off."

"What kind of vehicle are you driving?"

"That's it," I said, gesturing past him, baffled by this new direction his questions had taken.

Sheriff Grumman didn't bother to look. "The one parked at the curb? The white one?"

A little spark of concern flared in my belly.

"Yes," I said.

He nodded, as if he'd had a weighty problem on his mind and just figured out how to handle it.

"Miss Chandler, I'm going to ask you to—"

"Ed? Ed!"

He turned and I looked past him to see Sarah hurrying up the walkway, clutching her cell phone, slightly out of breath and looking somewhere between outraged and alarmed.

"Ed, what in the world are you doing?" she demanded, then waved her cell phone at me. "I called you."

To warn me, I realized, warn me that the sheriff was coming here.

"Now, Sarah, I'm in the middle of an investigation," he said, sounding more reasonable than when he'd spoken to me. "I have to—"

"You can't actually think Abbey was involved with Iris's accident," Sarah declared. "She was inside the bakery with me when it happened. I told you that already. Earlene told you that, too. Abbey didn't see what happened in the alley. And besides, it was an accident."

Sheriff Grumman listened patiently, let a few seconds go by, then said, "I don't know that it was an accident."

"According to who?" Sarah asked. "Earlene? Oh, Ed, you know how she is. She's worked at the café for years and still can't remember the menu or keep an order straight."

"Earlene insists that vehicle hit Iris on purpose," he said.

Sarah gasped softly; I felt that spark of alarm in my belly flare a little larger.

"Do you mean Iris was—" Sarah's eyes widened and her fingers covered her mouth.

"Murdered," I realized.

Sheriff Grumman turned to me. "I know you weren't driving that car, Miss Chandler, but the facts are that you suddenly left your home, left your job, in the middle of the night, and drove hell-bent to get here, and arrived minutes before Iris got run down."

"I didn't even know Iris," I said.

"Maybe you didn't come here alone. Maybe somebody came with you, somebody intent on murdering Iris, making you an accomplice," the sheriff said. "Nobody knew much about Iris's past. There's a good possibility she had an enemy. Maybe it was somebody who knew you, got you to bring him here so he could kill her."

Sarah shook her head. "That's too far of a stretch, Ed."

"I don't think so," he told her, and nodded toward the street. "Miss Chandler's car is white, just like the one that hit Iris, according to Earlene."

"This town is full of white cars," Sarah said.

"But how many of them have a dent in the right front fender in the exact spot where Iris was struck?" Sheriff Grumman turned to me again. "I'm taking your car to the crime lab."

"What?" I exclaimed. "But I need my car."

"Why?" he asked. "So you can leave town, suddenly, in the middle of the night? Again?"

I'd come here for some peace and quiet. Instead, I'd witnessed a gruesome death. But not just a death, a murder. And now I was a *suspect*?

CHAPTER 3

I'd watched—along with most of the neighbors—as the sheriff towed my car away yesterday, so this morning I was on foot, heading down Hummingbird Lane to Sarah's Sweets on Main. I'd slept in and rose to find fresh-baked blueberry muffins and a note from Sarah on the kitchen counter; both were welcome sights. Still, I couldn't shake the troubled feelings that I'd brought with me to Hideaway Grove, compounded now by Sheriff Grumman's suspicion that I was involved with Iris's death.

Not even Sarah's blueberry muffins could make those things better.

Nothing improved as I reached the mouth of the alley that ran behind the Main Street businesses where it intersected with Hummingbird Lane. I didn't want to look and once more recall the hit-and-run that had taken place there yesterday, but I couldn't help myself. I paused and took a quick glance. No cars, no gawkers, no flowers or candles, not even yellow crime-scene tape to mark the death of Iris Duncan.

I lingered for a moment and thought about Iris's decision to cut through the alley yesterday. Of course, she had no way of knowing what awaited her. None of us could predict the future. A little chill slithered down my spine thinking about how one seemingly innocuous choice could end your life—or send it in a totally different direction.

The reasons I'd left L.A. yesterday crowded out thoughts of Iris. I didn't want to think about those, either. I picked up my pace.

When I reached the corner and turned onto Main Street, a flash of movement off to my left caught my eye, and I saw a man on the sidewalk, barreling straight at me. I whirled away and he jumped aside to avoid colliding with me.

"Whoa! Sorry!" he said, stopping. "You okay?"

It took me a few seconds to collect myself and realize he'd been jogging. He had on sweatpants, a T-shirt, and running shoes. Rivers of perspiration ran from his dark hair and soaked his shirt.

"Yeah. Yeah, I'm okay," I managed to say.

He stepped closer, his breath still heavy. "Sure?"

"Yes," I insisted, even though I wasn't. Because in those few seconds I'd realized he was young—probably only a few years older than me—tall, incredibly fit, and really good-looking in a rugged sort of way. Mentally, I zoomed back in time to my fifteen-year-old awkward self.

"We don't get too many pedestrians in this area in the mornings." He smiled. It was the kind of smile that curled up one side of his mouth and caused a dimple to appear in his cheek.

"I was headed for Sarah's Sweets," I said, and managed to nod in the right direction.

"Good choice," he said. "Are you in town for the festival? We get vendors in ahead of time to check things out."

"No," I said. "Just visiting."

He nodded. "Where are you from?"

"Los Angeles."

"Plan to stay long?" he asked.

He had that look on his face, the one that suggested maybe he intended to invite me out, perhaps offer me a personal tour of Hideaway Grove, or at least ask me to have coffee with him. But before he could, somebody called my name.

A woman standing two doors down in front of Anna's Treasure Thrift Shop paused as she hung blouses on a sidewalk display rack, and waved at me.

"Abbey! I'd heard you were in town!"

A few seconds passed while I tried to match her up with a memory from my summers here. I figured her for mid-forties, pleasant looking, sensibly dressed.

"Anna." The owner herself, I recalled, as I walked closer. "You're still here."

"You bet I am. Still in business, still loving it," she declared. "Sarah must be thrilled to have her favorite niece here again."

Heat still radiated from the guy who'd been jogging as I realized he'd walked over with me.

"You're Sarah's niece?" His smile vanished, taking my goofy teenaged mental state with it.

"I have something for you. Wait right here," Anna declared, and dashed into the thrift shop.

"You're Abbey Chandler?" he asked, his voice heavy with concern.

Did everybody know who I was? Were they all aware that the sheriff considered me a possible suspect in Iris's death? Had the entire town found out my car had been towed to the crime lab?

"For Gretchen, when she gets back." Anna came out of the shop carrying a large brown shopping bag. She plopped it into my arms. "Now, Zack, what is going on with Iris? I can't believe what people are saying. Have you been into the station yet and gotten an update from Ed this morning?"

I froze, an ugly knot of suspicion blooming inside me.

"Are you a deputy?" I managed to keep my voice even but couldn't control the accusatory expression on my face.

"Oh, I thought you two knew each other," Anna said. "Yes, this is Zack McKenna, one of Hideaway Grove's finest."

"So what was that?" I asked, glaring at him, as I jerked my chin toward the corner. "Some sort of off-the-record interrogation session?"

He didn't say anything and I felt Anna's startled gaze pass back and forth between the two of us. I wasn't going to provide her, or passersby, with another opportunity to gossip about me so I forced a smile and said, "Good seeing you, Anna. I'll make sure I leave this bag for Gretchen."

I headed down the street, my blood boiling, and made it to the entrance of Sarah's Sweets when Zack caught up with me.

"Look, Abbey, I—"

"Stay away from me," I barked.

"I didn't know who you were," he said.

"Oh, really? In this small town? You had no idea?" I asked. "So it was just an incredible coincidence that we met on the corner. You just happened to be jogging through that exact spot, at the exact time. You oh-so casually almost ran into me so I'd have to stop. Then you proceeded to ask me where I'm from, what I'm doing here, digging for more information. Why? So you can catch me in a lie? Tell the sheriff about it?"

Zack drew a calm breath. "Okay, I can see why you might—"

"Stay away from me," I told him again, and pushed my way into Sarah's Sweets.

"Good morning," Sarah called as I stepped inside. She stood at the work island in the kitchen and gave me a huge smile.

I glanced behind me almost wishing Zack McKenna had followed me into the bakery so I could yell at him. He hadn't. Nor was he peering in through the display windows. I should have been glad but instead I was—something. I didn't know what.

"Busy morning?" I asked.

"Like you wouldn't believe," Sarah said, gesturing around the kitchen. "I got a rush order for sugar cookies, which I'm always glad for, of course. But Jodi wasn't scheduled to come in today—you haven't met Jodi, she helps out several days a week—and I couldn't reach her to ask her to come in."

"I'll pitch in," I said.

"I got it handled, despite the fact that everyone in town, it seems, has been coming in, talking about what happened in the alley with poor Iris."

I wanted to ask Sarah if everyone had also been talking about me and my car's suspected involvement in the hit-and-run, but didn't. Sarah and I had talked about it yesterday and she'd assured me nobody would take Sheriff Grumman's concerns seriously. As much as I'd like to believe her, I doubted she was right.

"Did any other witnesses come forward?" I asked.

"There's just Earlene and, well, most everyone expressed doubts about her assertion that it was deliberate, not an accident. She's always been . . . well, to put it as pleasantly as I can, she's always been a bit dingy."

"Nobody thinks she's a reliable witness?" I asked.

"I'm afraid not," Sarah said. "Plus, none of the merchants want to believe something so horrible could actually happen in Hideaway Grove, especially now. The festival is coming up and bad publicity could ruin the entire event."

The town's annual arts and crafts festival drew hundreds of tourists from miles away to check out the art galleries, enjoy concerts in the village green, shop our stores and specialty vendors, and eat in our restaurants—all of which brought tons of money to local merchants.

"The festival is the town's second biggest income producer, after the Christmas season," Sarah said. "I hope Ed will get this investigation wrapped up quickly."

I hoped so, too. I'd like to have my car back—and no longer be considered a possible accomplice to a murder.

"And as if that weren't enough, we had some mischief in the alley last night," Sarah said. "Sassy Fashions next door. Geraldine—she's the owner—came in first thing this morning and told me what happened. She was livid. Her dresses come wrapped in plastic, inside big cardboard boxes, and she always stacks them outside her back door until she can take them to the recycler. Well, when she came in this morning, boxes and plastic were strewn all over the alley."

"Had somebody tried to break into her store?" I asked.

"No, the door was still locked, just like she left it last night," Sarah said.

"Is the sheriff investigating?"

"Kids," Sarah said, waving away my words. "Just some kids acting up. It happens from time to time. Besides, Ed's got enough on his plate with Earlene's wild notions about Iris's death. He needs to concentrate on putting an end to that whole thing. And the quicker, the better."

"I couldn't agree more." I held up the bag I'd brought in with me. "This is for Gretchen, from Anna."

Sarah frowned for a few seconds, then nodded. "Oh, yes. Pillowcases. Anna always holds them back for Gretchen."

I glanced down at the bulging bag. "Pillowcases?"

"One of Gretchen's causes," Sarah explained. "Gently used pillowcases that she makes into dresses and donates to the church. Several times a year the pastor and his wife and a team of volunteers travel to villages in Africa and distribute the dresses to the girls there."

I glanced at the bag again. "Dresses? Made from pillowcases?"

"Let me show you."

Sarah wiped her hands on a towel as she came from the kitchen, and slid open the pocket doors across the room. I followed her inside—back in time to my childhood. Memories flooded my mind.

Muted sunlight filtered in through the windows that faced Main Street, now covered with cheap plastic shades. A desk and several folding banquet tables sat at odd angles around the room, most of them stacked with cardboard storage boxes. A dozen or so white folding chairs filled one corner. Bolts of fabric sat on a worktable alongside trays of sewing notions, and beside them was a sewing machine.

"I remember playing in here," I said, and couldn't help smiling. "I was, what, six when I started spending summers with you?"

"You were seven," Sarah said. "You made friends right away. There were so many little girls in town who were your age."

Images floated through my mind, faces, a few names.

"We had so much fun in here," I said.

The mash-up of furniture had lent itself to great hiding places, secret clubhouses, and treasure hunts. One summer we'd come across a box of old sheets and blankets, and had draped them strategically over the furniture around the room to form a tent. We'd played with toys and dolls on days when it was too hot or too rainy to go outside, all under the watchful eye of Sarah, and with the delicious scent of baking goods in the air. As we grew older, we'd used the room to listen to music, practice dance moves, read fashion magazines, and plan our futures. I'd been fourteen the last summer I'd spent here before my parents had taken positions in England, and I'd been doomed to touring European museums.

Older now, I saw the space in a different way.

"It would take quite a bit of work, and money, to

turn this into a usable space," I said, and gestured around the room, trying to imagine the bakery seating area and gift shop Gretchen and Sarah had wanted.

The two big windows that faced Main Street would need curtains, the cracked and peeling linoleum floor would have to go, and fresh paint and extensive cleanup would be required.

"You'll start on it when Gretchen gets back?" I asked, recalling how Sarah had explained Gretchen had to leave and care for her grandchildren while her daughter underwent cancer treatment.

"That might not happen," Sarah said. "Every time I hear from Gretchen she tells me how thrilled she is to be there—worried about her daughter, of course—but so happy to be part of her grandkids' lives every day."

"So what's up with these?" I asked, and dropped the bag stuffed with pillowcases onto the closest table.

Sarah pulled a long, narrow cardboard box from under one of the tables; beside it was another box stuffed with what looked like fabric remnants. Sarah held up a small garment. It was a bright pink, sleeveless dress with over-the-shoulder tie straps. I could see the pillowcase at the core of the simple design.

"It really is cute," I said, surprised.

Sarah dug through the dresses that remained in the box, and frowned.

"There're only five dresses here. I thought Gretchen had finished more of them," Sarah said. "The volunteers at the church are leaving to distribute them soon."

The bell over the front door chimed. Sarah

folded the dress into the box and dashed out of the room. I followed, making sure to close the pocket doors, and spotted a young woman with two little girls gazing at the cookies inside the display case.

"I think we're going to need a few minutes to decide," the mom said.

"No rush," Sarah said, and headed into the kitchen.

I joined her there, in the epicenter of the warmth and aromas.

"What can I do to help?" I asked, and reached for an apron hanging on the cluttered pegs beside the back door.

"Well, let's see." Sarah's gaze swept the kitchen as she headed for the sink. "Oh, I know. I heard Earlene is taking this whole thing with Iris very hard. In fact, she didn't even go to work at the café this morning. I think it would be nice to take her some cookies. Would you deliver them to her?"

"Sure," I said.

"These are her favorites." Sarah washed and dried her hands, then placed a dozen sugar cookies into a bakery box and handed it to me. "Earlene lives on Blue Bird Lane, just off Main. The pink house, two down from the corner. You can't miss it."

No freeway to take, no exit ramp to watch for, no traffic to contend with. I definitely wasn't in Los Angeles anymore.

"Give her my best," Sarah said.

Delicious smells wafted from the box and bright sunlight beamed in through the windows as I headed for the door. A wave of contentment passed through me.

It shattered when I stepped outside.

Deputy Zack McKenna, now in uniform, stood on the sidewalk, waiting, watching the door—watching for me, I realized.

His gaze sharpened when he saw me, and he stepped closer. "We have to talk."

CHAPTER 4

"No, we don't," I told him, and headed down the sidewalk.

I couldn't believe how annoyed the sight of Zack McKenna made me, even though he did look kind of hot in his uniform, with his baseball-cap style hat set just high enough on his head to make me realize he had gorgeous brown eyes.

He fell in step beside me.

"Look," I said. "I told you—"

"I came to apologize."

I hadn't expected to hear that and I should have been glad about it, but for some reason I was still riled up. I kept going.

He stepped in front of me and walked backward.

"I didn't know who you were when we nearly collided at the corner. I was just being friendly." He touched his badge. "I swear."

I rolled my eyes. "Really? You're swearing on

your badge? Like that's supposed to mean something to me?"

"We didn't see each other in the alley yesterday. You were gone by the time I got there. Remember?"

Yes, I would have remembered seeing him, which annoyed me further.

Behind Zack, coming out of a shop, was an elderly couple. I grabbed his arm to keep him from backing into them. A jolt shot through my hand and up to my shoulder.

"Would you stop doing that?" I demanded, and glanced around. "People are staring."

He stopped and eased closer. "Would you rather sneak off somewhere more private?"

Another wave of heat hit me. It hit me so hard I couldn't answer. A long, uncomfortable moment passed until I finally came up with something to say.

"The only thing I'm interested in hearing from you is that my car is being returned," I said. "Today."

Zack drew in a troubled breath and shook his head. "You're not going to get your car back today. More like weeks from today."

"You're kidding." My shoulders slumped. "There must be some way to hurry up the process."

Zack shrugged. "That dent in your front fender isn't helping."

I cringed at the memory of how it had happened.

"That dent is little more than a scrape, and has nothing to do with Iris," I insisted. "It was nothing. An accident. A one-car, I-didn't-hit-anybody accident—no, not even an accident. An incident."

"So what happened?" Zack asked.

"It's really none of your business."

"Actually, it is," he pointed out.

Yes, it was, which irritated me further.

"Must have hurt when you heard that scrape," Zack said, and winced. "A BMW. Nice car."

Yes, it was a really nice car—and an expensive one, too. Part of the lifestyle I'd tried so hard to fit into in Los Angeles.

"Okay, fine." I drew in a big breath and huffed slightly, just in case any doubt lingered that I wasn't happy about sharing the details. "I was in a parking garage and I cut the corner too sharp, and scraped a support column."

He gazed at me as if he somehow knew there was more to the story and was waiting for me to explain further. I pressed my lips together.

"That's it?" he finally asked.

"Yes."

No. I'd left the office midafternoon that day.

"You just bumped into a support column?" he asked.

"Yes."

No. I'd been crying when it happened and wasn't paying attention.

"You were the only one involved?" he asked.

"Yes."

No. My supervisor was involved—albeit a few minutes earlier—when she'd screamed at me in front of the whole department.

With effort, I shook off the memory of that awful day.

"So now that I've confessed," I said, "could you persuade the sheriff to release my car? Today, maybe?"

He shifted his wide shoulders and shook his

head. "There's lots of scrutiny on law enforcement these days, especially in a small town. Sheriff doesn't want a mistake to come back on him, especially since Earlene is claiming it wasn't an accident."

"You don't believe her?"

"I don't think she'd lie," he said. "I think she's confused."

The memory of Sarah and me rushing into the alley—along with the sounds I'd heard—zipped through my mind again.

"Where are you taking that?" Zack gestured to the bakery box in my hand.

"I'm not obligated to tell you."

"Smells like cookies." He sniffed. "Sugar cookies."

"Is that one of the investigative skills you learned in the Sheriff's Academy?" I asked.

"Self-taught," he said. "Can I have one?"

"No." I shifted away.

He grinned. "Okay, for the record, you accept that it was a simple coincidence that we met on the corner this morning."

"Okay," I said. "However, for the record, that misunderstanding wouldn't have happened if you'd been in uniform. There should be a town ordinance that you're required to wear your uniform at all times."

He leaned in, and a grin I hadn't seen before pulled at his lips. "Any time you want to see me without it on, let me know."

My cheeks flamed. He touched the brim of his hat and sauntered away.

"Terrible. I'm terrible. Things are terrible. Everything is terrible," Earlene declared.

She'd started talking the instant she let me into her house and headed down the hallway, leaving me to follow.

"I can't believe what people are saying. Have you heard what people are saying?" She went on before I could respond. "They're saying I'm making it up. They say I'm wrong."

Earlene looked worse than when I'd seen her in the alley yesterday. Bags and dark circles were under her eyes, and frown lines creased her face. I was pretty sure she had on the same pantsuit.

"How would they know? They weren't there." She wasn't angry or resentful, more befuddled and confused.

I trailed behind her as we reached the kitchen. Several cupboard doors stood open and a brown grocery bag sat on the counter by the sink.

I held out the bakery box. "Aunt Sarah sent these for you."

Earlene stared as if she wasn't sure what I'd offered.

"Sugar cookies," I said. "Your favorite."

Earlene's gaze pinged around the room, then she waved both hands in the air and turned to the counter. She grabbed a box of granola bars from the cupboard and dropped it into the grocery bag.

"They say I'm wrong." She pulled a package of doughnuts from another cupboard, opened the refrigerator, and put them inside. "They think I didn't see what I know I saw."

"You're confident about what happened?" I asked.

"Like I would make it up?" She yanked a loaf of

bread and two cans of peas from the cupboard, and tossed them in the bag. "Like I don't have sense enough to know what I saw?"

Earlene darted from the counter to the refrigerator, then cut back to the stove, then went to the fridge again. She opened it, grabbed a six-pack of water, and tossed it into the bag on top of the bread and peas.

"And they're blaming me if the festival fails. All the negative publicity they claim I'm causing. They're saying it will be my fault if it's a flop this year."

"Somebody actually said that to you?"

"No. But I see the way people look at me. I see them whispering. I know what they're thinking. Everybody in town is thinking it. I can tell." Earlene twisted her fingers together. "I can't believe everybody doubts my word. I thought they were my friends. I can't stand everyone staring at me, thinking those awful things about me."

"I'm sure not everybody thinks those things," I offered, and wished I could put more enthusiasm into my words.

Earlene pointed to the hallway that led deeper into the house. A suitcase sat there. Next to it were snow boots and a bathing suit.

"That's why I'm leaving," she told me.

"You're leaving Hideaway Grove?"

She took the water bottles out of the shopping bag and put them in the oven.

"I'm going to visit my sister in San Francisco— San Diego." She froze, frowned, then said, "San Diego."

"You're coming back, aren't you?"

"Maybe. Maybe not. I don't know."

Earlene noticed the bakery box in my hand and took it. She shoved it into the refrigerator, then unfurled a half dozen paper towels from the spindle beside the sink.

"Here. Take this. Please." She used the paper towels to pick up a canvas tote bag hanging on a peg beside the back door. "It's Iris's."

She thrust it into my arms. I looked down at the tote bag and felt kind of icky knowing it belonged to a dead woman.

"It flew right at me." Earlene dropped the paper towels, plastered both hands over her eyes, then yanked them away. "It fell at my feet. I picked it up. I mean, it was automatic. A normal response. I picked it up."

I remembered seeing Iris's purse and all of its contents strewn across the alley.

"And then you and Sarah came out. And Iris . . . Iris was there . . . like that," she went on. "I was so—so—"

"Upset," I said.

"Exactly." Earlene pulled the bakery box out of the refrigerator and put it inside the microwave. "I should have given it to Ed. I should have. I know that. Now. Now I know that. But I didn't even realize I had it. Not until I got home."

"I'll give it to the sheriff," I said.

"No. No, no, no." She whirled toward me, her eyes wild. "He'll want to talk to me again. He'll be mad I didn't give it to him yesterday. Then the whole town will find out. They'll say I kept it on purpose. They'll say I was hiding it. They'll make something awful out of it."

I couldn't disagree with her reasoning.

"It's just library books," Earlene implored.

From the weight and shape of the tote I could tell books were inside.

"Please, just take them to the library. They need them back—but don't tell them where you got them," she said. "Please."

"I'll take care of it," I promised. "I'll drop them in the book return slot. Nobody will know."

Earlene drew an exhausted breath. "If only . . . if only I could unsee what happened yesterday."

"What did you see? Exactly," I said.

I thought she'd cringe but instead she turned to me, as if grateful I'd asked.

"I'd just come around the corner, you know, from Main Street, heading toward Hummingbird Lane," she said, and gulped hard.

I knew people sometimes used the alley as a shortcut to and from Main and the residential neighborhoods.

"That car," Earlene said softly, as if seeing the whole, horrible event again. "I saw it sitting at the other end of the alley. It drove forward. It sped up. It swerved toward Iris. She was staring at her phone. She didn't even see it until . . ."

The memory of the sounds I'd heard yesterday flared in my mind. Then it bloomed. It got bigger and bigger.

"The engine revved," I mumbled. "The tires, they squealed."

A wave of nausea hit me. Earlene was right. It

was no accident. The driver of the car was lying in wait. He saw her, gunned the engine, took off so fast the tires spun. He'd hit Iris deliberately. The driver had intended to kill her. Iris had been murdered.

And Earlene and I were the only two who knew it.

CHAPTER 5

"San Diego," I said. "You're sure your sister lives in San Diego, not San Francisco?"

"Yes. I'm sure," Earlene said.

We were standing in her driveway beside her car. I'd helped her repack her suitcase and I'd filled the grocery bag with reasonable snacks for her trip, and loaded everything into her car. I was concerned that she'd be able to actually get to her sister's house.

"Do you know the way?" I asked.

"I've driven there before. And I know how to use this." She held up her cell phone. "It will give me directions, if I need them."

I didn't feel confident Earlene could—or would—use her GPS.

"Let me give you my number," I said. "Just in case."

I took her phone and put my number into her contacts list, then sent myself her info.

"Call me," I said, handing her phone over. "If you need something or if something happens, call me. Any time. Day or night."

"Thank you, Abbey. You're being so sweet to me. It means so much," Earlene said.

"Is somebody checking on your house while you're gone?" I asked.

"Oh, dear." She frowned and her anxiety spun up again. "I hadn't thought of that. I just want to get going. Who on earth can I call?"

"I'll do it," I offered. The job wouldn't require much more than an occasional spritz of water on her few houseplants, and cleaning out the refrigerator if she was gone for an extended visit.

"That would be wonderful. The key is under the pink flowerpot beside the back door," she said.

The same location Sarah used. I guess it was the go-to spot for hiding extra keys in Hideaway Grove.

"And keep the water bowl beside the back door full, too," she said.

"You have a pet?" I hadn't seen signs of an animal inside her house, except for a calendar with cats pictured, set to the wrong date.

"No, but I look after everyone else's as much as I can. So many—especially cats—run free. Traffic, you know. It's very dangerous. I worry."

"I'll handle it."

Earlene sighed and looked at her house, as if this might be the last time she saw it.

"My husband and I, we bought this place together," she said, and tears pooled in her eyes. "He passed three years ago."

"I didn't know you were a widow," I said, and realized that I knew very little about Earlene and most everyone else in town. All I had were memories, and they were the memories of a child.

"He was good with money. He left me well-off. I don't really have to work. I just do it to get out, you know, see people, talk to people."

Someone had mentioned Earlene worked at a café.

"The Parliament Café," she explained. "Near the village green."

When tourists read the name they usually thought of the governing body in the U.K., but even the youngest child in Hideaway Grove knew "parliament" was the term for a group of owls.

"I love living in Hideaway Grove. At least, I used to. Now I don't. All because of Iris Duncan." Earlene blinked away her tears and her expression hardened. "I never liked her."

"You didn't?" I asked, surprised.

"Not really. There was something about her. Something. I don't know what, exactly. Just something," Earlene said. "I'm not the only one who feels this way, you know. I hear things. At the café. My customers, they talk and they think I can't hear what they're saying just because I'm a waitress."

"People mentioned they didn't like Iris?" I asked.

"Oh, yes." Earlene nodded broadly.

"I don't suppose you recognized one of those people driving the car that hit Iris?" I asked.

"It's all a blur. Like I told the sheriff, all I know for sure is that it was a car, not a truck or an SUV. A car. And it was white." Earlene opened her car door. "White. Like my car."

I'd never realized how many white cars were in

Hideaway Grove until now. Since the hit-and-run, I'd seen them everywhere.

Earlene slid in behind the steering wheel, started the engine, and buzzed down her window. "Thank you again, Abbey, for everything."

"I'm sure all of this will be straightened out by the time you get back," I said, and sincerely hoped it would be.

Earlene shrugged. "I'm not sure it matters to me. After the way everybody has doubted my word, I don't know if I'll ever feel the same about living here."

She gave me a sad smile, and backed out of the driveway. I walked to the curb and watched as she stopped at the corner of Main Street, signaled for a left turn, then turned right and disappeared.

I felt a little sad at how things had so unexpectedly changed for Earlene. Her life had been going along pleasantly, everything was running smoothly, she was happy. Then something happened that was completely out of her control, and everything had turned against her.

I felt a kinship with Earlene.

I walked down the driveway toward the back of the house, my own anxiety spinning up.

I knew she was right about what she'd seen happen to Iris. I knew she wasn't mistaken about what she saw in the alley. I'd heard the car's engine rev and the tires chirp. I couldn't let everyone go on thinking Earlene was wrong, and I certainly couldn't let her bear the blame if the bad publicity ruined the upcoming festival.

But even if I went to Sheriff Grumman and corroborated Earlene's story, would it do any good? Would he believe me? Probably not. I wasn't an eyewitness, he'd surely point out. I wasn't in the alley. I could provide no evidence—black marks left by the squealing tires could have been there for ages, and the sound of a revving engine could have come from anywhere. And even if, by some miracle, he listened to me, it wouldn't erase the damage all the gossip had done to Earlene.

Only one thing could do that.

I'd have to prove Earlene was right. And the only way to accomplish that was to prove Iris had been murdered—and find her killer myself.

How would I do that? I wondered as I left Earlene's house. I'd gone back inside and made sure everything was turned off, and I'd retrieved the extra key from under the pink flowerpot on the back porch; I still had enough of Los Angeles on my mind not to leave a house key in a spot anyone would likely check. Now, as I headed toward Main Street, the problem of figuring out how to solve Iris's murder presented itself. How would I do it? Start with the victim, maybe?

Of all the things Earlene had told me, the one that surprised me the most was that she didn't like Iris. Others in town, according to Earlene, didn't like Iris, either. But Iris was a librarian. What's not to like about a librarian?

I'd have to find out.

I'd have to find out, too, who those people were and why they didn't like Iris.

The image of the alley, the crime scene, floated through my head. Iris's purse had been open and its contents spilled out—wallet, comb, sunglasses, tissues, all the usual things. Her cell phone was lying nearby. Earlene had mentioned that Iris had been on her phone. Was she texting? Making a call? Accessing a website? And whatever she'd been doing, was it connected to her death?

I paused on the corner and gazed up and down Main Street. Off to my left, several blocks away, was the village green and Hideaway Grove's government center, including the courthouse and Sheriff's Department, the post office, and the library. To my right was Sarah's Sweets and other businesses.

Why had Iris been in the alley? It led to nothing significant. It was just a shortcut from Main to the residential neighborhoods where Sarah lived. Where could Iris have been going?

More questions stacked up in my head, then dissolved when I heard someone call my name. I spotted a young woman dashing across Main Street—narrowly missing two white cars—and waving at me. She was blond, about my age, and for an instant I thought it was Brooke something-or-other again. But when she hopped up on the curb next to me and I saw her smile, I couldn't help smiling in return.

"Caitlin!"

"Abbey!"

We hugged, and the sudden onslaught of memories made me giddy. We'd been friends—best friends—during the summers I'd spent here. We'd lost touch after my parents moved us to England, but seeing Caitlin now made me feel as if we were kids again and all the years hadn't passed. It's like that with certain people, a connection that time and distance can't break. She'd hardly changed at all, still tall, fresh-faced, and looked great in jeans and a white T-shirt.

"I just heard you were back," Caitlin said, and gestured across the street to Barry's Pet Emporium, the store her parents apparently still owned. "Are you staying long? Please tell me you're staying a long time."

"For a while," I said, thinking maybe, somehow, she hadn't heard that my car had been towed to the crime lab, leaving me marooned in Hideaway Grove for the foreseeable future.

"We have to catch up," Caitlin insisted, and glanced at the pet store. "But not now. I have to get back over there—"

A horn tooted, drawing our attention down the block.

"Oh, no . . ." Caitlin said. "Not again."

A car—white, I noticed—cut the turn from Dove Drive too short, rocked over the curb, and kept going, causing a driver in oncoming traffic to stop quickly. The white car continued down Main Street.

"Miss Merriweather," Caitlin said, shaking her head. "She does this kind of thing all the time."

Only a few seconds passed until I made the connection. Miss Merriweather was the granddaughter of Hideaway Grove's founder. She lived in the family home, a huge, graceful old Victorian, on Owl Avenue at the other end of town.

"She's still alive?" I asked, stunned.

"And still driving, unfortunately," Caitlin said.

"She must be what—eighty?" I asked.

"At least," Caitlin said. "She's such a sweet lady. Everyone in town adores her. She lives alone so most of the merchants deliver to her house to keep her off of the streets."

I figured it was equally for the town's safety as well as Miss Merriweather's.

"We all keep hoping her niece or Mr. Schwartz, the family attorney, will insist she surrender her license, but so far, no. Somehow, she keeps passing the driver's test." Caitlin's smile returned. "I have to get back to the shop. I'm so glad you're here. We'll get together soon. I want to hear everything you've been doing."

I wasn't sure I was ready to divulge *everything* to Caitlin, despite our history together.

"And I want to know what you've been up to," I said.

She shrugged. "Not much. Not in Hideaway Grove."

We exchanged contact info, and she dashed back across Main.

I moved on toward Sarah's Sweets, then nearly stumbled when I spotted Zack McKenna across the street; I was slightly annoyed with myself for noticing him, and how good he looked in his uniform. He must have seen Miss Merriweather's near-miss at the corner and, obviously, hadn't done anything about it. I suppose the granddaughter of the town's founder still had some clout.

Since it appeared he was patrolling Main Street, did that mean Sheriff Grumman and the other deputies were investigating Iris's death? I hoped so. But I didn't feel strongly that they were. I agreed with Zack that Earlene didn't seem to be the most reliable witness, especially after seeing how scattered and confused she was earlier when I'd been at her house. All the more reason for me to figure a way to clear my name myself.

Zack turned his head and looked at me, as if he sensed I was watching him, as if he could somehow read my thoughts and know of my intention to solve Iris's murder on my own. I jerked my gaze away and continued on to the bakery, sure I could feel him staring but refusing to make eye contact again.

The bell chimed when I walked inside and the delicious scent of baking goodies engulfed me. Sarah was at the display case waiting on customers. A woman I was sure was Jodi, Sarah's assistant, was taking a pan of cookies out of the oven.

Sarah had mentioned Jodi in her emails. I would have known her anywhere from Sarah's description—thirtyish, dark hair, curvy figure, and an unmistakable aura of competence. She was a perfect complement to Sarah's work ethic. They shared an almost compulsive degree of care for their handcrafted baked goods, their carefully selected ingredients, and the inviting neighborhood environment the tourists and locals flocked to.

Sarah sent her customers away with a bakery box of cupcakes and a smile on their faces. Jodi looked up from her work; we introduced ourselves as I rounded the display case.

"Everything alright with Earlene?" Sarah asked.

"Not really," I said, and squeezed my things onto one of the hooks beside the back door already crowded with jackets, handbags, a raincoat, aprons, and two umbrellas.

"You should hear the gossip," Jodi said, shaking her head. "Almost everyone who's been in here today has something to say about Iris."

My attention perked up. Maybe I'd get a clue to Iris's killer.

"Such as?" I asked.

"They can't believe she's dead, can't believe she was killed, can't believe that sort of accident could happen here," Jodi said.

"Nobody believes Earlene's statement that Iris was hit on purpose?" I asked.

Jodi and Sarah exchanged a sad look.

"They don't," Sarah said.

"Or that somebody didn't like Iris?" I asked. "Didn't like her enough to deliberately run her down?"

"Who wouldn't like Iris?" Jodi declared. "She was new in town but she had fit in right from the start, making friends, helping out with things."

"And she'd developed new programs at the library that everyone was crazy about," Sarah said.

"Yes. That children's story hour. All the young mothers loved it," Jodi agreed. "I saw a notice posted outside the library that Iris was starting a new readers' group for adults. She was even arranging visits by authors to talk about their books. Everyone was excited."

"She was letting the arts and crafts festival planning committee use the conference room at the library at no charge," Sarah added.

I had to agree that based on what I'd just heard, it seemed unlikely anyone would have disliked Iris enough to deliberately run over her, even though I knew the truth.

Sarah gasped. "Oh my goodness, wasn't Iris heading up one of the festival committees?"

"She was," Jodi declared, then shook her head. "Who's going to take over for her? You know how hard it is to get anybody to oversee a committee."

"Everybody wants the festival, but nobody wants

to do the actual work to make it happen," Sarah said.

"And I'm afraid filling those spots is going to get more difficult," Jodi said, "with all this talk going around about Earlene's claims."

"I wish she hadn't said those things," Sarah said.

"Everybody knows how she is," Jodi said, a sympathetic note in her voice, as she moved the cookies onto cooling racks.

Again, I felt bad for Earlene and slightly annoyed that no one believed her. I was tempted to mention that she'd left town to escape the gossip, but I didn't want to give everyone something else to talk about right now. They'd figure it out soon enough.

"We've had more business owners in here today worried about the festival than we've had customers," Jodi said.

"Why do people insist on thinking the worst?" Sarah said. "All this bad talk just brings on more bad things."

"Well, more bad things may be on the horizon," Jodi said. "The festival committee has to deal with losing Iris—and they haven't even found Gretchen's replacement yet. We're down two volunteers."

"You're right. And we desperately need those positions filled." Sarah sighed heavily. "The committee will have to come up with someone soon."

"The next meeting should be a trying one." Jodi untied her apron and hung it beside the back door. "Since it's quiet now, I'm going to run to the bank. I'll be back in a flash."

Jodi left and Sarah started rearranging the cupcakes in the display case. I stood there watching, a new concern creeping over me. I could hardly bring myself to express it aloud, but I knew I had to.

"Do you want me to leave?" I asked.

"Sure. I can handle things until Jodi gets back."

"No," I said. "I mean, maybe I should leave Hideaway Grove."

Sarah's gaze came up. "What on earth are you saying?"

"Everybody in town is talking about Iris's death, and they're talking about Earlene. I think they're probably talking about me, too," I explained.

"Nobody thinks you're involved in any of this," Sarah said.

"The sheriff towed my car to the crime lab," I reminded her.

"Ed's just being overly cautious. Everyone knows that."

"I'm afraid that my being here will reflect badly on you. The last thing I want is for my presence to damage your business. So maybe I should leave. I can rent a car."

As badly as I felt for Earlene, and as sure I was that she was telling the truth and Iris had been deliberately run down in the alley, I couldn't stay and defend her at the expense of my aunt's reputation and business. I had to put Sarah first. I would, of course, go to the sheriff, tell him what I knew, and do everything in my power to convince him before I left that Earlene was, in fact, right about Iris's death.

"I'm not concerned about what people think. I don't want you to leave." Sarah paused. "Are you anxious to get back home?"

"You mean back to Los Angeles?"

"You don't feel as if Los Angeles is your home any longer?"

"Well . . ."

Sarah drew in a breath and looked at me, as if she could see my thoughts and knew something more was going on than what I'd told her.

"I think it's time you explained exactly why you left Los Angeles."

CHAPTER 6

"So tell me about *everything*," Sarah said.

I didn't want to make a big deal out of it—mostly because I thought it wouldn't hurt so badly if I told it quickly—so while Jodi was still at the bank and no customers were in the bakery, I blasted through the worst thing that had happened.

Sarah nodded sympathetically as I told her what I'd done.

"The mistake was mine. It was my fault. I totally overlooked a key component," I admitted. I'd made the same admission when my supervisor had cornered me in the office that day, but it didn't stop her from humiliating me in front of everyone in the department.

"Sounds as if it was a big project with a lot of moving parts," Sarah said.

I could tell she was on my side, which was nice, but in a marketing campaign for a major, international corporation, the mistake I'd made was glaring—and likely unforgivable, since I'd been put on administrative leave pending further review by upper management.

"Yes, it was a big project," I agreed. "But the mistake I'd made was costly and, well, things hadn't been going so great even before that happened."

I'd been struggling to keep up. The supervisor of my department didn't seem to like me, which never helps, and I didn't get much support from anyone else. The office atmosphere was very competitive, almost cutthroat. I'd realized pretty quickly after taking the job that it was beyond me. I guess that's the part that hurt the most. I'd gone to Los Angeles and secured the prestigious position with high hopes and big dreams, so I kept pushing, working long hours, trying to fit in, trying to figure everything out. I might have survived there if everything else hadn't happened.

"Then I found out I was being evicted," I said.

"Oh, dear," Sarah gasped.

"One of the men I worked with told me about a woman he knew who was looking for a roommate to share a condo she was renting. You can't believe how expensive housing is in L.A., and how hard it is to find something decent," I said. "It was a nice place and I figured I was lucky to have it, until I learned that the woman I'd been paying my rent to for six months had pocketed my money instead of paying the landlord. We were being evicted."

"You were losing your job *and* your home? At the same time?"

"Then I found out the one good friend I'd made was transferring to Denver, and a guy I'd met online turned out to be a complete jerk," I said. "It was a perfect storm of troubles. I couldn't take it any longer, so I came here."

"So it really was *everything*." Sarah gave me a quick hug. "You might get your job back, right?"

"The woman in HR told me they'd let me know when they'd made a decision." I gave myself a mental shake, anxious to focus on something else. "So, what can I do to help around here?"

Sarah seemed as if she wanted to discuss my situation further, but she let it go, thankfully, and turned to the work schedule and calendar posted beside the coffee maker.

"Looks as if everything is handled for today and most of tomorrow," she said.

I needed to stay busy, especially with the thoughts of my embarrassing, humiliating failures in Los Angeles fresh in my mind.

"How about if I organize the storage room?" I asked, waving my hand toward the pocket doors. "So when Gretchen comes back, the space will be ready if you two want to go ahead with the gift shop and dining room."

Sarah considered it for a few seconds, then nodded. "I think that's a good idea."

I slid the pocket doors apart and stepped inside. Dust motes floated through the air, highlighted by the muted sunlight. Looking at the jumble of old furniture and storage boxes, I hardly knew where to start, so I headed for the one area that was organized.

The sewing machine that belonged to Gretchen sat atop a folding banquet table. It looked expensive and complicated to operate, with all sorts of dials and knobs and even a small computer screen. Next to it were boxes containing spools of thread, bobbins, straight pins, and other things I didn't recognize. On an adjoining table were four bolts of pale green gingham fabric. Next to them was the shopping bag of pillowcases Anna at the thrift shop had given me.

Sarah had told me that Gretchen made dresses out of them and donated them to the church whose volunteers took them to Africa for distribution. It seemed that, like the gift shop and dining room conversion, the project would be on hold until Gretchen returned, if she returned at all.

I dumped the pillowcases out of the shopping bag and sorted through them. Many of them had colorful patterns, some were striped, a few were solids. Several had ruffled borders. They'd all make adorable dresses.

I used my phone for a Google search and found a nonprofit that collected and distributed the same style of dresses. I tapped on the photo tab. The pics had been taken in African villages and showed girls, from toddlers to teens, accepting the gifts, their smiling faces lit up with joy at having a new dress.

I heard a familiar voice in the bakery and spotted Caitlin at the display case chatting with Sarah, who pointed in my direction. Caitlin came into the storage room and we hugged.

"I came by to see if you want to make a delivery with me," Caitlin said, and held up a shopping bag from her parents' pet supply store. Before I could answer she gestured to the pillowcases, fabric, and notions on the worktable. "What's all this?"

I showed her the photos on my phone. "They're pillowcase dresses for girls in Africa."

"You're making them?"

"No, Gretchen was." I pulled one of the finished dresses from the cardboard box under the work-table that Sarah had showed me earlier, and held it up.

"Cute," she said. "Are they hard to make?"

I shrugged. "I don't know."

Caitlin grinned. "Remember when we took that sewing class at the rec center when we were twelve?"

Sarah had kept me and my friends busy during those summers with all sorts of lessons and activities.

I giggled. "It certainly went better than the cooking class we took the next summer."

"The fire was very small," Caitlin pointed out. "But the smoke detectors were awfully loud."

"Too bad some hot firemen didn't show up."

We laughed, then Caitlin said, "Come on. Make this delivery with me. I can't promise we'll see any hot firemen, but maybe a hot deputy sheriff."

My heart did a tumble.

"Surely you've noticed him," Caitlin said. "Zack McKenna. Tall, great body, good-looking."

"We met," I murmured.

"We'll walk and talk," Caitlin declared, heading for the door. "I've got to get this delivery done and get back to the shop before Dad has a stroke."

I remembered Caitlin's dad being intense and kind of hard on her when we were kids. I was surprised to see that nothing had changed even now that Caitlin was an adult.

"I'll be back in a bit," I called to Sarah. "Do you need anything while I'm out?"

"Not a thing," she replied, waving. "You girls have fun."

We left the bakery and headed west on Main Street.

"I want to hear what you've been doing," Caitlin said. "Sarah told me you were working for a huge company, living in Los Angeles. Sounds awesome. Tell me everything."

I couldn't bring myself to tell her *everything*, so I hit the highlights and omitted the trouble I'd experienced and the distinct possibility that very soon I'd likely be unemployed.

"How exciting," Caitlin declared. "Much more exciting than living here."

I detected a yearning in her voice I hadn't expected.

"You're not happy in Hideaway Grove?" I asked.

"Happy enough, I suppose," Caitlin said. "Dad's been making noises about retiring at the end of the year, but now he's in a panic about the festival being a failure."

"Because of the bad publicity about Iris's death?"

"If the tourists stay away it will be a hard financial blow. Dad might have to rethink his retirement plans," Caitlin said. "He's so annoyed with Earlene for claiming it wasn't an accident and causing this mess."

We paused on the corner of Hummingbird Lane, then crossed when traffic cleared.

"The whole thing is ridiculous," Caitlin went on. "No one would have done what Earlene claimed she saw happen. Everybody liked Iris."

"Everybody?"

"Everybody."

"Come on," I said. "There must have been someone who didn't like Iris."

"Not that I ever heard about. Besides, Iris had lived here only a few months. That's hardly enough time to make an enemy." Caitlin hoisted the Barry's Pet Emporium shopping bag a little higher. "This delivery is for Miss Merriweather."

I gasped, feeling like my twelve-year-old self again.

"You've been inside her house?" I asked.

"Many times," Caitlin said.

"And you lived to talk about it," I said, still in awe.

During my summers here, stories about the big old house had been rampant. All the neighborhood kids had been alternately enchanted by it—the kitchen walls were said to be made of chocolate—and terrified by the grizzly creatures rumored to live in the attic.

"Miss Merriweather is a really sweet lady and she likes to have visitors," Caitlin said. "She lives alone."

"What about her niece?" I asked, remembering Caitlin had mentioned her earlier.

"Joyce lives over in Parker. She works at the convenience store near the freeway exit," Caitlin said. "You passed it coming here."

I didn't recall seeing it, but I'd been so upset and tired I didn't remember much about my trip.

"Like I said, Miss Merriweather is lonely so she likes to chat. A lot," Caitlin said, as we turned onto Owl Avenue. "I have to get back to the store so we'll try to keep it short."

The house built by the founder of Hideaway Grove, Miss Merriweather's grandfather, sat on an oversize lot surrounded by flowers, trees, and shrubs. It was a three-story Victorian that featured a wraparound porch and circular rooms on the second floor, one of them topped with a turret. Like most homes of that era it was embellished with arched windows, scrollwork, and gingerbread; the white and pale yellow trim were perfect accents to the house's rich blue color. A matching detached garage was set on the rear of the lot.

There was a noticeable quiet, dignified feel to the place as we headed up the curved walkway and climbed the steps onto the large porch. Caitlin rang the bell; I heard it chime through the house. The door opened a few minutes later and Miss Merriweather appeared. She was short and round, as some women got in their later years, and she had on a yellow housedress and flats. Her hair was snow white and twisted into a soft bun atop her head. She looked almost the same as I remembered from my summers here years ago.

She smiled up at us, projecting the same quiet, dignified aura as the house itself.

"Oh, Caitlin, dear, it's so good of you to come by. What a lovely surprise."

"I brought supplies." She indicated the shopping bag, then me. "And this is Abbey Chandler. She's back in town visiting for a while."

Miss Merriweather frowned slightly, then smiled. "Oh, yes, of course. Little Abbey. Sarah's niece. My, what a lovely young lady you've become. Come inside, girls."

She stepped back and opened the door wider, allowing Caitlin and me into the entryway.

"My little sweeties will be so glad you came," Miss Merriweather said as she headed down a wide hallway.

Caitlin and Miss Merriweather moved along but

I took my time, anxious after so many years to see what the inside of the house looked like.

I felt as if I'd been teleported back in time a hundred years or so. The grace and elegance of a bygone era were evident in the dark paneling, the tapestries, and the coffered ceilings. Each room I passed boasted furnishings in a different jewel tone—a sitting room in amethyst, the parlor in emerald, the grand dining room in garnet. Down another hallway I caught a glimpse of a library.

After all the European libraries my parents had dragged me through, I couldn't resist a closer look.

I peeked inside and saw massive shelves that reached nearly to the ceiling filled with what looked like hundreds of books. At one end of the room a row of octagonal stained-glass windows let in colorful light. There was a fireplace and a small table and lamp situated between two green-leather, wingback chairs.

The room did, in fact, remind me of the sort of place my parents had taken me, and I stepped inside with the odd feeling of missing them. Images filled my thoughts, drawing me farther into the room.

When we'd moved to England and I'd been forced to spend my summers with them instead of Sarah, I'd been subjected to just this sort of place. While I'd mostly been bored beyond reason, I had come to appreciate the knowledge stored in libraries such as this one, preserved in the books, maps, and other publications. I wondered now where in the world my parents were, at this very moment. I wondered if they remembered the times I'd been with them, if they were thinking about me, if they missed—

"Hey!"

I jumped and spun around. A woman I'd never seen before stood in the hallway glaring at me.

"I don't know who you think you are, but you'd better get out of here before I call the sheriff!"

CHAPTER 7

A few seconds passed as the woman's threat to call the sheriff hung in the air. Granted, wandering through the house alone wasn't the proper thing for me to do, but her hostility seemed like an extreme overreaction. Still, I hardly needed another run-in with local law enforcement. Better to defuse the situation.

"Hello," I said, using my most pleasant voice but not stepping closer. "I'm Abbey Chandler. I'm here with Caitlin from the pet shop, making a delivery."

"Then what are you doing in *here?*" she demanded, and waved her hand toward the shelves of books.

My take-the-high-road attitude had done nothing to appease her, I realized. I guess I shouldn't have been surprised. She looked as if her thirty years of life hadn't been easy. Aside from the frown, the turned-down lips, and the scowl she wore, she had on faded jeans, a plaid work shirt, and well-worn athletic shoes. No makeup, I noticed, and unkempt dark hair threaded with strands of gray that hung past her shoulders.

Before I could respond, voices drew closer. Caitlin and Miss Merriweather appeared in the hallway.

"Oh, there you are, dear," Miss Merriweather said, smiling at the woman. "I thought I heard your voice."

"Aunt Tilly, what are you doing?" the woman demanded. "You have to stop letting people into the house."

Caitlin and I exchanged a troubled glance.

Miss Merriweather smiled pleasantly, as if the harsh words didn't penetrate, or perhaps she was used to them.

"This is Abbey. You remember Abbey, of course. Her aunt is Sarah of Sarah's Sweets." She turned to me. "And this is my niece Joyce."

I looked closer at Joyce, trying to remember her from my summers here. Nothing about her seemed familiar. I figured she was too old to be part of the friends I hung out with back then.

"You can't let people parade through here anytime they want," Joyce said to Miss Merriweather, ignoring me.

"One doesn't refuse callers," Miss Merriweather pointed out politely. "And everyone is so lovely. I do so enjoy visitors."

"Not everybody is nice," Joyce barked.

She sounded more like a bully than a concerned niece. Miss Merriweather didn't seem to notice.

"Why, the most lovely people come by. Caitlin,

of course, and Phoebe from the drugstore. That nice young fellow from the market, too. And dear Mr. Schwartz—"

"That lawyer isn't supposed to drop by. I told you," Joyce said, her voice rising.

"Iris, too." Miss Merriweather's smile dimmed. "Iris, from the library. I so enjoyed her visits. She had extensive knowledge of books, of course, and we had such lively discussions."

"She's somebody else you let have the run of the place," Joyce complained.

At the mention of Iris's name, I spoke up.

"You didn't like Iris?" I asked.

Joyce turned to me, as if really seeing me for the first time. She drew a breath and forced the scowl from her face.

"Of course I liked Iris. Everyone liked Iris," she said.

The mental tally I was keeping now showed five for five. Sarah, Jodi, Caitlin, and now Joyce and Miss Merriweather. Everybody liked Iris. Everybody but Earlene—and the people Earlene had overheard at the Parliament Café, whoever they were.

"You have to be careful about who you invite into the house," Joyce said, frowning at Miss Merriweather again. "You might think people are nice, that you know them, but they could have an ulterior motive."

"I guess you can't be too careful," Caitlin commented. "Especially after what happened to Iris."

Joyce uttered an ugly half laugh. "What nonsense. Even suggesting it was something other than an accident is irresponsible."

"Enough of this unpleasantness," Miss Merri-

weather said. "Do come, Abbey, and meet my little
sweeties. They're all atwitter with dear Caitlin's
surprises."

I followed her and Caitlin out of the library, relieved that Joyce didn't join us.

We moved through a series of hallways, past the
parlor, sitting room, and dining room we'd passed
earlier. I'd been so entranced with the house when
I'd first arrived, I hadn't looked closely. Now I noticed the furniture and drapes showed their age;
worn and thin spots were visible here and there in
the fabric. The air smelled slightly musty.

At the back of the house Miss Merriweather led
us into a sitting room alive with floral print furniture, a television, racks of magazines, and stacks of
books, the section of the house, it seemed, where
she lived her daily life. Through a doorway I spotted the kitchen, a large room with turquoise floor
tiles and white appliances and cupboards that
seemed to have been last updated before I was
born.

"Look at my little sweeties. They are so enjoying
the treats you girls brought," Miss Merriweather
said.

She stood in front of a huge birdcage that sat
atop a sturdy table near the windows. Inside, a half
dozen blue and green parakeets fluttered from
perch to perch or turned to tilt their heads at her.
The cage was furnished with a miniature Ferris
wheel, hanging mirrors, swings, and ladders. Water
bottles, feed cups, and cuttlebones were fastened
to the sides.

"Adorable," I said, as I joined Miss Merriweather. "They look so happy."

"Miss Merriweather takes excellent care of them," Caitlin said.

"My little sweeties brighten my day," Miss Merriweather said.

We stood there for a few minutes watching the birds before Caitlin caught my eye and nodded toward the door.

"I'd better get back to the shop," Caitlin said.

"It was good seeing you," I said, following Caitlin as we backed away from the cage.

"So lovely of you to come by," Miss Merriweather said as we walked through the house to the front door. "Come back again soon, won't you?"

We promised we would as we left the house. At the bottom of the steps I glanced back and saw Miss Merriweather lingering in the doorway; she offered a final wave and went inside.

"That niece of hers is quite a piece of work," I commented as we moved down the curved walkway toward the street.

"Joyce is a tough gal," Caitlin said. "I guess you could call her the black sheep of the family."

"How so?"

"Something to do with her parents," Caitlin said.

When I'd first seen Joyce, I'd judged by her appearance that life wasn't going great for her. Now, spotting a car parked in Miss Merriweather's driveway which must have belonged to Joyce, I figured I'd been right. It was a blue Chevy sedan with faded paint and an array of dents and scrapes. The license plate started with the number five, and according to California's DMV numbering system, it indicated the vehicle was well over ten years old.

"Does Miss Merriweather have other relatives nearby?" I asked, hoping there was someone in the family that could check on her and was actually pleasant.

"Nope," Caitlin said.

"What about that Mr. Schwartz I heard Miss Merriweather mention?" I asked.

"He's been the family attorney for . . . well, forever, I think," Caitlin said, as we turned onto Main Street. "Joyce is it, for family."

Miss Merriweather's house, though it showed signs of aging and needed updating, was expensive to maintain, which meant she had money. Old family money, a trust fund, or something set up by her grandfather, probably. Juxtaposed to that was Joyce's older car, her unkempt appearance, and what was likely little more than a minimum wage job at the convenience store. The disparity between their lifestyles was glaring.

"Maybe Joyce wouldn't be so grumpy if she lived with Miss Merriweather?" I suggested.

"It wouldn't help. Mom and Dad, and most of the town, have known Joyce all her life. She's always been like this," Caitlin told me. "Only worse, at times. Angry. Lashing out."

"The situation with her parents?" I asked.

"I guess," Caitlin said. "So, look, we have to get together and talk. How about we hit the Night Owl one evening?"

I'd seen the sign for the local bar just off Main Street on Eagle Avenue.

"Sounds great," I said.

I waved goodbye to Caitlin as she continued toward the pet shop and I crossed Main Street. As I stepped up on the curb my cell phone vibrated in my pocket. I fished it out and saw the name on the ID screen. Madison. A girl I knew from my job in Los Angeles.

The humiliation and hurt I'd experienced there hit me full force. My whole body tensed and my stomach rolled.

I'd met Madison in the employee breakroom and we'd become friends right away. It was like that with some people; you just hit it off. Madison was a few years younger than me, full of energy, and very social. She worked in the accounting department. I knew that if I was hearing from her, word of my major screw-up and administrative leave had spread through the whole company.

Tempted as I was not to subject myself to a re-hash of my ordeal and the details of how it had grown even worse since my departure, I decided to buck up and face it. Madison was a friend, one of the few I'd had there, and dodging her wouldn't have been right. I stepped aside in front of Anna's Treasure Thrift Shop and answered my phone.

"I just called your department to see if you want to go to lunch and they said you weren't there, and they didn't know when you'd be back," Madison said, her voice high with confusion and concern. "What's going on? Are you okay? Are you sick or something?"

While I was slightly relieved, my situation hadn't reached her department yet, I didn't want to get into the whole thing with her. But I knew she'd find out sooner or later anyway, so better to hear it from me.

"I screwed up," I told her.

"What do you mean?"

"My supervisor put me on leave."

"She did that? Oh my God, I can't believe she did that. Over one mistake?"

"It was a pretty big mistake."

"Yeah, but still," Madison said. "I mean, geez, you haven't worked here very long. She couldn't have cut you some slack?"

"I guess not."

"I can't believe she did that," Madison said again, then lowered her voice. "Nobody likes her."

That made me feel a little better.

"So when are you coming back?" she asked.

"Never, probably."

"Over one mistake?" Madison was outraged, which was nice to hear.

"Yep."

Madison paused for a few seconds. "That's not right. I'm going to find out what's going on."

"What? No, wait. Madison, really, it's okay. They'll let me know what they decide."

"Don't worry. I'm on it." She ended our call.

I couldn't help smiling. Though I was slightly alarmed at what possible trouble Madison could stir up on my behalf, she was in my corner and that felt good.

"Talking to your friends in L.A.?"

A warm tremor shot through me as Zack appeared in front of me. He had on his uniform and looked great, which annoyed me for some reason.

"Were you spying on me?" I demanded.

"Couldn't help it." He jerked his chin down the block. "You're the only person around here smiling today."

I glanced around. The few people who were out looked a bit grim.

Zack nodded toward my phone. "I figured that

must have been one of your L.A. friends you were talking to. Missing the big city already?"

"Not yet—not that it would matter since I don't have a way of getting there." I tucked my phone into my pocket. "Am I getting my car back any time soon?"

"No way. Not if you're planning to skip town." He grinned and leaned closer. "That's my personal position, not an official one."

He sauntered away leaving me feeling flushed and . . . something. I knew he'd likely look back to see if I was watching him, so I moved down the sidewalk and ducked into the bakery.

Sarah looked up from behind the display case and smiled. Jodi, in the kitchen, waved. Warm, delicious aromas comforted me. Zack popped into my head. How wrong he was, suggesting I missed my life in Los Angeles. I was perfectly happy here. For now.

"Can I help out with something?" I asked.

Sarah shook her head. "Not right now. How about you, Jodi?"

"I've got everything covered," she answered.

I was a bit disappointed but not surprised. Sarah had been managing her bakery just fine without me for decades. She really didn't need me. Still, I had to stay busy.

"I'm going to work in the storage room, get it cleaned up," I said.

Sarah called her thanks as I parted the pocket doors open and walked inside. I stood there for a few minutes assessing the situation and coming up with a plan. While I wasn't sure what was in all the storage boxes and would have to rely on Sarah to sort through them, I could stack them neatly in one corner of the room and arrange the haphazard placement of the furniture to clear some floor space. After that I could get down to serious cleaning.

But what was I going to do about Gretchen's sewing machine, her notions, supplies, and the fabric remnants? What should I do about the pillowcase dresses she'd made?

I pulled one of the finished dresses out of the box under the table and held it up. It really was cute. The image of the little girl in Africa who'd surely be thrilled to receive it flashed in my head. It seemed a shame the dresses would just sit here in a box until Gretchen came back—if she ever came back.

I decided I'd give them to the pastor's wife whom Sarah had mentioned, who accepted donated dresses. She'd probably take the pillowcases Anna had donated, and all the thread, pins, and other notions, too, so someone else in Hideaway Grove could make them into dresses.

I left the storage room and joined Sarah and Jodi in the kitchen.

"I was looking at the pillowcase dresses Gretchen was making," I said. "How can I get in touch with the pastor's wife?"

Sarah looked up from the pink icing she was swirling onto cupcakes, and seemed somewhere between startled and pleased.

"You're going to make the pillowcase dresses?" Sarah asked.

"What a wonderful idea!" Jodi said.

"Well, no," I said. "Actually, I was just thinking—"

"Good for you!" Jodi said.

"It's such a worthwhile cause," Sarah said.

"No, I only wanted—"

"Oh, and you can sew the new curtains Gretchen was going to make. The place surely could use them," Jodi said.

"Curtains?" I exclaimed. "I couldn't possibly—"

"Don't be so modest," Sarah said. "I remember that skirt you made in sewing class. It was lovely."

"Your aunt paid good money for that fabric. The green gingham for the curtains," Jodi said, and waved toward the storage room. "All that fabric—four bolts of it—and Connie didn't even give your aunt a discount, not one cent."

"Connie at Connie's Fabrics," Sarah explained to me. "And I didn't expect a discount. Most of the businesses here in town are barely eking by, lucky to earn even a small profit, and Connie is no exception."

"Well, she could have done a little something," Jodi complained.

"I'll send Gretchen a text and ask if it's all right for you to use her sewing machine," Sarah promised.

"I haven't sewn anything in years. My sewing skills are—they're nonexistent," I said. "And that machine looks really complicated. I can't possibly figure it out."

"Oh, of course you can." Sarah pulled her phone from the pocket of her apron and started texting.

My idea to donate the dresses had gotten completely out of control, well-meaning though it was. I noticed the trash bins were full and this seemed like a good time to leave. I pulled the bags out, tied them off, and pushed through the door into the alley.

The door slammed shut and memories of seeing Iris lying dead a few yards away assailed me. Sounds echoed in my head—an engine revving, tires screeching, Earlene screaming. A strange flash of *something*. I doubted I'd ever set foot in this alley again without remembering that awful incident. Maybe if Iris's killer was found and punished, I'd feel better about it.

Of course, that might never happen, I realized, as I headed toward the Dumpsters.

I hadn't made any progress finding the murderer. So far all I'd discovered was that everybody liked Iris—everybody but Earlene and the mystery people she'd overheard while waiting on their tables at the café. And that meant, really, the only person who I knew for a fact disliked Iris was Earlene.

Only Earlene.

I stopped and looked down the alley in the direction the hit-and-run driver had come from. I'd wondered about Iris and why she'd been here.

I wondered now why Earlene had been here.

Earlene's house on Blue Bird Lane was on the other end of Main Street, as was the Parliament Café where she worked. Why was she here in the alley? Where was she going?

A wave of unease passed through me.

Earlene was the only witness.

Earlene didn't like Iris.

There were so many questions, but I couldn't learn the answers. Not now.

Earlene had left town.

And I'd helped her go.

CHAPTER 8

I didn't like to think that Earlene had been involved in Iris's death, but the idea stayed with me all night and still lingered as I headed for Sarah's Sweets the next morning.

Was Earlene an unwitting accomplice? Had she somehow drawn Iris into the alley under unforeseen circumstances?

Or had she purposely lured Iris into the alley? Was she the lookout for the driver of the car? Had Earlene gone along with the plan, then gotten cold feet and claimed it was a murder to keep suspicion off herself in case the driver was identified?

I could see Earlene being duped into getting involved, but that was based on my limited experience with her and the comments I'd heard others make about her.

Maybe she was more diabolical than I—or anyone—realized.

I had to learn the reason Earlene and Iris had been in the alley in the first place. I wasn't sure how I'd find out why Iris was there, but getting the truth from Earlene was easier. I pulled my phone out of my pocket.

I'd gotten her number when I'd given her my contact info as she'd headed out for San Diego to visit her sister. I accessed it now and listened as her voicemail picked up. I left a message saying I wanted to make sure she'd arrived safely at her sister's place, and asked her to call me.

It wasn't a giant leap forward in a murder investigation, but hopefully it would point me in the right direction by eliminating Earlene as an accomplice—or not.

I turned onto Main Street. Several cars—three white ones—drove by and a dozen or so shoppers strolled the sidewalks. Compared to Los Angeles, so few people out and about might indicate a possible impending zombie apocalypse. Here, it was normal.

Jodi was busy in the kitchen and Sarah was waiting on several customers at the display case who were deciding which muffins to buy, when I walked into the bakery. I felt slightly guilty coming in after the shop was open, while Sarah and Jodi got here somewhere around dawn. But Sarah had insisted I sleep in while I could because she was confident my employers in Los Angeles would come to their senses at any moment and want me back. I sincerely doubted that would happen but I took advantage of the extra sleep and leisurely mornings just the same since I'd eventually leave Hideaway Grove for a job somewhere—provided some company would hire me after that last screwup.

I slipped into the kitchen, skirted around Jodi at the work island, looped my handbag over one of the crowded pegs beside the back door, and poured myself a cup of coffee. Unlike the customers at the counter, I had no trouble selecting an apple muffin still warm from the oven.

"Anything I can do to help?" I asked Jodi.

"Thanks, but no thanks," she said. "Not right now."

"Busy morning?" I asked, settling onto the tall stool nearby.

"Mostly a lot of talking, not a lot of buying," Jodi said, keeping her voice low. "Iris's death, the festival, crowds staying away, businesses closing. Everybody thinks this could spell the end of Hideaway Grove."

"That couldn't happen. Could it?"

Jodi shrugged. "Everybody would be better off spending their time planning the festival. We've still got two committees that nobody is heading up, and that's not the kind of thing that can wait until the last minute."

"Any word on the sheriff's investigation?" I asked.

Jodi's expression soured. "Ed's taking it seriously, for some reason, which just prolongs the ordeal, and leaves everybody to wonder and speculate and worry."

Again, I felt uncomfortable knowing that Iris had, in fact, been deliberately run down, but still didn't see how sharing that information with Sheriff Grumman would help anything. He was already going all-out with his investigation, basing it on Earlene's word that Iris had been murdered. And if I did come forward supporting Earlene, it could make things worse by causing him to focus more attention on me and his notion that I was somehow involved, rather than finding the real killer.

I finished my muffin and coffee, hopped off the stool, and put my dishes in the dishwasher.

"I'm going to get started cleaning the storage room," I said, and grabbed one of the white aprons from the peg.

In the supply closet at the rear of the kitchen I gathered a mop and bucket, the broom and dustpan, feather duster, cleaning cloths and products, and went into the storage room. To keep the dust and dirt I was going to stir up from drifting into the bakery, I closed the pocket doors behind me. I selected a rock & roll mix on my phone, starting with Bob Seger's "Old Time Rock & Roll," put in my earbuds, and went to work.

"Ta-da!"

I pushed open the pocket doors for my big reveal, and both Sarah and Jodi gasped in delight.

"It looks great," Jodi declared.

"I can't believe you did this." Sarah shook her head in wonder.

I'd spent hours sweeping, mopping, scrubbing, and rearranging the storage room, and was pleased with the result. I gestured grandly, and followed them inside.

On the left side of the room I had strategically placed all the odd pieces of furniture and arranged the storage boxes on top of them.

"I placed them so you can get to them easily, when you're ready to go through them, or if you need something," I told Sarah, gesturing with my best Vanna White impression.

At the other end of the room I'd set up tables, one for Gretchen's sewing machine. Next to it I'd put the boxes containing the sewing supplies, notions, and remnants.

"Everything is spotless," Jodi said, and gasped. "You even cleaned the windows."

I'd opened the shades and gone over the panes a half dozen times until they sparkled in the sunlight.

"I don't think we should let Abbey go back to Los Angeles," Jodi said, grinning. "I think we should keep her here!"

Sarah gazed around the room in awe. "I wish Gretchen could see this—oh, that reminds me. I heard from her. She said you can use her sewing machine, no problem."

"I'm not planning to do any sewing—" I began.

"How's her daughter?" Jodi asked.

"The same," Sarah said. "Still no idea when Gretchen will come back."

"I'm so glad you're taking over her project, Abbey," Jodi said. "Sewing those pillowcase dresses is a very worthwhile cause."

I'd already said that I didn't intend to take over making the dresses, but Jodi seemed to have it set firmly in her mind that I would. I was about to protest again when Sarah slid her arm around my shoulders and pulled me in for a hug.

"You did a fantastic job in here," she said. "Thank you so much for taking it on."

"Happy I could help," I told her, and couldn't hide my smile.

"I guess we can't call this a storage room anymore," Sarah said.

"Oh, I know." Jodi rushed into the bakery and

returned with three cake pops. She passed them out. "We'll christen it *the sewing studio.*"

"To the sewing studio!" Sarah and Jodi chimed in unison. I went along with it, mostly because I couldn't resist the cake pop.

The bell over the front door chimed and voices drifted in from the bakery. Sarah and Jodi hurried out to wait on the customers. I gathered the last of the cleaning supplies and put them back into the closet, shoved the white apron into the hamper with the other soiled ones, then washed up in the bathroom.

I returned to the newly christened sewing studio and surveyed my work. The room did look better, a massive improvement. It felt good to take on a project, figure out the steps, and accomplish it with help from no one. And, of course, knowing that Sarah appreciated my work gave my spirits an even bigger boost.

I turned in a slow circle. The room was finished. Now what?

Not much was on the horizon for me. Sarah didn't need my help with the bakery. I didn't have a job to go to every day. I'd have to update my résumé and apply for some jobs, and I needed to push ahead with solving Iris's death—but how much time would those things take?

I wandered to the box of pillowcase dresses, pulled one out, and looked it over. Making the dresses would fill my days—plus it was a good cause. But I'd have to figure out how to operate Gretchen's sewing machine.

I eyed it sitting on the worktable. All sorts of buttons and dials, plus a computer screen. It was much more complicated than the Singer I'd learned on years ago during my classes at the rec center.

Searching through one of the boxes of supplies, I found the instruction manual. I sat down, flipped through it, got overwhelmed, and put it away. I pulled out my phone and found a YouTube video on how to operate this particular model. I watched the first two minutes of it and got even more overwhelmed.

I sighed and sank back in my chair. My old job, my days at my office in Los Angeles, flashed in my head. What would my coworkers and supervisors think if they saw me now? What would my college professors say if they knew what I was doing with my business degree? And my parents? Well, no need to wonder what they'd think. I already knew. According to them, nothing *artistic* was worth spending too much time on.

Well, maybe I'd prove them wrong—someday.

I tidied up a bit and went into the bakery. Customers sat at two of the little tables by the front windows enjoying brownies and what looked like oatmeal cookies, along with cupcakes. My stomach growled.

"I'm going to grab something to eat," I called.

Sarah glanced away from the three women she was helping at the display case. "Making progress on the pillowcase dresses?"

"You're sewing?" one of the women remarked. "I haven't sewed anything in years."

Two of the women seated at the tables looked up at me, along with everyone else in the bakery, so I couldn't admit that all I'd done was read the instruction manual and check out YouTube—then quit.

"She's taking over for Gretchen," Jodi announced.

All the women nodded their approval.

"You should eat at the Parliament. Their special today is chicken-fried steak," Sarah said. "Give Earlene my best."

I asked if she or Jodi wanted me to bring something back for them, but they didn't. As I headed for the door, the two women seated at the tables glanced my way, then leaned closer and whispered. Talking about me, no doubt. But were they gossiping about my sewing pillowcase dresses, or the sheriff's suspicion that I was involved in Iris's death?

I hurried out of the bakery.

Traffic moved along Main Street at a steady pace—would I ever stop counting white cars?—and tourists window-shopped among locals. Two people waved. I didn't know who they were, but I waved back anyway; hopefully I'd been recognized as Sarah's niece, not the person whose car had been towed to the crime lab.

My gaze swept both sides of the street, checking out each face I saw—until I realized I was looking for Zack. Annoyed with myself, I locked my line of sight on the village green and kept walking.

The Parliament Café had an ideal location steps away from Hideaway Grove's government center, the village green, and many popular shops. I pushed my way inside and froze for a few seconds. The place looked much the same as I remembered from all those summers ago—two rows of booths, a lunch counter with stools, all done in warm shades of yellow, brown, and green, and decorated with photographs of owls.

Back then, Caitlin and I had raced into the café

on hot days, scrambled onto stools, and ordered sundaes served in big, fluted glass cups and coated with gooey fudge. We'd laughed and giggled—about what, I have no idea now—and chatted with folks who knew us, knew my aunt and Caitlin's parents. Then we'd be off again, finding friends, playing, loving every minute of our summer.

"Welcome," someone called as the door closed behind me.

I spotted a waitress wiping down the lunch counter. She wore the uniform I remembered, tan with a yellow apron tied around her waist; a name tag above her breast pocket identified her as Melinda. Her dark hair was pulled back in a bun. I guessed her age as approaching forty.

"Hello," I said, and walked over.

She looked me up and down. "Sorry, we're not hiring."

I wondered if my colossal failure at my L.A. job had made the rounds of Hideaway Grove and everybody knew I needed to find work.

"Although we could use the help," she complained, and shoved a menu into the slot behind the napkin dispenser.

No one was seated at the counter. I glanced to my left. One booth was occupied; a woman dining alone, fixated on her phone lying beside her plate.

Melinda seemed to read my thoughts. "It'll get plenty busy in a few minutes, as soon as the early birds start pouring in."

Through the pass-through behind the counter I saw a cook in a white T-shirt and chef's beanie at the flattop.

"You're covering the café alone?" I asked, and slid onto a stool in front of her.

"I'm not supposed to be, but yes, I am," she grumbled. "What will you have?"

Sarah had recommended today's special, the chicken-fried steak. A laminated photo clipped to the front of the menu showed it served with mashed potatoes, smothered in country gravy, and, surely, loaded with calories. I'd never have eaten this kind of meal when I was out to lunch with the women I'd worked with in L.A., but I was starved and I'd surely worked off hundreds, probably thousands, of calories turning the storage room into a sewing studio.

"I'll take this," I said, and pointed.

"Special!" Melinda called to the cook.

"So where are the other waitresses?" I asked.

"Just one." She poured a glass of water and sat it in front of me. "Earlene. She didn't show up."

A little jolt hit me. Earlene hadn't told her employer she was leaving town?

"She didn't call and explain?" I asked.

"Nothing to explain. She got her schedule mixed up—again. She does it all the time. I phoned her house but she didn't answer. Goodness knows what she's thinking." Melinda shook her head in disgust. "It's just as well. We don't need any more trouble around here."

"From Earlene?"

"All that talk about how Iris was murdered. I don't know what Earlene was thinking, carrying on like that," Melinda complained. "Well, let me tell you this—Iris certainly wasn't murdered, even if not everybody liked her."

I sat up straighter, startled by what seemed to be a clue to Iris's murder falling into my lap.

"Somebody didn't like her?" I asked, and tried to sound casual.

Melinda glanced toward the rows of booths. I looked that way, too. The woman seated alone seemed to sense our stares and looked up. I recognized her—Miss Merriweather's niece Joyce.

"Can I get you anything?" Melinda called, forcing more sweetness into her voice than I'd yet heard.

Joyce shook her head.

"You're sure?" Melinda smiled broadly. "I'm right here if you need anything. Just let me know."

Joyce focused on her phone again, ignoring us.

Melinda heaved a relieved sigh and murmured, "She ties up a table for hours playing on her phone, wanting refills and extras, sending her food back, and has yet to leave a decent tip."

"But you still give her great service," I noted.

"I don't dare do otherwise. Not for Joyce."

"You were saying you'd overheard people talking who didn't like Iris," I said, anxious to get back to a possible clue.

Melinda shrugged. "I hear things."

I leaned in. "Who? Who didn't like Iris?"

Melinda paused, frowned, then sighed. "Good gracious, I wait on so many customers I can't remember which one said what. But it was somebody. I'm sure of it."

So Earlene was right. There was, in fact, somebody in Hideaway Grove who didn't like Iris.

I definitely had a suspect.

I just didn't know who it was.

CHAPTER 9

In her haste to leave Hideaway Grove, had Earlene simply forgotten to call the café and let them know she wouldn't be coming to work? Or had she deliberately not told them because she didn't want anyone to know she was leaving and where she was going, because she was hiding out?

Hiding out from the town gossips—or something more sinister?

I left the Parliament Café with my head as full of questions as my belly was of the daily special, wishing I had some answers—and that I hadn't eaten so much.

Of course, if Earlene had returned my earlier phone call I could have gotten some info from her. I'd like to think she was simply having a pleasant time with her sister and didn't want to be reminded of her troubles by calling me back. But another part of me wondered if she had other reasons for ignoring my call.

I had to find out.

I stopped in front of the Eagle Art Gallery and pulled out my phone. Now that Melinda had confirmed Earlene's story that someone in the café had said they didn't like Iris, I was even more anxious to find out who it was. Maybe Earlene had calmed down enough now to talk about it. I called her. Again, her voicemail picked up. Once more I left a message and tried not to think she was deliberately ignoring my calls.

My phone chimed as I shoved it into my back pocket. I jerked it out, thinking it was Earlene, but saw Madison's name on the ID screen. A little wave of nausea hit me; I didn't know if it was the sudden reminder of my humiliation in L.A. or too much chicken-fried steak.

"What did you *do*?" Madison demanded when I answered.

I froze, too stunned to speak.

"Oh my God! It's all over the building! The building! Not just our floors—the entire building!"

"What?" I managed to say.

"You really had a major catfight with that supervisor of yours?" Madison asked.

"Well, no, not major—"

"You two were *screaming* at each other?"

"I wouldn't say we raised our voices—"

"And, oh my God, security was called?"

"Security? No—"

"And you had to be escorted from the building?"

"*What?*"

"That's *all* everybody is talking about," Madison told me.

"It didn't happen that way."

"I can't believe you did that," Madison said,

sounding testy. "And you didn't even tell me *first?* I had to hear it from *other people?*"

"Listen, Madison, everything you heard is a huge exaggeration. The entire incident is being blown completely out of proportion," I insisted.

"Yeah, right. I gotta go." She hung up.

I stood there, my mouth open, staring at my phone.

That's what people were saying about what happened? About *me?* That overblown, erroneous version had swept the entire building?

And I thought gossip was bad in Hideaway Grove.

I moved down the sidewalk, my head spinning, as I slid my phone into my pocket. Though I'd always known only a small chance existed that I could return to my job and prove I was worthy of the position, at least there'd been that small chance. I wanted that opportunity. But with that kind of thing being said about me—even though it wasn't true—there was no way upper management or HR would allow me to come back. Ever.

I paused, realizing I was at the corner. Up ahead was Sarah's Sweets. I could go there, pour out my heart and soak up Sarah's kindness and support. Across the street was Barry's Pet Emporium. Surely Caitlin would stop whatever she was doing and listen. All I had to do was ask. For a quick second Zack popped into my thoughts along with the fantasy that he'd lend a shoulder and comfort me.

But I couldn't bring myself to do any of those things. Instead, I went to Sarah's house, collapsed onto the bed, and fell asleep.

My so-called nap had stretched for hours, I realized, as I woke up in the pitch dark. I climbed out of bed and walked to the bedroom door. A weak glow shone from the night-light in the hall. The house was silent except for the gentle snoring coming from Sarah's room. I must have been more tired than I'd realized. Yet, somehow, I was still tired and wanted . . . something. I didn't know what, exactly, but decided some fresh air would help.

I slipped into the bathroom, splashed my face, whipped my hair into an updo, found my shoes and handbag, and left the house.

The night air was cool and still as I walked down Hummingbird Lane. Only a couple of houses had lights in the windows. No one was outside. A car glided past and turned right onto Main Street.

As I passed the entrance to the alley where Iris had been killed, I tried not to look but couldn't help it—not that I could see much. A single security light flickered from Sassy Fashions, the dress shop next door to Sarah's bakery, doing little more than deepening the shadows. I kept walking.

Apparently, I was the only person in Hideaway Grove who wanted some fresh air at this time of night. Not a soul was on Main Street when I rounded the corner and turned left.

For a few seconds I thought about texting Caitlin. She might still be awake. She'd suggested we meet at the Night Owl. But I wasn't really up to chatting. I had a little headache threatening and I felt kind of weird from sleeping so much. It didn't seem like the best time to do a lot of in-depth thinking, though I certainly had plenty to contend with—my job, my future, solving Iris's murder, and trying to come up with a good reason Earlene hadn't returned my calls.

Maybe I'd stop in at the Night Owl. While it wasn't like me to do much drinking—a glass of wine with friends was as wild as I usually got—having a beer seemed like just the thing at the moment.

I strolled down Main Street, taking in the peace, the solitude, the quiet. Every business was closed and most had only a dim light inside. When I paused on the corner to cross Main, I was surprised to see headlights in the distance headed my way. I darted across the street and hopped up onto the curb as the car swept past behind me. I whirled and watched as it made the quick turn onto Dove Drive.

A white car, I realized—or at least light-colored; it was hard to be sure under the street's old-fashioned security lamps. Nothing unusual about that. But was it my imagination, or had it sped up as I crossed the street? I stood there for a moment, thinking. Was it also my imagination, or was that the same car that had driven past me on Hummingbird Lane when I'd left Sarah's house?

My imagination, surely.

Still, I picked up my pace as I continued down Main Street and turned right onto Eagle Avenue.

Neon lit the night from the Night Owl's sign just ahead, about halfway down the block. Several cars sat at the curb.

Guess I wasn't the only person in town who wanted a beer tonight.

As I drew closer, two people walked out of the dark parking lot that adjoined the bar. Two men, I realized, as they headed for the Night Owl entrance. But not just any two men.

One of them was Zack.

I jumped back into the shadows and watched as the guy Zack was with opened the door and went into the Night Owl. Zack caught the door but didn't go inside. Instead, he turned in my direction.

I pressed myself flat against the wall of the building I was standing beside.

Zack stood there holding the door, his gaze sweeping the street and the sidewalk.

I refused to let myself move. I barely drew a breath. I was afraid he'd see me and come over. Not that I was doing anything wrong. I wasn't. But I looked awful. No makeup, my hair in a messy updo, wearing clothes that I'd—literally—slept in.

Bathed in the neon light, I saw that he was dressed in civilian clothes. But he might as well have been on duty the way his gaze probed the shadows. Did he sense my presence? Was that even possible?

I held my position, determined to wait him out. Finally, after one more visual sweep of the area, Zack went inside the Night Owl.

Breath left me in a single huff and I relaxed to the point of nearly collapsing onto the sidewalk. Then I got annoyed—at myself.

Why did I care what Zack thought of my appearance? I didn't, I decided. I couldn't have cared less, actually. I'd have been distressed about the way I looked no matter who it was. Right? Well . . . no. After all, I'd intended to go into the Night Owl knowing how bad I looked. Seeing Zack— well, seeing Zack made it different because . . . because . . . Actually, I knew why I cared—I just didn't want to think about it.

I spun around and headed back to Main Street, and stood there for a moment gazing up and down the street. Not another person was out. Every business was closed. The only places that might be open were the bars and all-night restaurants just outside of town. But since my car was still at the sheriff's crime lab, I had no way of getting there.

Still, I wasn't ready to give up and go back to Sarah's. I crossed Main Street and turned right toward the government center and village green.

Walking the streets alone at night in L.A. was unthinkable, of course. But I felt perfectly safe here. This was Hideaway Grove. Nothing bad ever happened in Hideaway Grove—well, yes, Iris had been murdered, but that was a rare, completely unrelated exception. It didn't mean the streets weren't safe.

Up ahead I saw Blue Bird Lane, the street Earlene lived on. I'd promised to keep an eye on her place so walking by seemed like a good thing to do, even if it was late. Turning the corner I saw that the neighborhood houses were dark. A few porch lights burned. Nobody was outside, not even a dog walker.

The street light closest to Earlene's house burned steadily, so much so that I felt exposed standing on the sidewalk. I headed down the driveway and stopped in the shadow of the house.

Earlene came fully into my mind. While I was annoyed she hadn't returned any of my phone calls so I could ask her for more info about Iris's death—and rid me of the nagging thought that she'd been somehow involved in the murder—I was also concerned that she'd gotten to her sister's house safely; San Diego was about a five-hour drive from here and anything could happen. It occurred to me then that I should have asked for her sister's phone number. It was probably inside

Earlene's house somewhere, in an address book or on a note stuck to the refrigerator. I thought about going inside and searching, but even with my best intentions the idea felt intrusive.

I looked at the front porch with the two white rocking chairs, barely visible in the shadows. Earlene had surely thought she and her husband would sit in those rockers together throughout their retirement. They'd bought this house with that in mind. They'd made a plan and followed it through. Now her husband was dead and she'd had to flee the town they'd both loved, under a cloud of suspicion.

The neighbor's dog barked, jarring my thoughts. Another dog nearby joined in, followed by a third. A wave of unease seeped through me, making me acutely aware of how alone I was. Everyone in the neighborhood was surely in bed, asleep. Would anyone hear me if I screamed?

I gulped down the unease that was threatening to turn into fright—irrational though it was—and hurried away from Earlene's house. Main Street was dark and lonely when I turned the corner and headed home. The barking of the dogs faded, then stopped, replaced by the sound of a car engine behind me. I glanced back and saw a sedan pull out of Earlene's street and cross Main.

My unease amped up. That car. It was the same one I'd seen earlier, the one I'd spotted twice tonight. I was sure of it. Well, pretty sure. I hadn't looked at the license plate. I'd noticed only that it was a light-colored sedan.

Maybe it was nothing.

I drew in a breath trying to calm down. Of course it was nothing. It *had* to be nothing.

Up ahead, the street seemed to stretch forever
into the darkness. Movement off to my left, on the
other side of Main Street, caught my attention. A
person stood in the shadows. A man? A woman? I
couldn't tell. Was I being watched?

I walked faster.

The engine sound came back, startling me as it
drew nearer from behind. The car—the same
sedan I'd just seen—cruised past me, slowly. My
heart beat faster. I chanced a look, but couldn't
see the driver. The car suddenly sped up and made
a quick left turn onto Eagle Avenue.

I looked around. No other cars. The one person—whoever it was—that I'd spotted in the shadows had disappeared.

Panic set in.

A strange car was stalking me. I was totally alone
on the street. Where was law enforcement? Where
was Zack when I could actually use his help—at
the Night Owl, that's where. Having beer with a
buddy, probably chatting up a waitress, laughing it
up with friends.

Headlights appeared at the intersection of
Eagle Way and Main Street. My heart pounded.
The car must have made a quick U, and now it was
back. I edged closer to the storefronts, trying to
stay in the shadows. I watched the sedan. It didn't
move, just sat there, waiting. Waiting for me to
walk past? And then what? Drive up onto the sidewalk and run me down, like Iris?

I gulped down my runaway thoughts. Nothing
bad had actually happened. I was probably making
something out of nothing. I needed to calm down
and get ahold of myself.

I repeated those words over and over in my mind, trying hard to override my rising fear.

I couldn't do it. Panic took over.

The entrance to the alley that curved around and ran behind Sarah's Sweets and the other businesses that faced Main Street was up ahead. I broke into a run.

Only minimum light from the security lamp lit the area, barely enough to keep me from falling over something. My feet pounded on the asphalt. The sound echoed off the buildings, trumpeting my presence. My ears strained for the revving of a car engine.

Should I look for a place to hide? Keep running?

Iris had cut through this alley, too. Was she being pursued? Was she afraid, looking for a safe place to hide, wondering where the sheriff and deputies were when they were needed? And why had I come this way? The question screamed in my mind. I should have stuck to Main Street, not run into this dark, isolated alley where somebody had actually been murdered.

Too late to turn back now.

Fear drove me faster through the alley, then to an all-out sprint down Hummingbird Lane, where I blasted through the gate in the picket fence, raced to the back of the house, grabbed the spare key from under the yellow flowerpot, and let myself inside. I slammed the door, turned the lock, and fell back against it, panting and shaking.

Maybe I should move back to Los Angeles—where it's safe.

CHAPTER 10

I'd let my imagination get the best of me. That's what had happened. That's all it was.

I closed the gate behind me and headed down Hummingbird Lane, the morning sun on my face, a gentle breeze ruffling my hair.

A mysterious car roaming the streets last night? Stalking me? Lying in wait to cut up onto the sidewalk and run me down? This wasn't Los Angeles. It was Hideaway Grove. Safe, sane Hideaway Grove. What had I been thinking?

I mentally admonished myself, remembering how I'd gotten to Sarah's house, crouched under the front window, and watched for the mysterious car to pull up. It hadn't, of course. The whole thing was silly, really. Why on earth would anyone be after me? Why would they want to run me down, like Iris?

Just to prove to myself that nothing was amiss, I paused and gazed down the alley where Iris had been killed. I gasped. A half dozen people were gathered there. I spotted Sarah and several Main Street merchants, all of them crowded around Sheriff Grumman.

This couldn't be good.

For a few seconds I was tempted to go back home, but Sarah spotted me and waved me over.

As I drew nearer, I saw that all the Dumpsters were open, and debris—trash bags, boxes, and general junk—was scattered through the alley.

"The Dumpsters were ransacked last night," Sarah said when I stopped beside her. "Would you just look at this mess?"

"Somebody was inside the Dumpsters?" I cringed. "Gross."

"Geraldine saw it this morning when she opened her shop, and called Ed," Sarah said.

Geraldine owned Sassy Fashions Dress Shop next door to Sarah's bakery, and she looked pretty sassy herself, going all-out to look less than what I suspected were the forty-plus years behind her. Her hair and makeup were done, she had on three-inch pumps, and a dress that nipped her waist and clung to her curves.

"This is twice something has happened here," Sarah said.

I remembered she'd mentioned that the boxes and plastic Geraldine had left outside her back door for recycling had been strewn through the alley a couple of nights ago.

Sheriff Grumman turned my way, then pushed out of the crowd of women surrounding him.

"Well, look who's at the scene of the crime," he said, glaring at me. "Our one-woman crime wave."

Everybody turned toward me.

"Since you arrived in Hideaway Grove," the

sheriff said, "a woman was killed and there've been two cases of vandalism right here in the alley behind your aunt's bakery, and Earlene's house was broken into. Nothing like this happened here until you showed up."

"Earlene's house was broken into?" I asked. "When?"

"Last night," the sheriff said.

"Earlene is missing," Sarah said. "Nobody can find her. She's not home, she's not at the café, and she wasn't there yesterday, either."

"She's not—"

"Where were you last night, Miss Chandler?" Sheriff Grumman asked, his booming voice echoing through the alley.

All the women crowded closer, eyeing me sharply.

"Oh, Ed, you can't be serious," Sarah said. "You can't think Abbey was involved in any of this."

"Either she is, or this is all one big coincidence," the sheriff said. "I don't put much stock in coincidences."

"But Ed—"

"Sheriff! Sheriff!" Anna from the thrift shop pushed her way to the front of the gathering. "Sheriff, all of this so-called mischief is getting worse. Where will it end? With a robbery? A theft? Someone injured—or worse? We need to know what you plan to do to protect our businesses."

"This can't wait," Geraldine insisted. "What are you going to do?"

The women pressed closer, all of them making demands at once.

"Now, ladies—"

I backed away, my heart pounding, only to bump into someone. Someone tall with a rock-hard chest, radiating a primal heat. I looked over my shoulder.

Zack frowned down at me. "Let's take a walk."

He reached for my arm but I pulled away. We walked through the alley while the chatter behind us escalated, and rounded the corner onto Hummingbird Lane. He planted himself in front of me, crowding me against the side of the building.

"You want to tell me what's going on?" he demanded.

I was unnerved by the sheriff's accusation and the questioning looks I'd gotten from the women watching. Now this? My fear morphed into anger.

"Why don't you tell me," I countered.

Zack glared at me for another few seconds, then took a breath.

"I saw you last night," he said.

Had he spotted me from the doorway of the Night Owl and somehow recognized me in the darkness? He couldn't have.

"That was you standing on Main Street in the shadows," I realized, and my simmering emotions boiled over. "Oh, well, thanks a lot! I was being stalked by some mysterious car and a crazed driver! Scared out of my mind, thinking I was going to be run over like Iris! And you saw it? And were just standing there? And did nothing?"

"Whoa, slow down," he said, sounding way too calm to suit me at the moment. "Slow down and calm down."

The very last thing I intended to do was calm

down. Zack must have read that in my expression because he moved a little closer and lowered his voice.

"Calm down. Tell me everything that happened so I can help you."

His tone was so soft, so reassuring, my emotions flipped and I could have easily burst into tears.

I guess he read that in my expression, too, because he grinned and said, "Okay, not that calm."

A little giggle bubbled up taking the edge off my emotions. I drew a breath and let it out slowly.

"Now," he said. "What happened last night?"

"I went for a walk."

"What time?"

"I don't know, really. Late. Everything was closed."

He frowned. "You were on the streets alone, after dark, when none of the businesses were open?"

When he said it like that it did sound kind of reckless, but I certainly wasn't going to acknowledge his point.

I told him about the car that I'd seen several times, how it seemed to be following me.

"Didn't you notice it when you were standing on the corner?" I asked. Surely he had. He was a trained observer. He'd have noticed the make and model, probably the license plate number.

"I saw it, but so what? A car driving down Main Street isn't unusual." Zack shook his head. "What I saw was you. Leaving Blue Bird Lane."

I paused, realizing what this little talk he wanted to have with me was really about.

"Earlene lives on Blue Bird Lane," I said. "Her house was broken into last night. You think I did it."

His expression gave nothing away. "Did you?"

"And then what?" I demanded. "You think I ran

into the alley, jumped in the Dumpsters, and tossed everything out just for the heck of it?"

"Did you?" he asked again.

"No! Of course not!" I rolled my eyes. "Did you see me go into the alley?"

I figured he had, but I wanted to know for sure.

Zack paused, looking uncomfortable. "I got a text. My dad's in the hospital. When I looked up again you were gone."

Earlene's break-in, the Dumpster vandalism, even Iris's death suddenly seemed unimportant.

"Shouldn't you be at the hospital?" I asked.

"Denver," he said. "The rest of the family is with him."

"Is he okay?"

"Two blocked valves." Zack touched his chest. "Everything went well. He'll go home soon."

"Scary," I said.

I thought of my parents. I couldn't remember the last time I'd heard from them. They were off on one of their research trips, likely some place where the inhabitants had never heard of cell phones, let alone the internet.

"So, last night," Zack said, bringing us back to the reason we were standing there.

"What happened at Earlene's? The break-in. What was taken?" I asked.

He hesitated a few seconds, then said, "This morning the neighbor noticed the window in the back door was broken. The place was ransacked. Didn't look like anything was taken, but we can't be sure."

This incident certainly wasn't going to encourage Earlene to return to Hideaway Grove anytime soon.

"Earlene is missing," Zack said.

"She's not missing."

He narrowed his gaze at me. "How do you know?"

Great, now he probably thought I'd murdered her and was about to confess where I'd hidden her body.

"She's in San Diego visiting her sister. I went by there to take her the sugar cookies. Remember? You saw me leave the bakery with them," I said. "She was in the process of packing. I offered to watch her house while she was gone. She told me to use her spare key under the flowerpot by the back door."

"People need to stop leaving their keys there." Zack uttered a disgusted grunt, then looked hard at me. "The key. Let me see it."

Now I was the one who uttered the disgusted grunt. I scrounged though my handbag and pulled out the key. I laid it flat in my hand and shoved it toward his face.

"Should we go over there now and try it," I challenged, "so I can prove it's actually Earlene's house key and that it will actually open her door so you'll know I'm telling the truth?"

Zack's sharp gaze stayed on the key and I knew he was considering doing just that.

"Why would I break in when I already had a key?" I demanded.

He paused for a long moment, then shrugged, the only acknowledgment I expected to get that my reasoning made sense. It wasn't much, but I was relieved by it.

I dropped the key into my bag again.

"So you went for a walk last night with the intention of checking on Earlene's house?" Zack asked.

I didn't want to get into the story of how my life had fallen apart to the point where I'd given up and taken a nap, and had awakened kind of cranky.

"I didn't *go* to Earlene's house. I wanted some fresh air so I went for a walk, and decided to check on her place while I was out," I said.

Zack seemed to be considering my reasoning so I pushed ahead before he could come up with something else to ask me.

"Why would someone break into Earlene's house?" I said. "I mean, why her house, of all the houses in Hideaway Grove? She didn't own anything of great value, did she? Not like Miss Merriweather's house."

Zack shrugged. "I think somebody wanted to scare Earlene, shut her up. All her talk about Iris's death being a murder didn't sit well with people."

"You think it was one of the town merchants?" I asked, and couldn't keep the surprise out of my voice.

"I don't like to think it, either. But there's a lot of worry among the merchants about the success of the festival. They feel their livelihoods are threatened. Can they keep their shops open, feed their families?"

"What about the Dumpsters getting tossed on the same night?" I asked. "Coincidence?"

I figured it had to be. What would Earlene's house and Dumpsters full of trash have in common?

"Coincidence? Maybe." His brows drew together, as if he'd just realized something. "Did you cut through the alley last night on your way home?"

I hesitated, knowing that admitting I was in the alley—present at both of last night's crime scenes—wouldn't look good. Still, I couldn't lie about it.

"Nobody was back there," I said. "The Dumpsters hadn't been tossed when I passed them."

Zack got quiet, seeming to digest everything I'd said. I saw a lingering look of doubt on his face, yet got the idea he wished I'd given him a different answer so my involvement wouldn't be questioned.

He sighed, resolved, and said, "You need to tell the sheriff."

I drew back a little, not wanting any more interaction with Sheriff Grumman, who seemed to twist my every action into something more than it was, something criminal.

"There's nothing to tell," I insisted. "I saw nothing going on when I was at Earlene's house. Nobody was there. Nobody was on the street. The neighborhood was silent. I'd have thought the whole area was deserted if the dogs hadn't started barking. I didn't—"

"Dogs started barking?" Zack leaned closer.

"You know how dogs are. One starts and others chime in—"

"They don't bark for nothing. The burglar must have showed up while you were there." I saw concern in his expression along with—was that fear? For me? "Abbey, you were in serious danger."

"If a burglar really was there at that exact moment, he was interested in the house, not me." Another thought flashed in my head. "The white car. The white car I saw, the one that I thought was stalking me. Do you think the driver was the burglar?"

I was relieved to realize that whoever was driving the car last night wasn't pursuing me. I just happened to be on Main Street and at Earlene's house at the wrong time. Still, I may have been in some danger, as Zack had said.

"Take my number," he said.

"I'm not calling the sheriff's station——"

"It's my personal number. Call me if something like that happens again, or you get . . . scared, or whatever."

I hesitated for a few seconds, then pulled out my phone and we exchanged contact info.

"Promise me you won't go out, alone, at night again," Zack said. "Promise me."

I didn't have a chance to say anything because at that moment Sheriff Grumman came around the corner from the alley. He glared at us as if he was the high school dance chaperone and he'd caught us making out behind the gym.

Zack walked over and spoke quietly with him, then they both came back.

"You have something you want to confess?" the sheriff asked.

I didn't like that he'd phrased it that way, but there was nothing I could do about it. I explained what I'd told Zack about Earlene's visit to her sister, my walk to her house last night, and the shortcut I'd taken through the alley because I thought I was being followed.

"Followed? By a car?" he wanted to know. "Who was it?"

"I don't know. I didn't see the driver," I said.

"What kind of car?"

"A sedan," I said. "Light-colored."

"Another white car, huh? That's convenient."

"I'm just telling you what I saw," I said, feeling a bit annoyed with him and his attitude.

"You make it sound like you're as innocent as the new-driven snow," Sheriff Grumman said. "But as far as I'm concerned, you're still under suspicion. Now more than ever because I know you're lying."

"I'm not—"

"You can't show up in a town like Hideaway Grove and think you can fool anybody. I know Earlene. I knew her husband. I've known them both for years." Sheriff Grumman leaned a little closer. "And I know for a fact that Earlene's sister lives in Phoenix, not San Diego."

My mouth dropped open but I couldn't get any words out.

The sheriff leaned even closer. "You're a liar, Miss Chandler. You're involved in everything that's happened here. I'm going to figure out exactly how you're involved and, rest assured, I'll make sure you go to jail."

CHAPTER 11

Had Earlene deliberately lied to me about her intention to visit her sister? Had she wanted to mislead me with her explanation that she was traveling to San Diego? Or was she confused, lost somewhere, trying to figure out whether her sister lived in San Diego or Phoenix?

That's all I could think of when I left Sheriff Grumman and Zack on Hummingbird Lane and headed for Sarah's Sweets. Well, that wasn't all. The fact that the sheriff seemed convinced I was responsible for every crime that happened in Hideaway Grove ranked pretty high up in my thoughts, too.

I pulled out my phone and called Earlene again. My call went to voicemail once more. I left another message.

Anna and Geraldine, two of the women who'd been in the alley grilling Sheriff Grumman about last night's vandalism, were in the bakery when I walked in. I'd stood out back with the crowd of merchants long enough to know that none of them had been happy with the sheriff's response to the vandalism, and judging from the expressions I saw on everyone's face, that hadn't changed.

"What a mess," Anna grumbled, motioning toward the alley.

"I'll call the crew that cleans my shop, have them come over and deal with it," Geraldine said, shaking her head. "More money spent."

"I'll contribute," Anna said.

"Me too," Sarah said. She plucked several muffins from the display case. "Anybody want a muffin? On the house."

"We certainly deserve something good this morning. But I'm going to pass." Geraldine planted her hands on her trim waist. "Anything that tastes as good as your muffins can't be good for my figure."

"I'll take one," Anna said, and grabbed one.

"I can't help thinking this is all Earlene's fault," Geraldine complained. "Somebody is trying to get back at her for her crazy talk about Iris's death being a murder, and we're paying the price for it. Why else would someone vandalize our alley where Iris was killed?"

"And somebody did break into her house. Broke the window in the back door to get in," Anna agreed, and pushed a large chunk of the muffin into her mouth.

"I hope the sheriff sent somebody to repair the damage," Sarah said.

Anna nodded, her cheeks puffed out with muffin.

"And where is Earlene anyway?" Geraldine asked,

her annoyance growing. "All this trouble she brought on, and where is she?"

Anna paused as she gulped down the muffin, and worry lines creased her brow. "You don't think . . . I mean, is it possible that whoever broke into her house . . . ?"

"Kidnapped her?" Geraldine asked, her eyes wide.

"Or . . . murdered her?" Anna asked.

All of them drew a breath in shock and horror.

"Earlene's visiting her sister in San Diego." I blurted it out. "I was there when she left."

"San Diego?" Sarah frowned. "Doesn't her sister live in Phoenix?"

"Why didn't she tell people her plans?" Geraldine demanded, and seemed more annoyed knowing Earlene was safe.

"I heard she didn't show up for her shift at the café yesterday," Anna said.

"Who told you that?" Geraldine asked.

I figured it was Melinda, the waitress I'd chatted with when I'd had lunch there. She seemed ready, willing, and more than anxious to let everyone know Earlene had missed her shift, leaving her in the lurch, so I was surprised when Anna spoke up.

"Joyce. Joyce Colby told me," Anna said. "She stopped by the shop yesterday and mentioned it, wanted to know if I'd seen her. She said Earlene didn't show up at the café. Not a call or anything. Melinda was really put out about the whole thing."

"Oh, that's just like Earlene," Geraldine grumbled. "She never thinks ahead."

"Why did she leave town?" Anna asked, biting into another muffin as she turned to me. "You were there when she left. What did she say?"

"Earlene was upset about . . . everything," I said, feeling the need to defend her for some reason.

"Seeing Iris killed." Sarah shook her head. "That was a terrible thing to witness."

"Earlene's feelings were hurt that everybody questioned what she saw, and nobody believed her," I added.

Anna and Geraldine had the good grace to look uncomfortable, though knowing Earlene wasn't in danger seemed small consolation.

"At least she's safe," Sarah pointed out.

"I don't know what is happening to Hideaway Grove these days," Anna said, finishing off another muffin. "Vandalism, a break-in, all on the heels of poor Iris's death. It's all so shocking, so unexpected."

"I guess we never know what our future holds," Geraldine said. "All the more reason to enjoy every moment."

"And just when things were looking up for Iris," Anna said. "Here she was in a new town, in a new job, with friends—even a man in her life."

Geraldine and Sarah both turned to her, eyes wide.

"Iris had a man in her life?" Geraldine exclaimed. "Iris?"

"I had no idea," Sarah said.

"I suppose Iris wanted to keep it quiet. You know how people talk," Anna explained. "They met secretly. I saw them together in the alley behind my shop several times. Not that I was spying, or anything like that, I just happened to see them there, together, out my back window."

"Doing what?" Geraldine demanded.

"Just standing there, talking," Anna said.

"Who is he?" Geraldine wanted to know.

"I've no idea," Anna said.

"So he wasn't a local," Geraldine concluded. "How did they behave? All lovey-dovey? Or something more . . . restrained?"

Anna thought for a few seconds. "They seemed comfortable with each other, familiar."

"Someone Iris had known before she moved here?" Sarah wondered.

"Oh, my. A secret lover!" Geraldine declared. "Who'd have thought it of Iris!"

Anna and Sarah both gasped at the idea.

"I'll bet he was married," Geraldine announced.

"Why would you think such a thing?" Anna asked.

"Why else would they be sneaking around?" Geraldine demanded. "Why meet in a back alley? Why not show themselves out in the open, on Main Street?"

The women fell into a stunned silence, which I was happy about since it gave me a chance to do some quick thinking. Iris had been seen meeting a man in the alley. Was that why she was there on the day she was killed? And if so, where was the man, her supposed secret lover, when she'd been hit by the car?

Just as I opened my mouth to voice the question, the bell chimed as the front door opened and Caitlin walked in.

"Heard you had some problems out back last night. Valerie told Dad first thing this morning," Caitlin said, and turned to me. "Valerie owns the Owl's Nest bookstore across the street."

"That must have gotten his morning off to a rough start," I said.

She shrugged. "You know Dad."

"Nobody was hurt and no damage was done," Anna said. "Just a lot of mess to clean up. Tell your dad he might want to have a word with the sheriff."

"I'm sure he will," Caitlin said.

I wanted to turn the conversation back to the man Iris had been seen with in the alley, but Geraldine drilled Caitlin with a suggestive smile and said, "So . . . how are things . . . *going?*"

"Fine. Business as usual," Caitlin said, ignoring the not-so-subtle innuendo in Geraldine's question.

"No. I mean, how are things going with—"

"Pillowcases." Caitlin held up the small shopping bag she'd brought in with her. "Mom sent them."

"Gretchen will be so happy to have those when she gets back," Anna said. "Any word from her?"

"Nothing definite," Sarah said. "She's loving spending so much time with her grandchildren."

"Well, I hope she gets back here soon," Anna said, shaking her head. "The pastor's wife dropped by my shop yesterday—even *she* was talking about Earlene. Anyway, she's getting anxious about the church making their donation quota with those dresses."

Sarah came from behind the display case. "Come look at our new sewing studio Abbey made."

She crossed the room, and with a grand gesture slid back the pocket doors and everybody went inside.

"Oh, my, what a change," Anna declared.

"I never realized this was such a big space," Geraldine said, gazing around the room.

Anna gestured to the sewing machine on the worktable. "You're sewing the dresses, Abbey? You're not waiting for Gretchen to come back?"

"Well, actually—" I began.

"You know, I've got all the bed linens from my grandmother's house in storage, and they're quite lovely," Geraldine said. "I'll pull the pillowcases out and bring them over."

The bell chimed in the bakery and Sarah hurried out to wait on customers.

"I've got to get back to the shop. I'll get those pillowcases to you soon," Geraldine said, and left the sewing studio.

"I'll spread the word," Anna promised, and followed Geraldine.

I watched them both go, feeling a bit scrambled. Caitlin blew out a heavy breath as she placed her shopping bag of pillowcases on one of the tables, making me think she felt something similar—but it went far deeper.

"What was Geraldine getting at?" I asked. "What kind of thing is *going on* that she wanted to know about?"

Caitlin twisted her hands together, intertwining her fingers, then drew in a big breath.

"She wanted to know about the wedding." Caitlin forced a smile. "I'm engaged."

"Engaged!" My mouth flew open. "That's wonderful!"

Caitlin managed a small nod.

"All these times I've seen you, and you never mentioned it?" I asked.

She gave me an apologetic shrug. "I know. I'm sorry. I should have. But, well, we never seem to have time to talk about much."

I realized I'd been dealing with my own situations and hadn't made a true effort to catch up, which didn't make me feel so good about myself.

"My fault, too," I said.

My gaze dropped to her left hand. No ring. She seemed to read my thoughts.

"I don't wear it when I'm working at the shop," she said. "I do the groomings and, well, I don't want to take a chance on it getting damaged or washed down the drain."

"Well, congratulations," I said. "Who's the lucky guy?"

"Scott Freedman. His family owns the tire shop out by the freeway. My dad is thrilled."

"When's the wedding? Have you chosen your colors? What venue?" I said. "I want to know everything."

Caitlin nodded toward the street. "I have to get back to the shop."

"Sure. But we have to get together and talk. I need to hear all the details," I said. "Tonight. Tonight we'll meet. How about the Night Owl? Eight o'clock?"

"Sounds good," Caitlin said.

I followed her out of the sewing studio and closed the pocket doors behind me. Caitlin waved and left the bakery.

Geraldine was gone but Anna stood at the counter helping herself to another muffin. Sarah was on the phone in the kitchen leaving me alone with Anna, and presenting me with the perfect opportunity to get more info from her about seeing Iris in the alley behind her store.

"So Iris must have been meeting that man, her

secret lover, in the alley the day she was killed." I tried to make my comment sound casual but concerned. "I wonder where he was when Iris was struck by the car. Did you see him?"

"I didn't, but I wasn't looking for him either," Anna said, the muffin halfway to her mouth. "I can only see into the alley when I'm in my office at the back of the store."

"Were you in your office that day? Did you see the car that hit her?" I asked.

Surely if she'd witnessed anything, the whole town would have known about it by now. But it never hurt to ask.

"I was arranging a display of Haviland teacups and saucers I'd gotten last weekend from an estate sale when it happened," Anna said. "Geraldine came into the shop and told me. You know how she likes to share gossip—I mean, news. We watched out my back window as the sheriff and paramedics arrived. Geraldine insisted—she wasn't going to miss all those men in action."

"And you didn't see the man Iris usually met?" I asked, bringing her back to the question I really wanted answered.

"I didn't see him. And if Geraldine had laid eyes on a strange man, she would definitely have commented," Anna said.

"Did you see him later, maybe?"

Anna paused for a few seconds, thinking. "I'm sure I'd have noticed if he was there. He always parks on Hummingbird Lane, near the entrance of the alley. It's the only car that ever parks there."

"What kind of car was it?"

"Nothing special. Just a car. Light-colored. White, maybe."

Another white car? Or was it *the* white car that had run over Iris in the alley?

"He couldn't possibly have been there," Anna insisted. "If he had been, he'd have gone into the alley to see about Iris. What else would a gentleman caller do? I mean, even if he was married he'd come forward at a time like that."

Anna's reasoning was sound—if, in fact, he was Iris's boyfriend.

"I'll put out the word that you're making those dresses," Anna promised. "I'll get you more pillowcases."

"Well, actually—"

Anna swiped the last muffin from the tray, waved, and left the bakery. I watched her go, thinking that she'd provided a little info about the day Iris was killed. But she'd also presented me with more questions. Who was the man in the alley? Was he involved in Iris's death?

I sighed and my shoulders slumped.

I was never going to solve Iris's murder.

CHAPTER 12

I grabbed the tray from the top of the display case that Anna had picked clean of muffins and took it into the kitchen, rinsed it, then slid it into the dishwasher. Sarah finished her phone call—an order for four dozen cupcakes, it seemed—and headed for the cupboard near the oven.

"What can I do to help?" I asked.

Her gaze took in the kitchen. "Everything is pretty well under control for today. I don't know of anything—oh, wait. The soiled aprons in the bin need to be washed. Can you take them home with you?"

A memory of my summers here flashed in my head, a big truck idling in the back alley and a man in a white uniform coming into the bakery.

"Don't you have a laundry service for them?" I asked.

"Used to. Their prices went up, so I decided I'd do them myself. Maybe I'll try them again one day," Sarah said.

"Have you ever considered doing something different with the aprons, maybe colored ones instead of white?" I asked. "Something in a soft pastel green or pink that would complement the bakery's colors?"

"Most of my creativity goes into my decorating." Sarah waved her hand toward the case displaying several gorgeous sheet cakes, and gave me a rueful smile. "I don't know what color or pattern would look best on a new apron—which is why I'm sticking with white."

I understood, since what little creative talent I had went into picking out clothes—or used to, back when I had a job.

"I'll take them home tonight and run them through with some bleach—they'll be the whitest white they can possibly be," I promised.

"That Anna," Sarah mused as she pulled canisters of ingredients off the cupboard shelves. "Thinking Iris was secretly meeting a man in the alley. And Geraldine egging her on, suggesting he was married. That's how gossip starts and runs rampant in this town."

"You don't think there's any truth to Anna's claim?" I asked.

"I'm sure she saw a man in the alley. But was he with Iris, or did they happen to be there at the same time coincidentally? And the rest of it—him being Iris's secret lover, and a married man. It's nothing but speculation."

I couldn't disagree, which did nothing to help my theory that he might be another suspect.

Sarah sorted through her mixing bowls, signaling she was finished with this topic of conversation. She'd never been one for gossip.

"Would it be okay with you if I went through some of those boxes stored in the sewing studio?" I asked. "I can organize them, make them easier for you to check out and see what you'd like to keep or maybe get rid of."

"That would be wonderful. Honestly, some of those boxes have been packed away for so long, I'm not even sure what's in them," Sarah told me. "Plus, several of them belong to Gretchen, things she brought over when we were planning to turn that room into our new dining area and gift shop."

I wasn't sure how I'd possibly know the difference between items that belonged to Sarah and those Gretchen had brought in, but I was glad to have a task that would occupy my time. While I'd thought that being in Hideaway Grove and enjoying tranquility, serenity, and peace and quiet would be a grand idea, the truth was that I needed more to do to fill my days.

It would help if I had my car.

The thought reminded me of Sheriff Grumman, then Zack popped into my head—which annoyed me, for some reason.

Determined to put them both out of my mind, I went into the sewing studio, closed the pocket doors behind me, and studied the mound of storage boxes stacked on the tables. But instead of pulling one down and diving in, my mind spun in a different direction—back to Iris and her relationship with this unknown man, her supposed secret lover. I'd like to think he and Iris were, in fact, happily involved with each other, but I wondered if that were true. If so, why did they meet secretly in the alley?

Maybe he was married, as Geraldine had suggested. Being involved in an extramarital relationship was bad—I'm old-fashioned like that. But maybe there was something more to it.

My thoughts rushed further, taking the possibility to a darker place. Maybe he'd decided to break it off. Maybe Iris, scorned, had threatened to tell his wife. Had he gotten rid of Iris to silence her? That scenario was a distinct possibility.

I definitely had another suspect. And, once again, I had no idea who it was.

I couldn't bring myself to open any of the storage boxes, so I sorted through the pillowcases Caitlin had brought over that her mom had donated. All of them were soft pastel colors, and two had ruffles on the hem. I imagined they'd been used years ago in Caitlin's room, remembering how her mom had doted on her, her only daughter.

Another memory popped into my head. Caitlin had an older brother. Tony had ignored us during those summers I spent here, which suited us fine. I wondered now what had happened to him, reminding me how I'd been out of touch with everyone here in Hideaway Grove for so many years. I realized, too, how little effort I'd put into catching up with everyone here since my return. I'd make sure to ask about Tony when I met up with Caitlin at the Night Owl tonight.

I turned my attention back to the pillowcases and added them to the stock on hand, then divided them up by color, solids, and prints. They'd make great dresses. Gretchen should be pleased with them when she returned.

But maybe there was no reason to wait. The idea flashed in my head. Sarah had contacted Gretchen and gotten her okay to use her sewing machine. I'd been overwhelmed when I'd tried before—not even getting past two minutes of the YouTube video or page three of the instruction manual. But I felt stronger now—or maybe it was just boredom. Either way, I could do this. I could figure out the machine and make the dresses myself. I had basic sewing skills. I was smart. I could do this.

I grabbed my phone and found the YouTube video on that particular make and model that I'd looked at before. My confidence in my big idea vanished three minutes in when I saw in detail how different this machine was from the one I'd used all those years ago during sewing classes at the rec center. According to the video, there was something called an arm and a hoop, and instructions on how to use a stabilizer, whatever that was, plus an explanation of the gizmo I'd need to download from the internet.

I watched for a few seconds more, then put my phone away, dismayed. Here was something else I didn't have a handle on—Iris's murder, my car, my old job, my life, my future. The list kept growing.

I drifted to the big front window that faced Main Street, pulled back the shade, and peeked out at the traffic. Cars, trucks, SUVs. All sorts of vehicles, all of them allowing their owners to come and go as they pleased.

I missed those days. I missed my car.

For a moment I thought about what I'd do if Sheriff Grumman hadn't towed my BMW to the crime lab. I could leave town, get out from under his accusations. I could just take off, drive north, maybe, see something new and different. Or I could—well, none of that really sounded as if I'd like it. I was more of a stay-in-one-place kind of person, thanks to my parents, who'd dragged me all over the world during my teenage years.

Sadness settled over me, and just as I was starting to feel even more sorry for myself, my phone rang. I was surprised to see Madison's name on my caller ID screen. She'd been upset with me the last time we'd talked, so I'd doubted I would hear from her again.

"This place is crazy," Madison declared when I answered. "Crazy."

From the tone of her voice I knew that she'd moved on from her anger with me during our last conversation. I felt as if I'd been tossed a lifeline, a chance to hang on to the one remaining thread that connected me to my previous life—the life I'd worked so hard to attain and I'd wanted so badly.

"I'm glad to hear from you," I told her. "The last time we talked you were definitely mad at me."

"Yeah, so? Friends can get mad and still be friends," Madison said. "Oh my God, listen. Have I got news for you."

"Let me hear it."

"That supervisor of yours," Madison said. "Oh my God, I'm hearing the craziest stuff about her. Crazy stuff, I tell you. Crazy."

I hoped that meant something good for me.

"What's happening?" I asked.

"Everybody knows her," Madison said. "Somebody in every department has had trouble with her."

"You asked every department?" I asked.

"Sure did," she announced. "And look, here's what else. I found out where she used to work and

I called there. I pretended it was for a job reference, you know, kind of sly-like. I talked to somebody in their HR department—"

"You actually called their HR?" I asked, stunned.

"Oh, yeah, sure. But the person I talked to wouldn't say much one way or the other—probably worried about some kind of lawsuit, or something. So I asked around some more and I got the name of somebody she'd actually worked with, and I called her."

"You did?"

"Get this." Madison drew a big breath. "Everybody hated her. Everybody. She was nothing but a backstabbing control freak. Nobody could stand her. She was always screwing over somebody to make herself look good."

Relief swamped me. "So it wasn't just me she turned against?"

"Oh, no. You were one of many," Madison told me.

The relief I felt edged toward anger.

"Too bad our HR department didn't find that out before they hired her," I said.

"They didn't push. I push," Madison said. "So, there you go. That's what I've got so far. Don't worry. I'm still on it."

She hung up before I could thank her.

"Wow . . ." I mumbled as I put my phone away. Madison was killing it. She'd brought her A-game to the investigation.

Maybe I should get her to come to Hideaway Grove and investigate Iris's death.

No, I decided as I turned away from the window. I needed to up my game. I needed to push, like Madison was doing.

What I really needed, I realized, was more information.

But where would I get it?

"I'm closing a few minutes early today," Sarah said as she slid open the pocket doors and peeked into the sewing studio where I'd spent the afternoon.

I looked up from the storage box I'd pulled from the stack and opened. It was the third one I'd gone through, so far. Most of what I'd discovered was linens—napkins, tablecloths, and placemats in a variety of colors and patterns. I figured they'd been intended for the dining area Sarah and Gretchen had wanted to add to the space.

"You're leaving now?" I asked, noticing she was holding her handbag. I'd never known Sarah to close early, so I said, "You're not sick, are you?"

"Oh, no. Nothing like that. There's a meeting for the arts and crafts festival tonight. We've got committee vacancies to fill and progress reports on preparations to hear about," she said. "Would you like to go? We can always use fresh ideas."

I glanced at the time on my phone. I was supposed to meet Caitlin at the Night Owl tonight.

"I just hope this meeting will be productive," Sarah said. "I really don't want everybody to get bogged down talking about Iris, speculating on what might have happened. And now that Earlene has left town, I'm afraid that's all everybody will want to talk about."

I thought about Earlene and how she still hadn't returned my phone calls.

Seeing my hesitation, Sarah held up the two bakery delivery bags I hadn't noticed.

"I'm bringing cookies—chocolate chip," she said, offering an enticing smile.

"I'm in." I hopped out of my chair. "I'll stop by the pet store and let Caitlin know I might be late meeting her tonight."

I left the bakery with Sarah. As she locked up, she explained where the committee met inside the courthouse near the village green.

"See you there," I promised.

I stepped off the curb to cross Main Street just as a car swerved across the double line. I jumped back. The car lurched right, then left, and finally straightened up. As it passed me I got a good look at the driver. Miss Merriweather. I glanced around. Other pedestrians watched, then turned away and kept walking.

CHAPTER 13

Barry's Pet Emporium hadn't changed much since I'd come here all those summers ago. The same bell clanged when I walked inside, and I was greeted by the same, not unpleasant smell of the dogs, cats, birds in their cages, and fish in their bubbling aquariums. The aisles were stocked with food, litter, and toys, and a small array of collars and leashes.

At the rear of the store I spotted Caitlin's dad standing behind the checkout counter, rifling through a stack of papers. He'd changed, I couldn't help but notice, even though the store hadn't. Gray hair, thinning on top, stoop shoulders, and a belly that pouched out attested to the years that had passed. The permanent scowl I remembered on his face was still there, however.

I'd thought Caitlin would still be here, since it was nearly closing time, but I didn't see her. The only other person in the store was a man studying an assortment of small dog figurines on a shelf

near the puppy pads. I saw him in profile and realized he was maybe a few years older than me. Tony,
I figured, Caitlin's brother.

I walked closer and saw that he was tall, with
broad shoulders and a strong jaw, dressed in jeans,
hiking boots, and a blue plaid shirt. His dark hair
was cut short and neatly styled. When he glanced
at me, I saw that he was—wow—quite handsome
in a rugged sort of way.

"Hi," I said. "Tony?"

"No," he said, and grinned. "I'm—"

Something caught his attention across the store,
and he seemed to tense and melt at the same moment. I followed his gaze and saw Caitlin as she
walked out of the stockroom.

I melted a bit, too. He was Scott, her fiancé.
That look on his face could mean nothing else. I
was simultaneously thrilled for Caitlin and envious
that she'd found a man who obviously loved her so
much.

Caitlin spotted us and froze. She seemed to melt
a little herself. Quickly she glanced at her father,
saw that he was focused on his paperwork, then
drew in a breath and walked over.

"Hello," she said, sounding somewhat formal.

"Hello," he murmured, and it seemed to take
extra work on his part to get the word out.

Caitlin glanced at me. "I see you've met Mitch."

Mitch? This guy was Mitch? I was sure she'd told
me her fiancé's name was Scott. Who was Mitch?
And why was he looking at her that way?

He struggled for a few seconds to break eye contact with Caitlin; the atmosphere between the two
of them was so thick I could hardly breathe.

"Mitch Delaney," he said.

I introduced myself.

"Abbey is visiting for a while. Her aunt owns Sarah's Sweets," Caitlin said. "Mitch makes custom furniture. His pieces are highly sought after. Internationally, actually."

"Impressive," I said.

Mitch shrugged modestly. "Caitlin's the one with the real gift."

She blushed. He smiled, as if her pink cheeks were the most delightful thing he'd ever seen.

"Did you know she painted these?" Mitch asked.

He gestured to the shelf where the dog figurines were displayed. There was a variety of breeds, all of them about three inches tall and painted in exquisite, realistic details.

"You did those? They're beautiful," I said, stunned. "I didn't know you did anything artistic."

"Well, not really . . . artistic. It's just something I enjoy," Caitlin said. "Dad prefers to focus the store's inventory on the pets' needs only, but he lets me sell a few of them here."

"They're very much in demand," Mitch said. "In fact, I'm here to get one."

"Another one?" Caitlin asked.

"A gift for my . . . grandmother," he said. "It's her birthday."

Caitlin frowned. "Didn't you just buy your grandmother one for her birthday a few weeks ago?"

"Oh. Well . . . yes, but that was my other grandmother."

She gestured to the figurines. "Which one would she like?"

"I'm trying to decide between the beagle and the shepherd," Mitch said. "What do you think?"

This seemed like the perfect time for me to leave.

I told Caitlin I was going to the festival planning meeting and I might be late meeting her at the Night Owl, but didn't add that we *definitely* needed to talk tonight. She nodded, but I don't think she heard me. I said good-bye to Mitch. I don't think he heard me, either.

I found the festival committee's meeting room on the first floor of the courthouse. The building was old, with dark wood, wide corridors, and tall ceilings giving it an air of stately dignity. A murmur of voices filled the meeting room as I stepped inside. Chairs were set up theater-style in front of a head table, backed by the American and the California state flags, and large framed photographs of people whom I guessed were Hideaway Grove government leaders, past and present.

Along the rear wall, refreshments were available. I spotted Sarah's cookies, a tray of sliced fruit, and a punch bowl of something orange and frothy surrounded by tiny cups. About a dozen or so people milled around, talking in low voices, helping themselves to the treats. Most of them were older women dressed in comfortable clothes and sensible shoes. A few were accompanied by men, husbands, I guessed, few of whom looked as if it was their idea to attend the meeting.

I spotted Sarah and Jodi across the room and was about to join them when a familiar warmth swept over me and a flash of gray caught my eye. Zack, in his uniform, stepped in front of me. My heart did a little flip-flop.

"I'm surprised to see you here," I said.

He shrugged. "Just checking on things."

"I can see why you're concerned. This looks like a rowdy crowd," I said. "I hope you already called for backup."

He grinned, which made me grin, too.

"Is this part of an official investigation?" I asked.

"Mostly I was hoping for a couple of those cookies," he said, and nodded toward the refreshment table.

"Iris's death, maybe?" I asked. "Her murder?"

Zack had told me that he doubted Earlene's assertion that Iris's death was deliberate, but I figured it wouldn't hurt to ask.

"There's a lot of knowledge in this room. You never know what you might overhear."

He'd said it in a casual manner, but something about his tone caused a wave of concern to sweep over me.

"So now you believe Iris was murdered?" I asked.

"I wouldn't go that far."

"Do you have a suspect? A person of interest?"

Zack didn't respond. His gaze roamed the room, leaving me with the feeling that, even though he was carrying on this conversation with me, he was also taking in everyone and everything around us.

"Somebody who's here? Now? In this room?" I asked.

A half smile pulled at his lips and he leaned a little closer, bringing a wave of heat with him.

"Or maybe I'm here to check out . . . somebody else."

His "somebody else" caused my breath to catch.

Zack gave me a final grin—complete with one dimple—and sauntered out the door.

My thoughts swirled around for a few seconds, as if the room were spinning.

Had he meant he was here to check out *me?* The notion made my heart beat a little faster and set a warm glow alight in my belly. Or had he said that for cover, so I wouldn't think he was actually here because the sheriff's office had identified a suspect—or a person of interest—who was here in this room, right now?

I looked around as Zack had done. More people had come in. I knew a few of them, but not many. And the few I knew hadn't been easy for me to talk to, to get info from, because they'd all been busy tending to their jobs and businesses.

Maybe I should attempt to eavesdrop, as Zack had been apparently doing, and uncover some clues. Still, I knew that wouldn't be enough.

Madison and my phone call with her earlier flew into my head. She'd gotten in-depth info about my supervisor in L.A. because she'd pushed for it. I had to push. I had to get closer to the folks in Hideaway Grove if I was going to find Iris's murderer. But how?

"Better grab a cookie before they're all gone," somebody said in my ear.

I turned and saw Jodi standing beside me, then checked out the refreshment table and saw that only a few of Sarah's chocolate chip cookies were left. There was, however, plenty of fruit still on the tray.

"That Anna," Jodi grumbled in a low voice.

"Eats everything in sight, then complains that her health is bad. Honestly, a woman her age ought to have more sense."

I spotted Anna with three cookies balanced on a napkin in the palm of her hand while she bit into another one.

"And you know Geraldine wouldn't be here tonight. Not when all our attendees are women and their husbands." Jodi uttered a disgusted grunt. "Oh, I swear. Never fails. Would you just look? There's Brooke Collins parading around in those yoga pants again."

I remembered Brooke from the summers I'd spent here and from my encounter with her the morning I'd arrived in Hideaway Grove. I hadn't liked her. Apparently, I wasn't the only one.

Jodi lowered her voice and leaned closer. "Brooke's married to Dr. Collins, the dentist. They've got a house in that new section on the other end of town. Very upscale, very expensive. And she doesn't let anybody forget it."

I had no idea Jodi was this wired into the town gossip. I'd have to spend more time with her.

"Attention," Anna called. "Could I have everyone's attention, please?"

The meeting hadn't been called to order yet, so most people were still milling around, chatting and eating. The three women gathered behind the head table looked up, confused and slightly annoyed.

"Attention," Anna called once more. "Could I have your attention for a quick announcement?"

The room quieted down and everyone turned to Anna.

"All of you who brought pillowcases to donate

should put them by the refreshment table," Anna
said.

I noticed then that several bulging bags were
piled up beside the table. Apparently, Anna had
spread the word about donations, as she'd promised. There must have been dozens of pillowcases
in the bags, to add to the dozens already accumulated in Sarah's storage room waiting for Gretchen's return.

"Or you can drop them off at Sarah's Sweets."
Anna pointed at me. "Abbey—Abbey Chandler, I
know most of you remember her from her summer visits here—will be making the dresses until
Gretchen returns."

I gasped, stunned.

Heads swiveled throughout the room until their
gazes landed on me. I opened my mouth but I
couldn't get any words out.

"And as you all know, the pastor's wife is anxious
to meet the church's donation quota that's fast approaching," Anna went on. "So let's all get those
pillowcases to Abbey. I know she'll do a beautiful
job on the dresses."

"Are you serious?" someone exclaimed.

Everyone in the room turned, their gazes hom-
ing in on Brooke.

"Abbey has no artistic ability," Brooke declared,
then uttered an ugly laugh. "I remember that
sewing class we all took at the rec center. That skirt
she made was . . . well, it was hardly recognizable
as a skirt."

If I didn't already dislike Brooke, I certainly
would now.

A grumble went through the meeting room.

"Abbey has been working on the dresses already," Anna declared, speaking up in my defense. "She's opened a sewing studio at the bakery. I'm sure she'll do a lovely job on the dresses."

"She took it upon herself to turn the storage room into the sewing studio," Sarah announced. "It's terrific."

A few heads nodded around the room, which I appreciated.

"All I meant was," Brooke said, backpedaling a bit, "that Abbey's chosen profession is in the business world, not the arts. I'm sure most everyone heard Sarah brag over the years about Abbey's master's degree and that international corporation she works for in Los Angeles. I think she'd be better suited doing something that draws on her experience and education, such as filling one of our committees' vacancies. Maybe the committee Iris was in charge of."

Heads nodded around the room, accompanied by mournful grumbles as everyone remembered Iris.

Jodi leaned close and whispered, "Say 'no.'"

"How about it, Abbey? Do you think you could handle working on that committee?" Brooke threw the words at me like a challenge.

"Say 'no,'" Jodi hissed again.

"Well?" Brooke asked. "You don't think working on one of our committees in little Hideaway Grove is beneath you, do you?"

Everybody stared, putting me on the spot. Despite Jodi's insistence, I couldn't back down.

"I'd be happy to take on running the committee," I announced. "No problem."

"Well, that certainly solves one major problem on our agenda tonight!" Anna declared.

"I'll drop everything off to you at the bakery," one of the ladies at the head table called.

A sigh of relief went through the room and everyone started chatting among themselves again.

Jodi shook her head mournfully and walked away.

"Sorry, I should have warned you," Sarah said quietly, suddenly appearing beside me.

I started to feel a bit icky.

"Iris was in charge of the donation committee," Sarah explained. "It's the committee that contacts businesses and individuals, and asks them to donate items for the big raffle at the festival. It's a major fundraiser."

"That doesn't sound so bad," I ventured, hoping it really wasn't.

"It's the worst committee to head up," Sarah said.

"How many other people are on the committee?" I asked.

"So far?" Sarah grimaced. "Well . . . none."

"But surely other people will volunteer—"

"They won't. Nobody likes canvassing Hideaway Grove, asking for raffle donations," she said. "The newest person in town gets that committee. That's why Iris had it. It's a tradition."

"A tradition to stick the new, unsuspecting person with the worst job?"

"Sorry," Sarah said again, then gave me a smile. "I'm sure you'll do a fantastic job."

"Let's get the meeting started," someone called.

I noticed that the three ladies at the head table were sorting through papers and taking their seats. As I followed Sarah toward the rows of chairs, I saw that Zack had come into the meeting room again. He stood at the back, beside the door, his hands resting on his belt, looking around.

It was hard to believe he was actually here to make sure there was no trouble; I'd never seen a more well-mannered group of people. I figured the worst that could happen was a polite squabble over who reached first for the last chocolate chip cookie. If anyone was going to actually cause trouble it would be me confronting Brooke for maneuvering me into heading up the festival's most dreaded committee.

So I was left to wonder again if, in fact, Zack was here to question someone in Iris's death. He'd denied it when I'd asked him earlier, but that was probably standard Sheriff's Department policy. He'd told me the folks in this room had a lot of knowledge about, well, everything in Hideaway Grove. He might be here to get that information—but I needed it more.

He didn't really believe Iris had been murdered, so I wondered how hard he'd try to question anyone here. Not that I doubted his ability, but if he wasn't committed to the investigation, how good a job could he do? If he wanted to discover something important, he'd have to push for it.

I'd push.

If I had a uniform and a badge, I'd question whomever I thought could help. If I had the backing of the Sheriff's Department, I'd—

It hit me then that, no, I didn't need those things.

Like a flash of lightning, I knew exactly how I'd get the information I needed.

"Excuse me," I called, and darted to the front of the room, the idea taking shape in my mind.

The three ladies at the head table looked troubled at my interruption, but I pushed ahead.

"I'm throwing a pillowcase party," I announced, and put all the enthusiasm into my voice that I could muster. "My aunt Sarah was so kind to donate her storage room for the sewing studio, and I'm committed to making pillowcase dresses, so I want to invite all of you to join me."

Many of the ladies in the audience perked up, interested.

"Bring your sewing machine and gently used pillowcases, if you have them. I'll have everything else we need to make the dresses," I explained, the whole thing coming to me in a flash. "We'll enjoy getting together, working on a project for a good cause—and I'll even make sure we have some of Sarah's delicious cookies for refreshments."

A happy murmur went through the gathering.

"All the details will be announced soon. See you then!" I declared, and headed for my chair.

I felt Zack's gaze on me—a frown, really, as if he suspected I was up to something.

I ignored him and made a point to smile at all the ladies who looked my way.

As Zack had said, everybody here had a lot of knowledge about Hideaway Grove. One of them—or more—knew something about Iris's death, and I was going to find out what they knew when I had them confined in my sewing studio.

I was going to solve Iris's murder—which, I was afraid, might be easier than figuring out how to operate Gretchen's sewing machine.

CHAPTER 14

When the festival planning meeting broke up I stayed behind with Sarah, Jodi, Anna, and a few other women to clear the room. While they wiped down the refreshment table and washed the punch bowl and other dishes in the adjoining kitchen, I stacked the chairs in the back corner of the room.

"Let me help." A young woman about my age grabbed one of the chairs. "I'm Phoebe. You don't remember me, do you?"

I paused and looked closer at her. Red hair, big blue eyes, and a scattering of freckles across her nose and cheeks. She had on jeans and a simple T-shirt that she'd accessorized with minimal jewelry. In my mind I aged her backward to when I'd visited here as a child.

"Phoebe. Of course," I said, remembering her. "One of the last summers I stayed with my aunt."

"My family had just moved here," she said.

I recalled that she'd been one of the girls Caitlin and I had hung out with in Sarah's storage room, listening to music, practicing dance moves, reading fashion magazines, and fantasizing over the hottest boy bands. I'd liked her.

"I was so glad to make friends," Phoebe said with a genuine smile.

I understood her smile. Having a friend, especially at that age, meant everything.

"We took the sewing class at the rec center," Phoebe said. "Remember?"

"Oh, yes. That skirt we all had to make."

"Mine wasn't that great," she said.

"Mine turned out really bad."

"Well, no, not really bad," she offered.

"It was awful."

"Yes, actually it was, but only a tiny bit more awful than mine," Phoebe admitted, and we both laughed.

"You still live in Hideaway Grove?" I asked.

"Yep. Still here. Are you visiting your aunt, or moving here permanently?"

"Visiting, for now."

"I think it's great you're making the pillowcase dresses."

"You should come to my pillowcase party," I said.

Phoebe shook her head. "My sewing skills are really basic."

"Since we're not making skirts, your skills should be fine."

We both laughed again.

"I work at the drugstore," Phoebe said. "If you want to make a sign announcing your party, I'll post it in our window."

"That would be great."

"You should ask Connie if she'll post one. Connie," she explained. "Connie's Fabrics. I'm sure she'll help."

I figured I might be asking Connie for help on a lot of things.

"Great idea. I'll do it," I said.

The ladies who'd been washing dishes came out of the kitchen, switching off the lights and gathering their belongings.

"Ready to go?" Sarah called.

Phoebe and I made quick work of putting away the last of the chairs, I grabbed the bags of donated pillowcases, and we all left the room, everyone chatting about what had been covered during the meeting.

Outside the courthouse the streetlights had come on, though it wasn't quite dark yet. The shops were all closed; a few people strolled the sidewalks, some walking their dogs. Several cars cruised Main Street.

I stopped when we reached Eagle Avenue; the glow of the Night Owl's neon sign down the block beckoned.

"I'll drop those pillowcases at the bakery," Sarah offered.

"Thanks. I'll be home later." I passed the bags to her, then turned to Phoebe. "We should get together and catch up."

"Come by the drugstore," she said.

"Come to the pillowcase party," I told her.

We waved and the group moved on. I stopped at the corner and dashed across Main Street, then froze when I stepped up on the curb. Zack stood in the shadows, still in uniform, waiting.

Waiting for me, it seemed.

I wasn't sure whether to be flattered, suspicious, or worried.

I compromised on cautious—then changed my mind. If I could push the ladies who'd show up at my new sewing studio for information, I could push Zack, too.

"Still out gathering clues for the crime you don't believe really happened?" I asked, stopping next to him.

"You never know when you might run into somebody worth taking a closer look at."

Judging by the playful grin on his face, I didn't think he was talking about a murder suspect, but I wasn't going to be distracted.

"Did you run into somebody with information while you were at the festival committee meeting?" I asked.

Zack shrugged. Obviously, he wasn't going to tell me anything about the investigation.

"Not saying, huh? Well, maybe you can tell me this," I said. "When will I get my car back?"

"Anxious to get back to Los Angeles?"

"Anxious to have my car back," I told him.

A horn blew. Tires squealed. Zack spun, instantly on alert, following the sound.

I turned with him and spotted a gray SUV that had stopped quickly as a white car pulled out from Blue Bird Lane onto Main Street. The white car motored along at a sedate pace, the driver seemingly unaware of the near collision. When it passed us, I saw that Miss Merriweather was behind the wheel. I also saw that the right fender was dented.

We both watched as the two vehicles disappeared down Main Street.

"Miss Merriweather shouldn't be driving," I said.

Zack sighed heavily, signaling that he agreed but there was nothing that could be done about it.

"I heard she keeps passing her driver's license renewal test," I said, recalling how Caitlin had mentioned it after we'd witnessed another close call caused by Miss Merriweather. "Her niece should do something."

"Joyce Colby? Won't happen. She's got her own problems to deal with." He turned back to me, a deeper frown on his face now. "So what's with all the questions about Iris's death?"

"I told you—I want my car back."

He narrowed his eyes at me and shook his head. "No, I think it's something more than that."

It was, so I didn't say anything.

"You think Earlene is right. You think Iris was murdered." Zack didn't pose his thoughts as questions. They were statements.

I didn't like that he'd figured out my intentions so easily.

"You're not denying it." Again, another statement from him.

His gaze hardened and I could see him shift into deputy sheriff mode.

"Look, Abbey, stay out of it," he told me. "Let the Sheriff's Department handle it."

"Frankly, the Sheriff's Department doesn't seem to be handling it—at all," I told him. "Sheriff Grumman doesn't really believe Iris was murdered. He's just going through the motions of the investigation so his department doesn't look bad."

Anger flashed across Zack's face, but he drew a breath and calmed down.

"The Sheriff's Department doesn't need or want your help," he said. "We know how to run an investigation. We know what we're doing."

"I don't know what it would hurt if I—"

"*You* could be hurt." His anger spun up again. "If you're right, if Earlene is right, that means there's a murderer in Hideaway Grove. Do you want him to know you're looking for him?"

His words brought with them a sobering dose of reality. Still, I wasn't ready to admit that the possibility had frightened me.

"Will you at least find out when I'll get my car back?" I asked.

Zack drew in a breath, tapping off his emotions.

"I will," he said. "Come on, I'll walk you home."

"I'm not going home."

"Where are you going?" he asked.

"You're so good at investigations," I said, and couldn't resist a smug grin. "You'll figure it out."

He gave me a smug grin of his own and nodded down the street toward the Night Owl.

"Tell Caitlin I said hi."

I spun away but felt his gaze on me all the way to the Night Owl. When I reached the door I glanced back. Zack stood at the corner watching me. I jerked my chin and went inside.

I was never inside the Night Owl during my summer visits with Sarah, of course, but when I saw the place I felt as if I'd been in a dozen other bars like it. The lighting was low, accented by neon beer signs behind the bar and fake stained-glass lamps over the booths. Tables were scattered across the floor and stools lined the bar that stretched across the back of the room. In an adjoining room I saw a pool table and dartboard. A jukebox sat nearby. The place looked clean and safe—like everything else in Hideaway Grove.

There wasn't much of a crowd—two men at the bar, a few couples at tables and another one at the dartboard. I spotted Caitlin easily, seated at a booth in the corner, a beer mug in her hand. She smiled when I slid in across from her.

"How'd the planning meeting go?" she asked.

"I got roped into heading up the donation committee," I said.

"Sorry. I should have warned you."

I glanced at the bar and saw the bartender watching us. He was a big guy with an apron tied around his belly and a towel tossed over his shoulder. He gave me a what-are-you-drinking eyebrow bob. I asked for a beer.

"Brooke what's-her-name was behind it," I said.

"I never liked her."

"Me either. I really don't like her now," I said. "But I'm okay working on the committee. It will give me something to do."

I glanced at the bartender. He waved me over. I grabbed the glass, thanked him, and sat down again.

"Oh, and I'm throwing a pillowcase party to sew pillowcase dresses," I said. "I announced it at the meeting."

"Something new is happening in Hideaway Grove?" Caitlin's eyebrows bobbed. "Tell me about it."

"Nope," I said, and sipped my beer. "Not until I hear about you and your fiancé. Where did you meet? What does he do? What's he like? When's the wedding? I want to know everything."

"There's not much to tell, really." Caitlin gave me a small smile. "Mitch is a great guy—"

"I thought his name was Scott."

"It is."

"You said Mitch."

"I did?" Caitlin shook her head as if to clear her thoughts. "Scott. His name is Scott. Scott Freedman. He works at the tire center near the freeway exit. His family owns it so he'll own it one day."

"What's he like?"

"Scott? He's a great guy. Great." She sipped her beer. "Both of our families are excited. They say we're perfect for each other."

"How long have you known him?"

"Forever. You know how it is in Hideaway Grove." Caitlin rolled her eyes. "We dated for, I don't know, something like two years. Getting engaged seemed like the next thing to do. Dad's thrilled. It's the only thing he's been happy about since Tony moved away."

"Your brother left Hideaway Grove?"

I was surprised and reminded, once again, how I'd been out of touch with everyone here for so long.

"Got married, moved to North Carolina. Tony was supposed to take over the pet store. Dad was crushed when that didn't happen. He always insisted he was building the business for Tony and me, his children. Tony wanted no part of it." She forced a smile. "Looks like it's up to me now."

"Is that what you want to do?"

Caitlin shrugged. "Sure. I guess. It's fine."

"It doesn't sound fine."

She straightened her shoulders. "It is. It's a

great business with a long history, profitable and stable. Mitch is totally on board."

"You mean Scott."

"Yes. Of course." Caitlin's cheeks flushed. She lifted her beer glass and uttered a quick laugh. "Too many of these things."

"So you're okay with taking over the pet store from your dad?" I frowned, recalling the talks we'd shared in Sarah's storage room all those years ago. "Weren't you wanting to move to Paris and paint?"

"I had a semester at art college, but Dad had a heart attack so I came home to help. He recovered, but Mom's still worried about him—me too, of course. So I decided to stay in town and . . . well, it just seemed like the right thing to do."

"Art school. That was a lot to give up," I said.

Caitlin shrugged indifferently. "I was probably never going to Paris anyway. Now Dad has this idea that Scott and I are going to form some sort of dynasty in Hideaway Grove. The pet store and the tire store are only the beginning."

I found myself slightly annoyed, for some reason, and decided to move the conversation to a happier topic.

"Your mom must be excited about the wedding," I said.

"She's all over it."

"When is it?" I asked.

"We haven't set a date yet."

"How long have you been engaged?"

She thought for a few seconds. "A little over a year now, I think."

"Why are you waiting to set a date?" I asked.

Caitlin shrugged. "We just haven't done it yet."

Another change in the conversation seemed in order.

"I was really impressed with the dog figurines you painted," I said.

"It's just a hobby." She waved away my compliment.

"Do you paint other things? Cats? Hideaway Grove's mascot, the ever-present owl?" I asked.

"Sometimes."

"They must sell well at the festival," I said. "Tourists love that sort of thing."

"No booth for me. Too expensive." Caitlin glanced at her phone and checked the time. "I'd better get going. I have to get up early in the morning."

We finished our beers, I paid our tab—Caitlin promised to get it next time—and we left the bar. Outside it was dark, just the streetlights and the Night Owl's neon sign illuminating the area. Another quiet night in Hideaway Grove. We agreed we'd get together again soon, and said good-bye. Caitlin headed down Eagle Avenue. I walked the other way toward Main Street.

At the corner, Zack stepped out of the shadows, startling me.

"Were you waiting here for me all this time?" I asked.

"Since you're convinced a murderer is on the loose in town, I figured you'd appreciate an escort home."

Considering how upset I'd been the night I'd thought a white car was stalking me around town, I appreciated his offer.

I looked up and down Main Street in both directions. There wasn't a car or a person in sight.

"Not exactly a wild night," I said.

"You never know when Miss Merriweather might show up."

The memory of how she'd nearly caused a crash earlier tonight flashed in my head—along with something I hadn't mentioned at the time.

"Did you notice there was a dent in the right front fender of her car?" I asked.

The right front fender. The same location as the damage to my car that had caused Sheriff Grumman to think I had struck Iris in the alley, the main reason he'd towed it to the crime lab.

Zack nodded slowly. "I noticed."

"How long ago was the fender damaged?"

"I don't know."

I didn't know either, but the possibility that it had happened recently filled my head along with the notion that maybe—just maybe—I'd found another suspect in Iris's death.

But Miss Merriweather? Sweet old Miss Merriweather?

Was it possible?

I'd have to find out.

CHAPTER 15

The dryer in the mudroom off Sarah's kitchen buzzed, pulling me out of my thoughts. I turned away from the back door where I'd been staring into the yard, and opened the dryer. Inside was the load of aprons from Sarah's Sweets that I'd promised to wash. I'd picked them up from the bakery earlier today, run another errand, and returned to the house to wash them. Luckily, it was a mindless chore because I couldn't stop thinking about last night.

Zack flew into my head, but only because he'd been standing beside me when I'd witnessed Miss Merriweather nearly cause another traffic accident—plus, he'd walked me home last night and waited on the front sidewalk until I waved from the living room window. I'd leaned against the glass and watched until the last second when he'd disappeared down Hummingbird Lane.

My imagination ran wild again, as it had last night, and I wondered once more what might have

happened between us if he hadn't been in uniform, hadn't been on duty, if he hadn't been concerned about the neighbors who might have been
watching us, if he'd held my hand or kissed me—I
was definitely picking up a vibe between us—or if
he'd asked to come into the house.

I posted a mental STOP sign in my brain, ending
those thoughts.

Better to think about Iris's hit-and-run.

Bad enough that Miss Merriweather's driving
had put another vehicle and driver, and herself, at
risk. But the thing I really couldn't get out of my
head was that dent in her front fender.

Had that dent always been there? Had I simply
not noticed it, or perhaps had never seen her car
from that angle?

Or was it new? New, since Iris's hit-and-run?

I pulled the aprons from the dryer, shook them
out, and folded them neatly into the big canvas
carryall Sarah had given me to use.

Was it possible that Miss Merriweather had
struck Iris with her car? The thought made me a
little queasy, but I stuck with it.

I'd seen her run up onto a curb, weave across
lanes, and pull out in front of another vehicle—
and goodness knows what other near-misses she
might have caused—and continue on her way,
seemingly not aware of what she'd done.

Could she have hit Iris with her car and not realized it? Maybe she'd gotten confused or simply
made a wrong turn and driven into the alley, then
had been so focused on finding her way out that
she hadn't noticed.

That alley. Mischief involving the Dumpsters
and boxes outside Sassy Fashions; Anna surveilling

the area out the back window of her thrift store; Iris there to meet a mystery man; Earlene there for reasons unknown—and which I may never learn since it seemed she had no intention of returning my phone calls. Who'd have thought the alley—of all places in Hideaway Grove—would be a hot spot for trouble, one that possibly involved sweet, kind Miss Merriweather in a hit-and-run.

"Oh, Miss Merriweather, you shouldn't be driving."

I whispered the words aloud as I gathered my things, looped the canvas carryall over my arm, and left the house thinking I might have another suspect—but not feeling so good about it.

Of course, I had other suspects. They paraded through my mind as I headed down Hummingbird Lane. There was the unknown person in Hideaway Grove who, Melinda at the café had told me, didn't like Iris. Next on my suspect list was the mystery man Anna had seen in the alley with Iris. I'd wondered, too, if Earlene had been involved.

Earlene—who'd disappeared—and two unknown suspects. Not much to go on.

I turned onto Main Street and Zack came to mind—but only because I was thinking about Iris's murder. He'd claimed the Sheriff's Department was investigating. I'd told him I doubted it, but he'd insisted. Maybe he was right. Maybe they had a suspect—with a name, unlike some of my suspects.

The little bell over the door chimed and the marvelous scent of vanilla hit me when I walked into Sarah's Sweets. Jodi and Sarah were both at the display case helping customers. I circled around them into the kitchen and started hanging the clean aprons on the pegs beside the back door. There was hardly room for them, thanks to the jackets, umbrellas, totes, handbags, and remaining clean aprons that hung there, but I squeezed them onto the pegs and put the carryall back where it belonged on the shelf in the stockroom.

When I returned to the kitchen Jodi was at the work island swirling chocolate icing onto dozens of cupcakes.

"Lots of clean aprons," I announced, glad I'd done something to help. "It's pretty crowded back here. More pegs would be good."

"I've told Sarah that over and over," Jodi said. "She just won't do it. Doesn't want to spend the money."

"How expensive is it?"

"I don't know." She gave me a slightly wicked smile. "But whatever it costs would be worth it to get that hottie Mitch Delaney in here to do the work. Have you seen that man?"

I couldn't help smiling—and I couldn't disagree. "I saw him at the pet store. He's good-looking."

"More than good-looking," Jodi declared. "He's got what I'm looking for in a man—I want to see him sweat, and I want to see him fix something."

Sarah finished with the customer at the counter and went to the sink.

"More pillowcases were dropped off for you," she said as she washed her hands. "I put them in the sewing studio."

"Everybody in town is talking about your pillow-case party," Jodi said. "It's about time people were talking about something positive."

I hoped they would still be saying good things

after they saw my struggle with Gretchen's beast of a sewing machine.

"Anna was in here this morning," Jodi said. "All she could talk about was what happened to Iris. She's put herself in charge of keeping watch in the alley, for some reason."

"Why?" I asked, wondering if something more was going on back there, and if I should question Anna about it.

"She's watching for that mystery man everybody thinks Iris was involved with, I suppose," Jodi said. "All she's seen so far is Joyce Colby back there, and I'm sure she's not having a secret rendezvous with anybody."

"The materials for the festival donations were dropped off," Sarah said. "I put them with the pillow-cases."

"Look what I had made." I pulled a stack of signs out of my tote bag that announced the pillowcase party. "I stopped by the office supply store this morning and had them printed. What do you think?"

I'd made the design myself on my laptop—an array of sewing notions surrounding the info about the pillowcase party. I'd picked a date and time for the party that would, hopefully, give me ample opportunity to learn to use Gretchen's sewing machine.

Sarah studied my sign with a critical eye, then nodded her approval. "I love the owl."

"Of all the owls in Hideaway Grove—and we've got dozens of them—I've never seen one quite like that one," Jodi said.

"My own creation," I said, and took a small bow. I'd cobbled it together from images I'd found online, a cartoon owl standing upright with slightly raised wings, rendered in pastel shades of green, pink, and yellow, outlined in tan.

"It's adorable," Jodi agreed, then huffed. "That Brooke has her nerve saying you can't do anything artistic, just because your sewing skills weren't so good—back when you were a child."

Another mention of sewing caused a tremor of anxiety to pass through me. Somehow—*somehow*—I had to figure out how to operate that complicated sewing machine *soon*.

"I thought you were very creative as a child," Sarah told me. "I wish your parents had encouraged it more. I suggested it to them several times but, well, you know how they were."

They were both academics. I'd had it drummed into my head since kindergarten that getting a lofty degree was expected, mandatory, really. My slight rebellion had been to pursue business.

I slid the stack of signs into my tote. "I'm going to post these in some of the shop windows. Is there anything I can do before I leave?"

Sarah glanced around. "Would you mind taking out the trash?"

I wasn't all that anxious to go into the alley where Iris had been killed, but I certainly wasn't going to refuse Sarah's request.

I pulled the trash bags out of the bins, tied them off, and pushed my way out the back door into the alley. I kept my gaze away from the spot where Iris had been killed, and hurried to the Dumpsters.

Something popped out from under one of the Dumpsters. I squealed and jumped back, then relaxed when I saw that it was a cat.

"Goodness, you gave me a fright," I said aloud, as if it could understand what I was saying.

It was a puffy, roly-poly ball of orange fur, with big green eyes, and seemed interested in my presence—or maybe just annoyed that I'd invaded its territory. Something about it seemed familiar; I must have noticed it around town somewhere before.

"You live around here?" I asked.

My first thought was that it was a stray, hungry, and had been hanging out at the Dumpsters hoping to find something to eat. I wondered what Sarah had in the bakery that I might fetch for it. But as I looked closer I saw that all its chubbiness wasn't fur. It was well fed, clean, and cared for.

I guess it had enough of me, because it scampered down the alley toward Hummingbird Lane. Concerned that it would dart out into the street and get hit by a car, I shoved the trash bags into the Dumpster and started to follow. But it pivoted, and with what looked like practiced ease, leaped onto the block wall that separated the alley from the neighborhood beyond, and disappeared.

My phone chimed as I headed toward the bakery's back door. I pulled it from my pocket and saw that Madison was calling.

"Oh, my God, girl. Are you sitting down?" she declared when I answered. She went on before I could say anything. "You have started something. I mean you have *really* started something—big-time."

I'd been in Hideaway Grove for days. How could I have started something in Los Angeles?

"What's going on?" I asked.

"You're not going to believe this. You're not

going to believe it! That supervisor of yours—the one nobody likes—well, upper management and HR just had a huge meeting about her."

"About what?"

"You."

"Me?"

"You and everybody else she's treated so bad," Madison said. "I heard they'd thrown around terms like 'hostile work environment' and 'retaliation,' like they were worried about a lawsuit."

I was stunned. "I never said I was considering a lawsuit."

"They think you might do it," Madison reported. "And if you do, I want to be the first to know."

Madison wouldn't want to miss out on a chance to spread that kind of gossip through the office, understandably so.

"So what was the outcome of the meeting?" I asked.

"I don't know. Details are still hush-hush. But it looks like you might be coming back to work here soon—I mean, really soon. Hang in there. I'm still on it." Madison ended our call.

I stood there for a moment, trying to take in what I'd just heard.

The notion that I'd be vindicated, welcomed back, restored to my position with the company stunned me. I'd never thought it would happen. I'd hoped for it, but it seemed like too much of a stretch.

The possibility floated through my mind—a phone call from a higher-up in management or HR telling me that my position was being restored, maybe even offering an apology, being welcomed by a, hopefully, new supervisor as I arrived at the office.

Then reality hit—if all that happened and I got my job back, how was I going to get there if I didn't have a car?

Somehow, after being in Hideaway Grove for less than a week, I'd gotten involved with so many things—things I couldn't leave hanging. I had to resolve them. Now.

CHAPTER 16

After Madison had rocked my world with the stunning turn of events that she'd reported during our phone call while I was in the alley taking out the trash, I'd grabbed my things, left the bakery, and headed down Main Street. I needed to get stuff handled, and a visit to Connie's Fabrics seemed like the best place to start.

The store was quiet when I walked in. A half dozen customers roamed the aisles, chatting softly. Display after display held bolts of fabrics in an array of colors, patterns, and prints. Low tables with comfy chairs held giant pattern books. Big cabinets held drawers of patterns. Notions were featured in a rainbow of colors, along with walls of other sewing necessities. A huge cutting table sat in the center of the store. Nearby were the sewing machines, everything from a basic model to one that looked even more intimidating than Gretchen's.

"Can I help you find something?"

I turned and spotted a woman looking at me with a welcoming smile. She was probably in her forties, I guessed, with short dark hair, and dressed in comfortable clothes.

"Connie." I read the name tag pinned to her blouse, and introduced myself. "You're just the lady I want to see."

She studied me for a few seconds. "Oh, of course. Abbey. I'd heard you were in town for a visit. Sarah must be thrilled."

"I remember you teaching the sewing class I took one summer."

"Oh, yes. At the rec center." Connie's smile soured a bit. "That—skirt, was it?—that you made."

My skirt was so bad she remembered it all these years later?

"It was supposed to be a skirt," I admitted.

Her smile brightened. "It was a good try. That was the end of your attempts at sewing?"

"No." I drew a fortifying breath. "Actually, I'm making pillowcase dresses for girls in Africa. I'm taking over for Gretchen until she gets back."

"You are?" she asked, slightly alarmed.

"And I'm hoping you can help me learn to operate Gretchen's sewing machine," I said.

Connie frowned, thinking. I was relieved she hadn't immediately told me I was a hopeless case.

"Sarah let me turn her storage room into a sewing studio and I'm throwing a pillowcase party so other people can make the dresses, too. So I'm kind of in a tight spot," I admitted. "I can't be the only person in the party who can't sew. But Gretchen's machine is so complicated. If you could help me figure it out—"

"No need for my help," Connie said, and waved away my concern. "Gretchen uses that machine mostly for embroidery. You don't need it. You can use a basic machine to make the pillowcase dresses, same as the one you used in sewing class that summer."

I felt a ray of hope well inside me. Could it be that simple?

"What kind of machine would I need to get?" I asked, glancing at the machines on display.

"You already have one. At the bakery. Gretchen took it there when she was going to make window curtains. It's simple to use. I'm sure you can pick it up again, easily."

I exhaled so hard I thought I might faint. The machine I needed had been at the bakery all along?

"Didn't you see it there?" Connie asked.

I shook my head, my thoughts racing. "It must be packed away in one of the storage boxes."

"Dig it out. I'm sure you'll be able to operate it with no trouble—just like riding a bicycle."

"Thank you, Connie. Thank you so much. This is such a relief."

"If you need help, just let me know." She gave me a big smile.

I pulled one of the signs I'd made from my tote bag and held it up.

"I'm spreading the word about the pillowcase party. Would you mind displaying it?"

Connie took the sign, studied it, then nodded. "That's an adorable owl. Very original. You know, you could make this with that embroidery machine, if you wanted to. And what a good cause you're taking on with those pillowcase dresses. Of course I'll display your sign. I'll put it in the front window."

Connie had been so sweet about everything I almost hated to ask her for anything else, but I figured that since things were going my way I should keep rolling.

"Thank you—again. And while I'm here, would you like to donate something for the raffle at the arts and crafts festival? I've taken over the committee from Iris."

Connie's smile vanished and she took a step back. The change was so sudden, so severe, it startled me.

"That Iris." Connie spoke the words as if they were bitter on her tongue. "What happened to her wasn't my fault. It wasn't."

I just looked at her.

Her expression morphed again, now to sadness.

"Well . . . honestly, I suppose it was," Connie said, and gulped hard. "Iris's death was all my fault."

I stood staring at her, too stunned to speak. Was she about to confess to killing Iris? Had I stumbled over Iris's murderer and not known it? And if so, what was I supposed to do about it?

Where was Zack when I needed him?

"So . . ." I said, unsure of how to proceed. The only thing I knew for certain was that I had to keep her talking. "What happened?"

Connie glanced around. I followed her gaze and saw that all the customers were clustered together on the far side of the store. She shrugged, as if dismissing them and her concern.

"I guess it doesn't matter if we're overheard," she said. "Everybody in town knows."

If Connie was about to confess to Iris's murder, fine. But that wasn't enough. I wanted to know what had happened, and why.

"I haven't heard," I offered, hoping to encourage her to keep going.

"I'll give you the short version," Connie said.

I'd hoped for the long version, but this was a place to start.

"Iris and I found each other on Facebook. Our old high school page. We were friends back then. I told her how happy I was living in Hideaway Grove, what a great place it was, and the next thing I knew she moved here." Connie shook her head. "How was I to know?"

"Know what?"

"All the problems she'd cause here." Connie flung her hands out, exasperated. "Everybody in town thought Iris was so wonderful. Everybody was singing her praises. Well, not everyone."

"Why not?"

"How do you think our hard-working, longtime librarians felt when Iris blew into town and started changing things? New programs, new hours, new this, new that, as if what was already in place wasn't good enough."

I could see how the librarians wouldn't be happy with Iris. Unhappy enough to kill her?

"And now . . . now . . ." Connie gulped hard and blinked away tears. "Now Valerie will hardly speak to me."

Valerie? Was she another suspect? Connie's accomplice?

"She blames me for Iris moving to Hideaway Grove." Connie sniffed. "And I suppose she's right. It's my fault."

Before I could ask anything, Connie turned her attention to the cutting table where a customer now waited. She hurried away leaving me with more questions, but with one consolation—if Valerie was a suspect, at least I had a name for this one.

I'd have to meet up with Connie again, away from her store and all the distractions there, and get more information. I had a good idea how I'd accomplish it. I also needed to find out who Valerie was, which should be pretty easy, and discover her connection to Iris's death.

I left Connie's Fabrics hoping Connie wasn't too distraught to remember to put my sign announcing the pillowcase party in her window. I had a number of other signs to distribute among the Main Street merchants, but decided I should run by Earlene's house and check on things since I was close. I crossed the street—after checking traffic twice in case Miss Merriweather was out and about—and headed down Blue Bird Lane.

Earlene hadn't returned my many phone calls and it seemed unlikely that she intended to do so, but I decided it wouldn't hurt to try again so I did. Sure enough, her voicemail picked up. I left a message. Either she was having a fabulous time with her sister, too busy to check her messages, or she simply wanted nothing to do with anyone from Hideaway Grove. I was sorry if she felt that way about me, but I guessed I couldn't blame her.

At Earlene's house, everything seemed to be in order on the front porch. No broken windows, no furniture overturned, no sign of another break-in. I headed down the driveway, then rounded the corner to the back porch—and froze.

A man stood at the back door, yanking on the board that covered the broken window.

"Hey!" I yelled, then realized how thoughtless, maybe even dangerous, my reaction was.

He looked over at me and smiled, and I realized it was Mitch Delaney. He had on jeans, work boots, a plaid shirt with the sleeves rolled back. A toolbox sat at his feet.

"Hey, Abbey," he said.

"Sorry," I said, exhaling heavily and feeling foolish. "I thought you were breaking in."

"Understandable." He nodded and stepped away from the door. "I'm just checking to make sure my repair is still holding."

I hadn't realized Mitch had been called on to fix Earlene's door after her break-in. But it seemed logical. He made custom furniture. He could nail a piece of plywood over a broken window with ease.

"No more trouble back here?" I asked, gazing around. Nothing looked out of place.

"Just pots overturned. I replanted the flowers. Should be okay. Deputies are keeping an eye on the place. I guess it was a onetime thing. Kids, probably," he said. "Anybody know when Earlene's coming home?"

"I haven't heard from her."

"Neither have I." Mitch shook his head. "I left her a message letting her know I'd fixed her door, although I guess the sheriff already did that. I didn't hear back from her."

I suppose that meant Earlene wasn't answering anybody's calls, but it didn't make me feel any better. I really wanted to talk to her, to quiz her about witnessing Iris's death and ask why she'd been in the alley in the first place. Maybe, somehow, she suspected that.

I grabbed the water dish Earlene kept on the porch for neighborhood pets, rinsed it at the spigot, filled it again, and put it back in its usual spot.

"I'd like to replace the window before Earlene returns," Mitch said. "I don't want her to come home to a plywood repair. A reminder of the break-in might upset her."

"If I hear from her I'll let you know," I said as I dug Earlene's house key from my bag. "I'm going to check inside."

When the sheriff had arrived here and gone inside after the neighbor reported the broken window in the back door, he'd found the place had been ransacked, according to Zack. I wanted to see how bad it was and straighten up before Earlene decided to come home.

Thankfully, the place wasn't in bad shape. No broken glass, no overturned chairs, no sofa cushions split open. It looked as if the burglar—kids, probably, as Mitch had suggested—had rifled through things looking for cash or other valuables. I put everything back in order, watered the plants, and brought in the mail. In the kitchen I checked the small corkboard that hung by the wall phone. Pinned to it were slips of paper with phone numbers on them. Only one had an area code I didn't recognize. Hopefully, it was Earlene's sister's number.

I pulled out my phone, accessed the internet, and looked up the area code. San Diego. I tapped the number into my contacts list and called it. A woman answered right away. I identified myself and asked to speak to Earlene.

"Oh, Abbey, you're that sweet girl who's watching the house," the woman said. "I'm Eileen, Earlene's sister. She told me all about you."

In my head I imagined the sisters looked just alike.

"You're in San Diego, right?"

"You bet. Lived here for two years now," she said.

Sheriff Grumman had insisted I was lying and that Earlene's sister lived in Phoenix. Now I knew his information was outdated.

"Is Earlene there?" I asked.

"She's getting her hair done."

"Would you ask her to call me when she gets back?"

"I'll ask her but . . . well, from what she's told me she's not all that happy about what went on in that town—except for you helping her, that is."

"I don't blame her," I said. "But will you ask her?"

"Of course."

I thanked her and ended the call.

I took one last look around the house, and left through the back door. Mitch was still there.

"Good timing," he said, and closed his toolbox. "I just finished."

"That's very thoughtful of you to help with the window."

He shrugged off my compliment and picked up his toolbox. "It's no big deal. Just helping out a neighbor. That's one of the reasons I moved to a small town."

"You're a city guy?"

"Big-city guy," he said as we walked down the driveway alongside the house toward Blue Bird Lane. "New York."

"Los Angeles," I said, feeling a bond with him.

"You're here visiting."

"And you're here to stay?" When he nodded I said, "It's a big change. You're okay with it?"

"Anxious for it. I had it all, or thought I did. High-paying job, expensive apartment, ambition."

"So what happened?" I asked. I knew it was awfully presumptuous of me to ask, but he seemed anxious to share his story.

"This guy I worked with, a friend, somebody who seemed to have everything . . . just ended it all."

I gasped.

"There was talk in the office. Suicide? Accident? Looking back I realized there had been signs of how stressed he was. I didn't see them because I'd been too busy, consumed with making the right moves, meeting the right people, clawing my way up to the next rung on the ladder." Mitch sighed. "I saw my future and I didn't like it. So I left. And here I am."

"Making custom furniture?"

"Doing what I love, the thing I should have been doing all along."

I thought about my job in Los Angeles, how I'd wanted it, the effort I'd put in to getting it, what I'd put up with, how devastated I'd been since it had been ripped away from me.

"So you just walked away?" I asked.

"Not *away*. *Toward* something. Something I really wanted to do."

It was hard to imagine. He'd had a life thousands of people would kill for, and he'd left it. Sure, living the quiet life in Hideaway Grove seemed appealing after what he'd been through in New York. But was this a *forever* place? Would he be satisfied with a life so different? Satisfied enough to stay? And would making custom furniture be an adequate substitute for the hustle and bustle, the drama and excitement, the prestige and extravagant lifestyle of living and working in New York?

"How's the custom furniture business?" I asked.

"It's coming along," he said, and seemed pleased with the progress. "I'm trying to get more local business. I hope the arts and crafts festival will bring attention to my work."

"You've got a booth?" I remembered someone mentioned how expensive a booth was at the festival. I hoped that meant Mitch had banked a large portion of that big salary he'd earned in New York.

"Yep," he said. "I'm making and selling miniature doghouses."

A jolt went through me, causing me to stop. "The size that will fit Caitlin's dog figurines?"

He stopped beside me and shifted uncomfortably. "I thought maybe she'd like to share a booth."

"Have you asked her yet?"

"No, not yet," he admitted. "But it seems like a natural fit, her dogs and my doghouses. She should get more recognition for her work. She's very gifted. She's got a great eye for color and she's—"

"—engaged. She's engaged."

Mitch looked away. "I know."

"Your interest in Caitlin is strictly business?" I asked. Again, it wasn't my place to question Mitch, but Caitlin was my friend and I didn't want Mitch to put her in an awkward situation.

"Of course. Of course," he said. "I think—"

Car tires squealed. I looked toward Blue Bird Lane expecting to see Miss Merriweather's white sedan involved in another near miss. Instead, a blue pickup truck slid to a stop in the middle of the street as an orange cat scampered in front of it and disappeared behind a house across the street.

"Cheddar," Mitch said, shaking his head. "That cat. She really does have nine lives."

"*Cheddar*? Cute name. It fits," I said. "I saw her in the alley behind Sarah's bakery. Who's her owner?"

"Beats me."

I wanted to get back to our conversation about Caitlin but when we headed down Blue Bird Lane, Mitch gave no indication he wanted to continue our talk. We wouldn't have had the chance anyway, I realized. Up ahead on the corner of Main Street, Zack was waiting.

CHAPTER 17

Zack and Mitch nodded at each other, the way men do. Mitch kept walking. Zack stepped in front of me. He wore his uniform. Apparently, he intended this to be an official meeting, but I wasn't going to give him the chance.

"What's up with Valerie?"

Instead of answering my question, Zack frowned. "Why do you want to know?"

I didn't answer his question, either. "Is it a secret?"

"Maybe. Why do you want to know?"

We could have gone round and round like this all evening. I huffed, signaling my annoyance, as if he didn't already see it.

"I'm heading up the arts and crafts festival raffle committee—"

"I heard. Sorry about that."

"I'm trying to contact all the businesses for a donation, and Connie mentioned Valerie," I said, pleased that it wasn't a complete, outright lie.

Apparently, Zack picked up on my partial outright lie.

"That's the reason Connie mentioned Valerie? You're sure?"

"Pretty sure." I sounded guilty, even to myself.

Zack squared his shoulders and his expression hardened.

"Has this got something to do with Iris's death? I told you to stay out of it."

"Well, maybe I could, if you'd tell me what's going on."

"It's none of your business."

"It is, as long as the crime lab has my car," I told him, and considered for a moment telling him that I knew Earlene was telling the truth and Iris had been deliberately hit by that car. Maybe then he'd be more forthcoming with information about the sheriff's investigation.

"Look," I said. "I just want to know what's going on."

Zack paused for a moment, as if considering what I'd said, then nodded.

"You want to know what's being said around town? Okay. People are talking about *you*."

"Me?"

He shrugged. "Rumors about why you came here."

"Such as?"

"You were left at the altar."

"You're kidding."

"Child Services took away your illegitimate baby."

I gasped. "Are you serious?"

"You had an affair with your boss."

"I never!"

"You embezzled money from your last job, then jumped bail."

"That's a complete fabrication—"

I stopped when I saw one side of his mouth draw up in a grin and that dimple appear in his cheek.

"I never did those things—but I'm tempted right now to swat a certain deputy sheriff for teasing me mercilessly."

A full smile bloomed on his face—complete with two dimples—and I couldn't help smiling, too.

"Is that some sort of clever questioning technique taught at the sheriff's academy?" I asked.

"Works pretty good," he said. "Usually."

"None of those crazy rumors are true. I'm here to visit my aunt. End of story," I said. "Now will you tell me what's up with Valerie?"

"She owns the Owl's Nest." He nodded down Main Street. "The bookstore."

"I know that. Connie told me Valerie would hardly speak to her now. Because of Iris."

"Connie and Valerie are sisters," Zack said, then rolled his eyes in who-knows-what's-really-going-on fashion. "Family."

"It seems Iris created more than a few problems in town," I said.

His expression hardened again. "You've been asking around."

"I have." He opened his mouth to tell me once more, I was sure, that I should stay out of the investigation. I cut him off. "I have an idea. Why don't we have an exchange of information?"

"I can't tell you anything about an active investigation," he insisted.

"Sure you can," I said, as if it would be easy, if he'd just go with it. "Look, I'm not asking for any super-secret classified information. But you've lived in this town a while. You know people. You know things. I've found out things. Maybe we can help each other out."

"You've found out things?" He raised a skeptical eyebrow. "Like what?"

"Exchange of info—yes or no?"

He drew a breath, slightly annoyed. "Yes. But not here. We'll meet tonight."

"Where?"

"You're so good at investigations. You'll find me."

"If you're lucky," I said, and walked away.

Halfway down the block I stopped and looked back. Zack stood on the corner watching me, grinning as if he knew that was exactly what I would do. Annoyed with him—and myself, really—I pushed into the nearest store I happened to be standing in front of.

It was the Flight of Flowers florist. The shop brimmed with flowers, plants, and decorator items. I found the manager, introduced myself—though, somehow, she already knew who I was—and asked if I could display my pillowcase party sign in their window. I got a hearty "of course" followed by pleasant small talk.

I continued down Main Street. Every business I popped into was the same, friendly, welcoming, already aware of who I was and my pillowcase dress project, and anxious to help. Most everyone asked about Gretchen's daughter's cancer treatment, and sent their regards to Sarah. Life in a small town.

When I got to the bakery Sarah and Jodi were

busy at the display case with customers. I asked if I could help out, but Sarah waved me away so I headed into the sewing studio and closed the pocket doors behind me.

For once, being inside this room didn't fill me with anxiety. Thanks to Connie, I could make the pillowcase dresses using Gretchen's simple machine instead of the beast that had terrorized me for days. I felt confident that I could master the basic machine. All I had to do was find it.

Dozens of storage boxes were stacked in the room. Sarah had told me some of them held things that belonged to her, and others were full of items that Gretchen had brought over when they were planning to make the space into a dining room and gift shop. I had no way of knowing which boxes belonged with which of them. None were marked with contents. Nothing to do but dig in.

One by one, I pulled boxes out of the stack, opened them, and checked the contents. No sewing machine . . . no sewing machine . . . no sewing machine. When I got down to the last three boxes—and genuinely feared Connie had been wrong—I found it.

"Thank goodness," I said aloud, and heaved a sigh of relief.

The machine was a Singer, inside its original box. Gretchen had taken great care in packing it away.

I carried it to one of the tables I'd set up and pried it out of its Styrofoam packaging. Memories rushed back. That sewing class at the rec center. Threading the machine. Winding the bobbin. Adjusting the stitch length. I remembered that I'd picked up operating the machine quickly, even if the skirt I'd sewn hadn't turned out so great.

The nearest electrical outlet wasn't close by, so I dragged the table closer, plugged the foot pedal into the machine, then plugged the machine into the outlet. I switched on the light. It worked. I'd figured it out—and I hadn't even had to read the instruction manual or search YouTube.

I dug a small piece of fabric out of the box of remnants I'd put aside, pulled a chair up to the machine, and sat down. The moment of truth. I drew a determined breath, positioned the fabric, lowered the presser foot, and touched the foot pedal with my toe. The machine sprang to life, laying down a row of uniform stitches in a straight line.

"Yes!"

So I'd lost my job, was on the verge of being evicted from my condo, didn't have my car, couldn't solve Iris's murder, and had no idea what lay ahead of me—but I'd sewed a seam!

I spun the fabric around and sewed another seam, then another and another. A sense of relief and joy came over me that I hadn't experienced in days. I could do this. I could host my pillowcase party—and not be the only one there who couldn't make a pillowcase dress.

Pulling out my phone, I accessed a website for a nonprofit that collected the dresses and whose volunteers took them to villages in Africa to distribute among the girls. I read over the instructions, which were pretty simple, even to my untrained eye. No pattern needed. The required length of the dresses and the templates for making armholes were included. Then I found a YouTube channel that demonstrated actually making the dresses, and offered tips and suggestions.

I knew there was no stopping me now.

From the stack of pillowcases that had accumulated I selected a blue print, then dug through the notions and supplies for bias tape, elastic, a tape measure, and pins. Gretchen had left her scissors, which, I suddenly remembered from sewing class, were actually shears because of their length, so I used them, too. The blades were eight inches long and sharp, and probably cost hundreds of dollars. I used them to cut armhole templates out of scrap paper, then worried that I should have used cheap scissors instead so as not to dull the blades.

Following along with the instructor on YouTube, I laid out the pillowcase, cut it to size—I decided making a size small to start with would be a good idea—then cut the armholes. I folded the tops over to make a casing on the front and back, pinned them in place, and sat down at the machine. My first official stitches for a good cause went great. Then I cut elastic to size, threaded it through the casing, and stitched it in place. I found a small pair of scissors among Gretchen's supplies and trimmed the loose threads.

Putting on the bias tape that would line the armhole and loop over the girls' shoulders to tie looked a little trickier. And it was. It took a few tries to pin it properly, then I stitched it super slowly to make sure my seams were in the right place. I finished it off by trimming the ends of the bias tape.

Done.

I sat back in my chair and held up the little

dress. I'd done it. I'd sewed a garment. I compared it to the example on YouTube. Pretty good, I decided—no, really good. Not only were my seams straight—well, mostly straight, considering it was my first attempt—but it actually looked like a dress. An adorable dress.

The stack of donated pillowcases suddenly looked different—alive with possibilities. I could add lace and rickrack, and all kinds of embellishments. I imagined the little girls in the villages standing in line to receive a new dress, and that mental picture made me want to make the dresses as lovely as I could for them.

Ideas popped into my head. I got out my phone and started a list on the notes app of all the trim I could get to enhance the dresses. Another trip to Connie's Fabrics was definitely in order—and this time I'd be there to actually buy sewing supplies.

My sewing studio needed some fixing up, too, I realized, and started another list. I'd have to make space at the tables for the women coming to my pillowcase party with their sewing machines, which meant I'd need extension cords and power strips. I'd need a designated cutting table, too, and an iron and ironing board. Maybe I could pick up an inexpensive sewing machine at Anna's thrift shop for anyone who didn't own one. I trapped my finger against my chin and turned in a slow circle. A design wall would be great. A few ideas of what it could look like spun through my head.

I went to the stack of pillowcases, anxious to start on another dress. Maybe, after more practice, I could add pockets to the dresses or sleeves. Maybe I could learn to operate the embroidery machine and really enhance the dresses.

"Abbey?"

Jarred out of my thoughts, I spotted Jodi standing at the pocket doors. I got the feeling she'd called my name more than once.

"Someone's here to see you," Jodi said, her eyes wide and questioning.

"Who?"

"A certain someone," she said, with an unmistakable I-want-details look on her face.

I thought for a few seconds.

"Zack?"

I'd been in the sewing studio totally immersed in pillowcase dresses for so long I'd lost track of time.

"Are you two dating?" Jodi asked, lowering her voice.

"It's just something casual," I said because it sounded nicer than saying we were meeting to discuss a murder.

CHAPTER 18

❧

Zack wore jeans and a black polo shirt instead of his uniform, so perhaps it appeared as if we were on a date, as Jodi had suggested. But the look on Zack's face definitely indicated otherwise.

"Bad afternoon?" I asked as we stepped out of the bakery.

With some effort, he relaxed his frown.

"Nothing unusual," he said. "Except for a certain civilian who keeps putting herself in danger over something that's none of her business."

"You could think of me as a confidential informant," I suggested.

"No," he said, frowning again.

Things were winding down in Hideaway Grove. Traffic was light. Few pedestrians were in town. I noticed Joyce walking out of Hummingbird Lane and turning right onto Main Street. I wondered if she was headed for a visit with Miss Merriweather. For a few seconds I considered talking with her and sharing my concern about her aunt's driving, but decided that with Zack next to me it might look like an official visit and I doubted it would be well received.

"I checked on your car," Zack said as we walked down Main Street.

Before I could ask if he had good news, he shook his head.

"The crime lab is still backed up?" I asked.

"No idea when it will be released."

I wasn't happy to hear the news, but I wasn't surprised, either.

Across the street I spotted Mitch exiting Barry's Pet Emporium. I wondered if he'd been there to ask Caitlin to share a booth with him at the festival.

"There's trouble," Zack commented.

I realized he'd spotted Mitch also.

"You don't like him?" I asked, concerned that there was some sort of illegal activity associated with him.

"Mitch is a good guy," Zack said. "But he's playing with fire."

Obviously, I wasn't the only one who knew that Mitch had designs on Caitlin. I was surprised Zack had noticed. He was a trained observer, but a possible budding relationship? Maybe Zack was more attentive than I'd realized.

"You think Mitch should back off, leave Caitlin alone?" I asked.

"Hell, no. If he loves her, he should go after her."

"What about Scott Freedman, her fiancé?"

"Theirs is not exactly a match made in heaven. It's not even a match Scott is committed to."

"Scott isn't being faithful to Caitlin?" I asked, surprised.

He ignored my question. "Scott's family is counting on him marrying Caitlin. Her dad owns land
adjacent to their tire store. There's a rumor going
around that Scott's family wants it. And what better way to get it than to marry into it?"

"It's a rumor. But is it true?"

Zack gave me a who-knows shrug.

I wondered if Caitlin had heard that unflatter-
ing rumor. In a small town like Hideaway Grove,
how could she not? But maybe she was okay with it.
Maybe her feelings for Scott were so great it didn't
matter.

We continued down Main Street. Zack touched
my elbow and steered me to the Parliament Café.
A crowded diner hardly seemed like the best place
to discuss a murder investigation.

"I'm hungry," he said, as if reading my thoughts.

Inside, the place was hopping. All the booths
were taken and only three of the stools at the
counter were vacant. Through the kitchen pass-
through I saw two cooks at the flat top, steam rising and burgers sizzling. Waitresses hustled
heaping plates of food to diners. I thought about
Earlene; it looked as if the staff could really use
her help.

Melinda, the waitress I'd spoken with the last
time I was here, spotted Zack. Her gaze bounced
to me, then to him again. She disappeared behind
the counter and presented him with a large brown
bag.

"Enjoy," she said, and smiled, as if she thought
we were on a date.

Several other diners took note of us as we left
the café.

"We'll be the talk of the town now," I commented.

"That's why I got this," Zack said, gesturing to the bag. "I thought it would be better if we weren't seen in the café together."

"So you parade us down Main Street instead?"

"Don't worry. I know a secluded spot for us."

"Oh, great. That's so much better."

The location he'd decided on was a picnic table on the village green, partially surrounded by trees, shrubs, and blooming flowers. No one else was there. The streetlights had come on casting the area in warm, golden light.

The Parliament had provided hearty sandwiches, chips, and sodas, probably at Zack's request. He'd gone to some trouble for the evening. This was the closest thing to a date I'd had in a while.

"How's your dad?" I asked, as we laid out the food. "Is he out of the hospital?"

"He's home," Zack said, as if surprised I remembered he'd told me his father had been hospitalized for heart trouble. "Doing well."

"Are you going to see him?"

"No plans yet." Zack shrugged and popped the top on our soda cans. "How about you? Going home to Los Angeles when you get your car back?"

I didn't have much to go back to, but I didn't want to tell him that.

"You don't talk about your past." He grinned. "Makes me wonder if some of those rumors about you might be true."

I rolled my eyes. "Believe me, nothing that interesting ever happened to me."

"So what did happen?" he asked, the playfulness gone from his voice.

"Nothing."

"Then why don't you want to talk about it?"

Good question, I realized. He seemed genuinely interested and concerned, and it hit me then that I trusted him. If I told him everything I'd gone through in Los Angeles, he'd listen and understand. Maybe those wide shoulders of his were figurative as well as literal.

"Okay, here's my story."

I told him everything as quickly as I could, trying to keep the emotion out of my voice so I wouldn't sound overly dramatic. He listened. He stopped eating and listened.

When I finished, he reached across the picnic table and covered my hand with his. His fingers were strong and warm.

"I'm glad we took your car. I hope we keep it forever," he told me, with an intensity in his voice I hadn't heard before. "I don't want you to ever go back to those awful circumstances."

I was touched, touched so deeply I had to gulp down my rising emotions.

"I doubt my employer will take me back anyway," I said. Madison's phone call had given me hope, but I knew it was really just a fantasy.

"So stay here." Zack bit into his sandwich.

"And do what?"

"What will you do if you go back to L.A.?"

I forced a smile. "Since I figured out how to sew a pillowcase dress, maybe I can get a job sewing something in the Garment District."

"You could sew something here."

I meant it as a joke, but his words floated through my head as we finished our sandwiches and chips.

"What I'd really like to do is solve Iris's murder

and get my car back so I'll have some options," I told him.

"Okay. Let's solve a murder." He sat back. "What have you got?"

After sharing with him everything about my personal life, it only seemed natural to tell him what I knew about Iris's death. No sense in holding back now.

"Iris was murdered. It wasn't an accident," I said.

He looked skeptical. "How do you know?"

"Because I heard an engine rev and tires squeal in the alley seconds before she was struck by the car."

He frowned. "Why didn't you tell the sheriff this?"

"I didn't remember it right away," I admitted.

"You could have come forward then. Why didn't you?"

"Because I knew the sheriff wouldn't believe me—just like you don't believe me," I said. "I see that look on your face. I know what you're thinking. But I'm telling you what I heard."

"What else did you hear or see?" he asked.

I shook my head. "That's it."

"Think about it. Sometimes details come back. You might remember an important clue." Zack thought for a few seconds. "Okay. Let's say you're right. A car was in the alley, waiting for Iris, with the intention of hitting her. How did the driver know she'd be in the alley?"

"She was meeting a man."

"What man?"

"Her mystery man, according to Anna."

"You talked to Anna?"

"Yes."

"She saw them back there?"

"Yes," I said. "And there's something else. Earlene. I think she could be involved."

"How?"

"Why was she in the alley? What reason was she there at the exact moment Iris was killed unless she was somehow involved?"

Zack just looked at me.

"Now she's suddenly left town, and she was really upset when she left and anxious to go. Plus, she won't return my phone calls," I said. "What about the mystery man? Was he Iris's secret lover, there to meet her for a tryst? Or maybe to break off their relationship and figured the best way to do it was to kill her."

"He's a suspect?"

"That's not all. The town librarians weren't happy with Iris, neither was Connie," I told him.

"You think all of these people are suspects?"

"I think Valerie was troubled by Iris, too, but I haven't talked to her yet."

Zack tilted his head, thinking.

"You look like you don't even know what I'm talking about," I told him. "Hasn't the sheriff done *any* investigation?"

Zack shifted uncomfortably.

"You must have turned up *something*," I insisted.

He hesitated a few seconds. "Iris led a quiet, simple life. She lived in one of the furnished studio apartments on Dove Drive. They're not very nice, but they're cheap. She could have afforded something better. She had no close family that we can find, no criminal record—not even a parking ticket. She had a nice-size nest egg in her bank account, considerably more money than you'd expect for a small-town librarian. She must have saved every extra dime she earned."

"What about her phone records?" I asked. "She's bound to have contact info for the man she met in the alley."

"The mystery man?" he asked, sounding skeptical.

"If nothing untoward was going on between them, why were they meeting in secret? Maybe he was there that day. Maybe that's why Iris was in the alley. And if he really wasn't involved in her death, maybe he saw who was."

"I'll check it out," Zack said. "That's it? Just those people? That's your list of suspects?"

"Joyce Colby," I said. "She was seen arguing with Iris."

Zack's frown returned.

"Look, I know this sounds thin," I admitted. "If I didn't know for a fact that Iris had been deliberately run down, I'd doubt it, too."

"Anything—anyone—else?"

I almost hated to name my last suspect, but at this point there seemed little point in holding back.

"Miss Merriweather."

Zack drew in a breath, as if he'd been expecting to hear her name.

"You think she hit Iris with her car, and kept going?" he said.

"Not on purpose. I think she might have been confused or maybe wasn't paying attention. You must have thought the same."

"Her car is the same color as the suspected vehicle. The dent in her fender. Her history of erratic driving. Yes, I think it could have happened."

A darker, more unwelcome thought came to me. If it hadn't been an accident it could mean only one thing—Miss Merriweather had hit Iris on purpose.

I didn't like to think either of those things could have happened, but both were possible. Yet it left me with a bigger question—why would Miss Merriweather want to kill Iris?

We gathered the remains of our meal, dumped it in the trash and recycling bins, and left the village green. It was dark now, only a few cars were on the street and a couple walking their dog.

We headed down Main Street together. I guess he intended to walk me home.

"So you're out of it now," Zack said. "No more investigating Iris's death."

"Because of the information I shared with you?"

"Let our department handle it."

"Are you going to tell Sheriff Grumman that I heard the engine rev and tires squeal in the alley?" I asked, hoping he wouldn't.

"I can't withhold information."

Great. Did that mean I could expect a visit from the sheriff? Not the outcome I was hoping for.

"But you believe me, right?" I asked.

"There's still a great deal of investigating to do," he said.

At this point it seemed I couldn't count on Zack to turn up the heat on Iris's murder investigation, even after what I'd told him. I wasn't sure he believed me. Of course, he was trained not to make a snap decision, to first analyze facts and evidence. Maybe that's what he was doing.

Or maybe he didn't really believe me and didn't want to stick his neck out supporting my theory, figuring the sheriff wouldn't believe me, either.

The shops we passed on Main Street were closed for the evening. Most had dim lighting inside offering a shadowy image of the interior. Zack rattled doorknobs as we walked, making sure locks were secure.

We turned onto Hummingbird Lane, and as we neared the entrance to the alley, an orange streak shot across our path. We both stopped short.

"Cheddar," I realized, seeing the cat tear across the street and disappear behind one of the houses. "She's always on the prowl."

"Or something scared her."

Zack turned the other way, gazing into the alley.

"Stay here," he said, with an urgency and command that galvanized me to the spot.

"Stop! Police!" he shouted.

In the shadows of the alley I spotted a figure outside Sarah's bakery, pulling on the door. Whoever it was—a man, I thought, though it was hard to tell since he wore dark pants and a hoodie—looked up, spotted us, and ran away. Zack took off running.

No way was I staying put. I followed.

Zack dug in, running impressively fast through the alley, but the guy had a big head start. He turned the corner that led to Main Street, and disappeared. Zack disappeared, too.

By the time I got to Main Street, Zack was standing on the corner visually searching the area, breathing hard and holding his cell phone. I looked, too, but there was no sign of the guy; neither was there the sound of a car speeding away. All was quiet. A typical night in Hideaway Grove.

I headed toward Sarah's bakery to check the front door, but Zack caught my arm and pulled me close.

"Stay here with me, where you're safe," he said to me, then turned back to his phone. He spoke to the police dispatcher, calm and composed, reporting an attempted break-in and requesting backup.

Gazing up and down Main Street I doubted the would-be burglar would be caught. The lighting wasn't great, there were several streets leading in different directions, lots of hiding places. It seemed logical he was a local, knew the area well, and was likely long gone by now.

Since I'd arrived in Hideaway Grove there had been a rash of crimes—Dumpsters vandalized, mischief outside Sassy Fashions, a break-in at Earlene's house and, of course, Iris's murder. And now this.

The only consolation was that this time Sheriff Grumman couldn't think I was involved. I glanced up at Zack. This time I had an alibi.

CHAPTER 19

❧

By the time I got to Sarah's Sweets the next morning a man was there working on the back door, reinforcing it and installing a stronger lock. Sheriff Grumman stood in the kitchen, hemmed between the work island and the refrigerator by Sarah, Jodi, Geraldine, and Anna. Word of last night's attempted break-in had spread already, it seemed.

"Again!" Geraldine declared. "Something happened again!"

"And what are you doing about it?" Anna demanded.

"Ladies—" the sheriff began.

"Where is the protection you're supposed to be providing?" Geraldine wanted to know. "If you can't ensure the safety and security of our businesses, what do you expect us to do? Hire our own private security?"

"I can't afford that!" Anna declared.

Sarah swayed and steadied herself by grabbing the work island. Jodi patted her hand.

"Ladies, if I may remind you," Sheriff Grumman said, "the break-in last night was only an attempt. One of my deputies stopped it."

He meant Zack. He wasn't here and I found myself wondering where he was. Investigating Iris's murder after our talk last night?

"But the burglar got away," Geraldine declared.

"He's still out there," Anna said. "He's probably planning another crime, whoever he is."

"All those patrol cars searching Hideaway Grove last night," Geraldine said, "and nobody saw who it was."

"One person saw who it was." Sheriff Grumman's gaze impaled me.

Everyone turned and stared at me.

I'd told the sheriff what I'd witnessed—which was nearly nothing—last night when he'd showed up in the alley, along with several deputies. He'd had little to say to me then. Now, he seemed anxious to put me on the spot.

"And she could have been injured—or worse," Geraldine declared. "Suppose that burglar had been carrying a gun."

"A gun? Oh, my word!" Anna moaned.

"There was no gun," Sheriff Grumman insisted. "No weapon of any kind."

"You can't be sure, since you didn't catch him," Geraldine told him.

"What is happening to Hideaway Grove?" Anna raised her hands, beseeching an answer from a higher power, it seemed.

"Thank goodness Abbey and Zack were there and stopped him," Sarah declared. "I hate to think what might have happened to my shop."

I'd never seen Sarah this rattled. I eased through

the throng of people squeezed into the kitchen and looped my arm around her shoulders. She gave me a weak smile.

"Tell us, Abbey," Geraldine said, deliberately turning her back on the sheriff. "Tell us. Do you have any idea who was trying to break into the bakery last night? Any idea at all?"

"Like I told the sheriff last night, the person was dressed in dark clothes, with a hoodie pulled up. I couldn't see who it was. I'm not even sure if it was a man or a woman." I looked at Sarah, feeling as if I'd somehow let her down. "Sorry."

"I'm just glad you weren't injured," she told me. "You or Zack."

"All done," the repairman announced, stepping away from the back door.

I realized it was Mitch. Sheriff Grumman forced his way out of the circle of women to inspect the repairs to the door. Mitch joined the ladies, diminishing the tension in the group considerably.

"Your door was in good shape," Mitch said to Sarah. "I doubt anybody could have broken in."

Sarah exhaled heavily. "That's good news."

"I reinforced it anyway, and installed a heavier lock," Mitch said.

Geraldine sidled up next to him, smoothing her dress down her hips. "Maybe you could come install something at my place?"

"I have to get to work," Sarah announced, and briskly clapped her hands, dispersing the crowd.

"Thank goodness you're here," Anna said as I walked with her to the front door. "This whole thing is terribly upsetting for Sarah. She needs you here now more than ever."

Anna left the bakery. Geraldine lingered for a

few seconds to offer Mitch a sultry smile, then left, with a noticeable swing of her hips.

Sheriff Grumman approached Sarah.

"I know this is scary for you, Sarah," he said softly. "But remember that nothing happened, really. No damage was done, nobody was hurt. That's the important thing."

"But he could come back," she said. "What are you doing to catch him?"

"Or to find out who ran down Iris?" I couldn't resist adding.

He hit me with a hard look and ignored my question, and turned back to Sarah.

"We're on it," he told her. "We're handling it."

I found myself more than slightly annoyed with the sheriff, so I was glad when Mitch picked up his toolbox and joined me by the front counter.

"Thanks for handling the repair," I said.

The bell on the front door chimed.

"Happy I could help—"

Caitlin walked into the bakery. They spotted each other. Both of them froze.

An awkward moment unfurled, urging me to break the tension.

"I guess you heard about last night?" I said.

Caitlin gave herself a little shake and focused on me.

"Dad is beside himself, as usual," she said. "Honestly, I'm afraid he's going to worry himself into another heart attack."

"Fortunately, nothing serious happened." I glanced around for Sheriff Grumman, hoping for some backup to ease Caitlin's dad's mind, but he'd left, presumably out the back door. "Still, it's worrisome."

"Tell your dad I can install a stronger lock on your doors at the shop, if he'd like," Mitch said.

"That would be really sweet of you," she said with a shy smile.

Mitch beamed, as if somebody had just told him he'd won the lottery.

"I'd better get back." Caitlin gestured to the pet store across the street but made no move toward the door.

"Actually, I wonder if you could help me with something," I said.

I'd added Caitlin's name to my list of things needed to prepare for my pillowcase party, and this seemed like a good time to enlist her help.

She glanced again at the pet store. "Well . . ."

"It's for the sewing studio," I said. "It won't take five minutes."

"Okay," she said.

"I heard you turned the storage room into a nice place," Mitch said.

I wasn't sure how everything I'd done had made the rounds of Hideaway Grove, but I wasn't surprised.

The three of us went into the sewing studio. I gestured to the wall in the area across the room, partially blocked by storage boxes.

"I was thinking of making a design wall, a place to display some of the dresses and ideas for different embellishments," I said. "I'm not sure how to make it come to life. I could use some ideas."

I knew, of course, that no matter what happened at my job back in Los Angeles, my time in Hideaway Grove was growing short. Still, I wanted to do my best on the sewing studio, make it an inspiring place to create dresses. Hopefully, after

Gretchen returned from helping her daughter, she would continue with pillowcase parties and make them a regular charity event.

Mitch set his toolbox aside. He and Caitlin moved together as if magnetized, both of them studying the wall, thinking.

"Maybe a large frame covered with fabric remnants," Caitlin suggested.

"How big?" Mitch asked.

She went to the wall and pointed. "Starting here, and going—"

Mitch grabbed the boxes blocking her path and set them aside. "Here, maybe?" he asked, pointing to a spot on the wall. He pointed again. "And running down to here?"

"Oh, yes. Perfect." She seemed to suddenly remember me. "What do you think, Abbey?"

"Looks great."

Mitch got a tape measure out of his toolbox and started making notes. Caitlin looked over the sewing supplies and notions I'd assembled on the table beside Gretchen's sewing machines.

"Looks like Gretchen left you pretty well stocked." Caitlin picked up the scissors I'd marveled at myself, and felt the weight of them in her hand. "These are awesome. Heavy-duty. They must have cost a small fortune. They'll make cutting the fabric so much easier."

Caitlin pulled the box of fabric remnants from under the table and laid some of them out. They looked like a jumble of patterns, colors, and textures to me, a chaotic rainbow. But Caitlin moved them around, turned them, switched them back and forth several times.

"You can sew these remnants together to make a

cover for the design wall frame," she suggested. "Maybe cut them into different shapes. I'm thinking . . . triangle, or maybe diamond."

I studied them for a few seconds, and finally, I could see what she had in mind. And I loved it.

Mitch came over and stood behind us. "Looks good."

We talked about the design, the construction, and what would be needed to get it ready.

"Talk to Connie," Caitlin suggested. "She'll know what kind of batting you'll need."

"And you'll help with the sewing?" I asked. "You have to help. I'll never get this pattern right without you."

Caitlin promised she would help, Mitch said he'd get started constructing the frame, and we left the sewing studio. Several customers were in the bakery talking to Sarah at the display case, asking about the break-in while they ordered. Sarah called her thanks to Mitch, and he and Caitlin left.

I stood at the window watching them. They lingered for a few seconds, talking, and finally Caitlin crossed the street. Mitch watched until she disappeared into the pet store, then moved along.

I caught Jodi's eye in the kitchen. She gave me a knowing nod and went back to icing cupcakes. Guess I wasn't the only one who saw the attraction between Caitlin and Mitch—for all the good it did.

Back in the sewing studio I stood for a moment contemplating the area that would become a design wall, feeling good about it. Nearby were the four bolts of mint-green gingham fabric Sarah had bought so Gretchen could make window curtains for the room. The fabric was perfect for the shop. It seemed a shame to let it lie there, unused.

Maybe my sewing skills would improve enough that I'd attempt the curtains. They would give the bakery a lift and, maybe, lift Sarah's spirits as well. I'd sensed mild, underlying stress from her but maybe it had always been there and I'd been too young to notice. Running a business and keeping it afloat wasn't easy.

I was anxious to dive in and continue the preparation for my pillowcase party but there was another chore I had to work on. Looking around I spotted the manila envelope Sarah had told me had been dropped off, the one with the information about the raffle donations for the festival that Iris had been handling.

Even though most everybody in town who knew I'd taken over this committee had expressed sympathy that I'd gotten stuck with it, I figured there would be little for me to do. After all, Iris had been working on it for weeks, and according to most everyone, she was efficient and organized. I was sure I could wrap it up quickly.

Handling the envelope that a dead person had used felt kind of creepy to me, but I forced myself to open it. Inside were what appeared to be receipts, tax forms, and instructions for the donors, and a master list for tracking the items that had been donated.

All the pages were blank. I turned them over, rechecked the envelope, and looked again. Not one item had been entered on the master list. Iris, obviously, had done nothing.

"Great," I mumbled aloud.

The festival was coming up soon, and she'd accomplished nothing? Absolutely nothing? This was a big job. It was a major moneymaker for the festival. The town was counting on her. Yet she'd ignored it, or intended to rush through it at the last minute and hope for the best. What could she have been thinking?

I'd have to reorder my priorities now and focus on the donations to get them done in time. I slid the documents back into the envelope, grabbed my things, and left.

As I headed down Main Street it occurred to me that I could solicit donations and finish prep for my pillowcase party at the same time. That meant my first stop would be Anna's thrift shop.

Zack came around the corner from Hummingbird Lane and headed my way. He spotted me. I paused as he walked over, and couldn't help but wonder why he'd been on that particular street.

I remembered seeing Joyce leaving Hummingbird Lane. The mystery man parked there and Iris met him there, of all places in town. Earlene had been in the alley headed that way. Cheddar had disappeared behind a house there. What was the big attraction on Hummingbird Lane?

"I have that information you asked about," Zack said, stopping beside me.

He wore his uniform. He smelled great.

"You found out when I'm getting my car back?"

He shook his head. "The mystery man. Iris's supposed secret lover. We found him."

CHAPTER 20

❧❧❧

My heart jumped. Zack had followed up on one of my leads. He'd believed me.

"You found him?" I asked.

"The sheriff had already checked Iris's phone records," Zack said.

This surprised me. Sheriff Grumman was actually investigating, after all, it seemed.

"He was interviewed," Zack reported. "The guy's an assistant manager at one of those home improvement stores back in Richland where Iris used to live. He told the sheriff that Iris called him when she wanted advice on something that needed repairing at her place."

"Her place here? In Hideaway Grove?" I remembered that Zack had mentioned Iris rented a furnished studio apartment on Dove Drive. "I wonder why she called him for help instead of her landlord."

"Could have been lots of reasons," Zack said.

I knew he was right. Some tenants didn't like repair people coming into their place if, like Iris, they had to work and couldn't be there, or their relationship with their landlord wasn't the best and they didn't want to ask for anything unless it was a major repair. But it still made me wonder if there was something more going on between the two of them, something romantic.

"He said he'd never been to Hideaway Grove," Zack told me.

"And the sheriff believed him?"

"No reason not to. He had no criminal record. There's nothing to indicate he'd been here— other than Anna's claim of glimpsing a man through her window which, really, is pretty thin— or that he was involved with Iris beyond what he said."

Anna had seen the mystery man in the alley with Iris. But was he *this* guy?

"You should be able to get his photo from his driver's license," I said. "Anna would recognize him."

"The sheriff is handling it."

By the tone of his voice I wondered if Zack had stuck out his neck, asked about the phone records because I'd requested it, then gotten into a bit of trouble with Sheriff Grumman for seemingly second-guessing the sheriff's actions.

"Do you at least know if this guy is married?" I asked.

"With kids."

I guess that explained why—if he was the man Anna had spotted—he was sneaking through the alley, meeting Iris out of sight of everyone in town.

"His name?" I asked.

"I can't give you that."

A few seconds passed while I mulled over what Zack had reported. It seemed like a dead end.

"Thanks for letting me know," I offered.

Zack nodded.

We stood like that just looking at each other until we both realized how awkward it was.

"I've got to go," he said, stepping back.

"Me too," I insisted, and dashed into Anna's thrift store.

No customers were inside. I spotted Anna at the rear of the store rearranging the books on display. There were three shelves of them. It reminded me of the library in Miss Merriweather's house and how she'd mentioned Iris's frequent visits that she'd enjoyed so much. It reminded me, too, of the conversation I'd had with Connie and her troubles with her sister who owned the Owl's Nest bookstore.

Anna looked up when she heard the bell over the door clang.

"Hello," I called, and walked back to meet her.

She didn't smile or offer a greeting, which surprised me. Maybe she saw the manila folder I carried, knew what it meant, and didn't want to be asked for a donation. I'd probably get that same response from several of the merchants as I made the rounds through town.

"I'm here to ask for a donation *and* shop," I said, waving the folder.

Anna gave herself a little shake.

"I guess I do look like a sourpuss," she admitted. "I just can't get over how that Geraldine acts around men. Her conduct earlier in the bakery was disgraceful, carrying on like that toward that nice young man Mitch. A woman her age! People notice. They notice and have opinions—and they're not always good."

I didn't know what to say and Anna didn't give me the chance anyway.

"Somebody is going to confront Geraldine one of these days," Anna predicted, her irritation rising. "It will get ugly. I'm telling you, it will get ugly. I've seen it myself. Right back here in the alley. Joyce Colby. Of all people."

Something else had happened in the alley? I opened my mouth to ask, but Anna kept going.

"Joyce and Iris were arguing at the end of the alley, right there at Hummingbird Lane. Arguing, I tell you. They were really going at it."

"Arguing about what?"

"Her mystery man," Anna declared. "I'd just seen him drive away and here came Joyce. She confronted Iris and told her in no uncertain terms that she should watch herself. She was a *librarian*, for goodness' sake. Her behavior was unbecoming a woman in her position."

I guess I had a different idea about librarians and their positions in the community. I was equally confounded to learn that Joyce knew about Iris's affair with the mystery man, and was so outraged by her supposedly unbecoming conduct that she'd confronted her.

"Is that what Joyce said?" I asked. "Exactly?"

"Well," Anna said, backpedaling. "I didn't actually hear what was being said. I only saw them through my window. But what else could it have been about?"

What else indeed? I wondered. Perhaps there was a romantic triangle between Joyce, Iris, and the mystery man? I'd suspected Joyce might have been involved in Iris's death, for no really good reason. Seems I had one now—even though it was pure speculation with no real facts.

"Anyway," Anna said, shaking off her irritation. "I'm happy to make a donation. In fact, I've put aside several items that I know will be well received."

I pulled documents from the folder and gave them to her. She told me what she planned to donate—table settings of antique china—and I wrote it on the master list. One down, who knows how many more to go.

"I need an iron and an ironing board for my sewing studio," I said, then gazed around the store. "And I don't suppose you have any used sewing machines that are in good condition?"

"I sure do."

I bought the items Anna recommended and made arrangements to pick them up later, then headed to my next stop.

At the drugstore two blocks down on Main Street, I spotted Phoebe behind the pharmacy counter wearing a white lab coat and explaining a prescription to a young mom holding a wiggly baby. Phoebe smiled when she saw me and held up a finger indicating she'd be with me in a minute.

I grabbed a plastic handbasket and roamed the aisles selecting the extension cords and power strips I'd need to set up the sewing machines in the sewing studio. Phoebe found me a few minutes later.

"I overheard several customers talking about your pillowcase party," she said.

"I hope that means they're coming," I said. "You're coming, aren't you?"

"Since your sewing standards are low, I'm definitely coming," Phoebe said and we both laughed. "I'll dig out Mom's old sewing machine and bring it."

I juggled the handbasket and envelope, and pulled out the documents for the raffle.

"Oh, yes, the donations," Phoebe said, taking the papers from me. "Sorry you got stuck with this, but at least Iris had been working on it."

"Nope," I said.

Her eyebrows bobbed up. "You're kidding."

"I wish."

"That's odd." Phoebe tilted her head, thinking. "Iris was so thorough about things. Like that travel program she came up with. She scheduled a lecture, had a travel agent give a talk, put books on Italian history in the library's entryway. She was even learning to speak Italian. She made it seem exciting. It made me want to go there."

I'd been to Italy but all I remembered were the musty museums and libraries, and wanting to leave while my parents were completely enthralled with everything.

Phoebe rose on her toes and peered over the aisles at the pharmacy.

"Got to go. Customer." She held up the donation documents. "I'll make sure this gets handled."

"Thanks," I called as she hurried away.

I paid for the items I'd selected, then hit Main Street again. I stood for a minute, debating which way to go. Anna's and then Phoebe's comments about Iris had brought her murder into my thoughts again, pushing away prep for my pillowcase party and the raffle donations.

My list of suspects was short. Even though I was

sure I had a good reason now to include Joyce, I knew one more person I could possibly add.

I crossed Main Street, and as I stepped up on the curb my phone vibrated in my pocket. I pulled it out and saw Madison's name on the ID screen.

"Update!" she announced as soon as I answered.

I moved out of the way of pedestrians, my heart rate picking up. When I'd last spoken to Madison she'd told me HR and upper management were having a meeting about my supervisor and my possible return to work.

"What's going on?" I asked, trying not to sound too anxious.

"Oh my God, girl. Oh my God. You are not going to believe this," she declared.

I waited, my future presumably hanging in the balance while Madison let the moment build.

"They called in another law firm," she announced.

"They—what?"

"Yes. They are consulting with an outside law firm. This thing you started is huge—mega huge. Everybody in the building is talking about it. I even heard—look, I've got to go. Don't worry. I'm all over this." She ended the call.

I stood on the sidewalk feeling as if I'd been buffeted by a small tornado. Gossip about my departure was still raging through the building? An outside law firm was being consulted? Were they looking for a way to fire me, or my old supervisor, or maybe both of us, without getting sued?

Madison was all over it. I figured I'd hear the answer from her before anyone at the company contacted me with an official decision.

I refocused my thoughts onto Iris's murder and my search for another suspect. Connie at the fabric store had been upset about the rift between her and her sister Valerie, caused by Iris. I needed to talk to her. Maybe Valerie would be willing to give up more information than her sister had been.

I continued down Main Street and went inside the Owl's Nest bookstore. It had a cozy, warm feel to it and a soothing vibe, as independent bookstores often do. The dark wood shelves were filled with a huge array of books. Printed signs, embellished with little owls wearing glasses, were posted over each section of fiction and nonfiction books. Magazine racks sat off to the right, and nearby was a small selection of stationery and gift items.

A young woman was at the register assisting a line of customers. I didn't recognize her but doubted she was Connie's sister. I roamed through the stacks until I spotted a woman coming out a door at the back of the store—a storage room, from the boxes I glimpsed behind her—while studying a stack of papers in her hand.

She resembled Connie vaguely—fortyish, stout, with a no-nonsense air about her—so I took a chance.

"Valerie?" I called, and walked over.

She looked up and managed a halfhearted smile. "Can I help you find something?"

I introduced myself and held up the donation envelope.

Valerie's halfhearted smile withered.

"I donate, I have a booth at the festival, I run a sale, everything. Any merchant in town who didn't would be crazy." She waved toward the front of the store while sorting through the papers in her hand. "Leave the forms at the register. I'll take care of it."

"Sorry for asking you to rush it," I said. "But I just took over the donations and they're way behind."

Valerie glanced up at me. "Took over from who?"

I had to solicit a donation, but what I really wanted was to get her take on Iris's murder. She'd given me the perfect opening.

"I inherited this job from Iris. She'd done nothing."

Valerie's expression soured. "I'm not surprised, considering everything she was doing at the library. Children's reading hour. Adult book club. Authors coming in to speak."

"I heard she was doing a travel program, too."

"Oh, yeah. That Italy thing. Iris couldn't find enough ways to get people into that library—and keep them out of my shop."

The anger in Valerie's voice surprised me. I let her keep talking.

"She didn't even tell people I had books on Italy right here in my shop. She had the book club check their selections out of the library—or read them online—when she could have told them to buy local, from me. That would have been the decent thing—the right thing—for her to do. But no."

"Did you talk to Iris about it?"

"Of course I did," she snapped. "Iris acted so surprised—like she'd never thought she was hurting my business. She knew. She knew exactly what she was doing, and she couldn't have cared less."

"Connie told me she and Iris were friends from school. Couldn't Connie make her understand?"

"Connie." Valerie uttered the word with a disgusted grunt. "You'd think you could count on family to do the right thing."

"She wouldn't help?" I asked, surprised.

"Oh, yes, Connie talked to her. Iris acted all sweet and caring. Connie believed her. She told me everything would be better, but it wasn't. Iris didn't change." Valerie shook her head, her anger growing. "That Iris. She was two different people. She acted like she was so sweet and kind, working hard for the community. But she didn't fool me. She didn't fool other people, either. You can ask Joyce Colby, if you don't believe me. She knows what Iris was like."

So Joyce's name had popped up again. Seems I'd been right adding her to my suspect list.

I remembered what Anna had mentioned earlier, and said, "I heard there was a confrontation between them near the alley behind the thrift shop."

"I'm not surprised, after what I saw," Valerie said. "Nobody needs another reason to dislike Joyce. It's no secret that she's ... trouble. She went up to Iris outside the library and blasted her about something."

Now I was confused. Anna had seen Iris and Joyce arguing near Hummingbird Lane. Valerie had witnessed them going at it outside the library. There'd been two confrontations between them?

"What were they arguing about?" I asked.

"Who knows? Joyce's behavior has always been erratic and, well, maybe it's not all her fault, her being related to all that Merriweather money but not allowed to have a penny of it," Valerie said. "And, of course, everybody felt sorry for Iris. Poor sweet, kind Iris being accosted by Joyce. Makes me sick, the way she fooled everybody."

"You must be relieved you don't have to deal with her anymore."

"Iris took business from my store—money out of my pocket, food off my table. She wouldn't stop even after I asked her to and when Connie asked her to. If she'd kept it up, I hate to think what might have happened."

I wondered if I already knew what happened.

Valerie seemed to run out of steam. "I'd never say I'm glad someone is dead. But I'm glad Iris isn't around any longer."

She disappeared back into the stockroom. I left the paperwork by the register and went outside.

I'd wanted another murder suspect.

Seems now I had one.

CHAPTER 21

My next stop was the fabric store. Connie greeted me with a warm smile when I walked in.

"How's it going with the sewing machine?" she asked.

"I'm getting the hang of it," I was proud to say. "My seams are straight, most of the time."

"Are you ready to move up and do some embroidery?"

I shook my head. "I don't think I'm ready for that yet."

"It's not hard," Connie insisted. "Come on. I'll show you."

I knew there was no way I could take on that beast of a sewing machine yet, or maybe ever, but I didn't want to be rude so I followed Connie across the store to the sewing center where all the machines were on display, ready to demonstrate their capabilities.

Connie sat down behind a machine I recognized as the same model Gretchen had, and held up a booklet. She fanned the pages showing me images of borders, plants, animals, all sorts of things.

"You pick what you want, program it into the machine, put in the right color thread, and off it goes," she said.

"It can't be that simple."

"Watch."

Connie demonstrated how to use the hoop that held the fabric in place, the stabilizer backing, and how to set up the machine. She hit a button, sat back, and the machine started stitching.

I moved closer, my mouth gaping open, as the machine stitched, cut the thread, moved to the next spot in the design that required that same color thread, and started stitching again.

"Wow," I said. "The machine does it all by itself?"

"Nothing to it," Connie said.

"It looks so easy. I can't believe I was so afraid of Gretchen's machine."

Connie chuckled. "You can get hundreds of designs in this book and online, or you can make your own and scan it in."

An unexpected surge of creativity bloomed in my head.

"Really? It can do any design I come up with?" I asked.

"Pretty much."

Connie rose from the chair. "Customers. I'll be back."

She crossed the store leaving me to stare at the sewing machine as it whirred along and the design materialized right before my eyes. It really was simple. All I'd have to do was learn how to program it, thread it, and off it would go.

The image of the little owl I'd come up with to decorate my pillowcase party poster popped into my head. Suddenly I could imagine it coming to life embroidered on—what?

I spotted the pattern books nearby, sat down, and turned to the craft section. I flipped through the pages until I found a pattern for a bibbed apron. It featured an adjustable neck, two pockets, and extra-long ties.

Since arriving in Hideaway Grove I'd questioned the white aprons Sarah used in her bakery. She'd seemed content with them and, really, nothing was wrong with them. But I couldn't help feeling that a new, colorful design would give the place a lift, and maybe lift Sarah's spirits, too, after all the problems that had been thrown at her lately.

I sat there for a few seconds, thinking, and the whole project came into focus. I could use the green gingham fabric for the apron. There were four bolts of it, which meant there would still be plenty to make the curtains, if Gretchen came back, plus it would look awesome with the bakery colors. I could embroider my cute little owl onto the apron's bib—I could even add "Sarah's Sweets" on it.

This surge of newfound creativity surprised me. Where had it come from?

When Connie finished with her customers I explained my idea. She helped me pick out the right kind of thread in the colors I wanted for the aprons, the lettering, and the owl, and nodded her approval when I found the right apron pattern in the big filing cabinet.

"Sarah is going to love this," Connie told me as we walked to the checkout counter.

"I'm going to surprise her and Jodi."

"My lips are sealed."

"Oh," I said, remembering the reason I'd come here. "I'm in charge of donations for the festival raffle."

"Heard you'd gotten stuck with it. Sorry."

I noticed she hadn't mentioned Iris, though I'm sure Connie knew she had been put in charge of the raffle.

"Give me the forms," Connie said. "I'll fill them out now."

I pulled the documents from the envelope and presented them to her. While she filled them out I wandered through the aisles. This store seemed so exciting now. All the colors, the patterns, the textures—the possibilities. My imagination came alive with the things I could create.

In a bin near the cutting table I spotted spools of lace. There were about a half dozen colors, varying in width from an inch to about three, four yards to a spool. I checked the price. They were downright cheap, and they would make nice embellishments to the pillowcase dresses. I loaded two of each color into a handbasket. I checked out the ribbon and trims on the next aisle, and took everything that was on clearance.

The nonprofit I'd read about online that collected and distributed the dresses in Africa had specifically stated not to use buttons or zippers in the construction of the dresses because there was no way for the girls to repair them if they broke.

But when I looked at the buttons on display and saw how adorable some of them were—rocking horses, bumblebees, teddy bears, all sorts of things meant for children's clothing—I decided I could sew them onto the dresses to fancy them up a bit.

I hadn't actually purchased anything in a while, I realized. Even though my financial future was unknown, I had money tucked away from my job, and it felt good to buy things that would help those girls so far away who had so little.

When I arrived back at the checkout register Connie had finished the donation paperwork.

"You know, you can embroider most anything," Connie pointed out. "How about trying your hand at tote bags? I'm ordering tomorrow. I'll get you some."

"Sure," I said.

Connie began scanning my selections.

"Oh, wait," I said, remembering something Caitlin had told me. I described the cover for the design wall frame. "Can you recommend some batting?"

Without a word, Connie plucked several large bags of it from the shelf and added them to my haul. I paid and headed for the door.

"Let me know if you need help with those aprons," Connie offered.

I called my thanks and left the store.

Since I was on this end of town and close to Blue Bird Lane, I decided to check on Earlene's house. I still hadn't heard from her, and after all this time and all my phone calls, it didn't seem that I would. I didn't know what to think. Was she having fun with her sister? Or hiding out?

Everything was quiet at Earlene's place, no sign

of a problem or another break-in. I used my key to open the front door and walked through the house to make sure a pipe hadn't burst and flooded the place, or any other catastrophe had occurred. All was in order.

Because I'd been in such a creative mode today, ideas for redecorating Earlene's house sprang into my head. There was nothing wrong with how she'd fixed up her place, but I couldn't help thinking of the changes that could be made.

On the back porch I refilled the water bowl and saw that the repair to the door that Mitch had done was holding, and thought about our conversation when I'd seen him here. I wondered if he'd asked Caitlin to share a vendor booth with him at the festival. Her painted dog figurines and the miniature doghouses he'd built made perfect companions. Maybe the two of them were perfect companions for each other. Or maybe Scott was the perfect one for Caitlin. Mitch seemed like a great guy. Maybe Scott was, too.

I double-checked to make sure I'd locked both doors, then left. As I stepped down off the porch I glanced around, afraid I'd find that little orange fur ball Cheddar lurking nearby, ready to dart out into the street again. I worried about her running loose in town, dodging traffic, causing almost as many near collisions as Miss Merriweather.

When I reached the bakery Jodi seemed rooted to the work island in the kitchen and Sarah stood like a statue behind the display case. I froze when I stepped inside, conscious of the odd, strained vibe in the room. Sarah's gaze shifted to the left and I saw Joyce Colby standing by the front window. She had on jeans, worn-looking athletic shoes, a black

T-shirt, and a yellow windbreaker that seemed out of place on her.

"Hi, Joyce," I said, and tried to sound friendly.

"Hello." She paced to the display case but gazed into the kitchen.

"Have you decided?" Sarah asked, straining to sound friendly, as I had.

Joyce took a step to the right and craned her neck to peer behind the counter.

"Huh . . . yes. Give me a cookie. Chocolate chip," she said.

Sarah opened the case. I headed for the sewing studio.

"What's in there?" Joyce asked, following me. "Is that the place you're making those dresses? I saw the signs around town."

"Yes." I know I should have invited her to join us for the pillowcase party, but I couldn't seem to get the words out.

"Good cause . . . I guess," she said.

I smiled, slid the doors open and went inside.

"Big room," Joyce said.

I spun and saw her standing in the doorway looking around, as if mentally measuring every square inch of the room. I dropped my packages on one of the tables, feeling uncomfortable about her being in here, for some reason. I headed toward the doors. Joyce held her position for a few seconds, and finally backed out of the doorway.

Zack and I had discussed the possibility that Miss Merriweather had accidentally hit Iris with her car, and if so, probably hadn't realized it. I'd seen several close calls with her driving. This would be the perfect opportunity to discuss my concerns with Joyce. But something about her was so off-putting I couldn't find the mental energy to talk to her.

"Anything else?" Sarah called.

Joyce turned slowly and went to the display case. She paid for the one cookie, and left.

"What in the world was that all about?" Jodi declared, joining Sarah.

"Seems Joyce is getting more and more odd every time I see her."

"Not that we've seen her in here much," Jodi grumbled. "When was the last time she was here? It's been ages—ages."

"It has," Sarah agreed.

"Then she shows up looking everything over like she's the health inspector trying to find a reason to shut us down," Jodi said. "And she buys one cookie—one cookie!"

"You never know what you're going to get from Joyce," Sarah said. "She can be . . . unpredictable."

"I hope she never comes back," Jodi said. "She's trouble. You remember that assault charge against her a while back. The charges were dropped, but still."

"I heard that Joyce got into a confrontation with Iris," I said, joining them at the display case.

"That figures." Jodi threw her arms out. "Iris was one of the nicest, sweetest, kindest people in town. And, of course, Joyce finds fault with her."

"What were they arguing about?" Sarah asked.

I shrugged. "I don't know for sure. Maybe something to do with Iris's secret lover she met in the alley out back."

"Oh, that." Sarah dismissed the notion with a wave of her hand. "Nonsense."

The bell over the door chimed and I jumped,

thinking Joyce had returned. Instead, Caitlin walked in carrying a sewing machine.

"My mom's. She never uses it anymore," she said. "I thought we'd get started on the design wall."

We went inside the sewing studio and spent a while getting things set up. I decided to go ahead and configure the place for the pillowcase party. We rearranged the tables so we could face each other and talk as we sewed. I broke out the new extension cords and power strips, and we got all the machines powered up.

"I'm thinking a diamond pattern for the design wall frame," Caitlin said.

"Love it."

Caitlin rifled through Gretchen's box of supplies and came up with paper, pencil, and a ruler. She drew a pattern and held it up.

"I think this size will fit perfectly on the frame," she said.

I studied it for a few seconds, feeling really creative and excited about what we were doing. I declared it perfect. Caitlin got started pinning the pattern on the remnants while I unloaded the rest of the things I'd bought.

"That lace is going to look adorable on the dresses," Caitlin said. "Gretchen never did anything like that."

"Here's my other project." I glanced at the doorway to the bakery—no sign of Sarah or Jodi— then laid the apron pattern beside her. "For the bakery. I'm using the gingham fabric, and I'm going to embroider the bib with Gretchen's machine."

Caitlin's eyebrows bobbed. "You're going to tame the beast?"

"Connie walked me through it. It seemed pretty simple, the way she explained it." I hesitated a moment, gathering a little courage. "And I'm going to add my cute little owl with the slogan 'Sarah's Sweets' and 'Look Whoo's Baking.'"

"That's adorable."

"I'm making one for Sarah and Jodi," I said. "I'm going to surprise them."

"They'll love it," Caitlin said. "You should sell them at the festival."

I shook my head. "I wanted to make it special for Sarah and Jodi."

"But it's such a cute concept."

An idea hit me. "Maybe I could do the owl design on other things. Connie suggested tote bags. I could change the slogan to . . . 'Look Whoo's Reading.'"

"I love it. You'll be the hit of the festival."

"Want to share a booth?" I asked. "Or are you sharing one with Mitch?"

She grabbed the scissors and started cutting out diamond shapes. "Don't tell me that story has made the rounds through town already."

I pulled up a chair next to her and started pinning the pattern onto the fabric remnants.

"Mitch told me himself. He said it was just business."

"That's what he told me. But, I don't know, it doesn't feel like business."

"Did you talk to Scott about it?"

"No."

"Do you think he'd mind?"

Caitlin shrugged as she expertly wielded the scissors. "I doubt it."

"Then why not do it?" I asked. "I mean, your

china dog figurines and his doghouses would be an easy sell. And if Scott wouldn't mind, why not do it?"

"It's not Scott I'm concerned about."

I realized then what her hesitation was.

"Your dad?"

"He gets so upset over everything—every little thing. Mom is always telling me not to disagree with him, not to cause a confrontation. She's afraid he's going to have another heart attack. I'm afraid he'd think there was a problem between Scott and me, if I shared the booth with Mitch."

"I know he's counting on you to stay in Hideaway Grove and take over the pet shop," I said.

She'd told me how devastated her dad had been when her older brother moved away. The burden of carrying on with the family business had fallen squarely on Caitlin's shoulders.

"So what are you going to do?"

She sighed. "Do I have a choice?"

We worked on the cover for the design wall frame, taking turns cutting diamond shapes and sewing them together. Caitlin's skills were good, and I was pleased to see that mine had improved considerably since that class at the rec center when we were twelve years old.

When Caitlin left with a promise to come back tomorrow and finish the project, I was a bit restless and wished I could do something to help her with the dilemma she faced. Should she go along with what her dad had in mind for her, keep the peace so her mom wouldn't worry he'd have another heart attack, or not?

I thought about my parents, how they'd driven

me to pursue my education. They'd wanted me to follow in their footsteps. I'd refused, disappointing both of them.

My rebellion hadn't worked out so great, it seemed.

I couldn't help Caitlin, of course. In fact, I was probably the last person she should take advice from. She had a tough decision to make, and she'd have to make it on her own since she was the one who'd have to live with the consequences. Like I was.

Shaking off those troubling thoughts, I remembered that I had to go back to Anna's thrift shop and pick up the things I'd bought, and that reminded me of what she'd said about seeing the mystery man in the alley with Iris, and Joyce's displeasure with her. Zack had said the sheriff didn't consider the man a suspect in Iris's murder. Maybe if he'd taken the investigation a step further, he'd have learned something valuable.

Of course, I could do it, even if the sheriff hadn't.

I fetched my laptop and started a Google search. Zack had said the man was an assistant manager at a home improvement store in Richland, a town north of Hideaway Grove. Richland wasn't a big place. How many of that kind of store could there be?

I found out pretty quickly—two.

I paged through both the sites and, sure enough, in small-town fashion, there were photos of the staff on the sites. I took screenshots, and went to find Anna.

It was late and stores were closing for the evening, but Anna was still in her shop.

"Ready to pick up your things?" she asked.

"Sure. But I wanted to show you something first."

She perked up, intrigued.

"Do any of these men look familiar?" I held up my phone and swiped through the photos. On the fourth one, she gasped.

"That's him. Oh, my goodness, that's him," she declared.

"Who?" I asked, just to be sure.

"Iris's mystery man."

"You're sure? You're positive? This is the man you saw out back in the alley, driving the white car, meeting Iris?"

"Absolutely. How did you find him?"

I couldn't answer. All I could do was think and try to sort out what I'd just learned.

This guy, this Gerald Avery, had been to Hideaway Grove. He'd lied to Sheriff Grumman.

I could think of only one reason he'd do that.

CHAPTER 22

Yesterday I'd thought there was only one reason Gerald Avery would lie to the sheriff about having been to Hideaway Grove—he'd murdered Iris. Today, I couldn't ignore the strong possibility that Gerald's motive for lying to Sheriff Grumman was simply to cover himself because he was cheating on his wife.

Most of my attention had been focused on pillowcase dresses this morning. I'd been in the sewing studio for hours cutting pillowcases to size— I added purchasing another pair of Gretchen's awesome scissors to my to-do list—so they'd be ready for the pillowcase party. I'd also made several dresses myself to perfect my sewing skills. My thoughts had wandered from Iris, to the festival, to my old job, to my idea of making tote bags, and aprons for Sarah and Jodi. Of all those things, making the aprons was the one thing I felt confident I could take on and make work.

The biggest part of my thoughts hovered over

Iris's murder. My mental list of suspects paraded through my mind as I stepped on the foot pedal and laid down an—almost—straight line of stitches. I'd come up with a list of suspects and had made a little progress narrowing it down, though with mixed results.

The elusive somebody-didn't-like-Iris suspect had been identified, sort of. It seemed several people didn't like her—Connie, Valerie, and Joyce. Connie and Valerie had a reason for disliking Iris, but I wasn't sure if it was strong enough to actually cause one of them to kill her.

Joyce had been seen in verbal confrontations with Iris. I didn't know what their arguments had been about so I had no way of knowing if their disagreement could have escalated into a full-fledged motive for murder.

If Earlene would return my calls I could likely cross her name off my suspect list. But since I still didn't know why she had been in the alley, of all places, at the exact moment, of all times, that Iris had been struck by the car, I couldn't stop thinking she was somehow involved. It didn't help that Earlene had admitted to me that she didn't like Iris.

That left me with the mystery man himself, Iris's possible secret lover Gerald Avery. I knew now that he'd actually been in Hideaway Grove. He'd lied to Sheriff Grumman about coming here so I figured the reason he'd given the sheriff for staying in touch with Iris—helping her with home repairs—could also be a lie. I also knew that he was married which meant, it seemed, that he was lying to his wife, as well. Maybe he was lying to Iris, too, and hadn't revealed he had a family.

I heaved a sigh and sat back from the sewing machine. There were lots of *maybes* surrounding Gerald Avery. I needed some definite info to either confirm or eliminate him as a suspect. No way would Sheriff Grumman tell me anything, and Zack had already refused to share any specific info with me. I'd have to figure out some other avenue to pursue.

For a moment I considered telling Zack that Anna had identified Iris's mystery man as Gerald Avery, and that he'd lied to the sheriff about his visits to Hideaway Grove. I hesitated to put myself in that position. First, because it was possible the sheriff already had that info and Zack hadn't wanted to tell me; he'd been adamant about me not involving myself in the investigation. Second, because I figured the more distance and less involvement I had with Sheriff Grumman, the better off I'd be.

Still, I couldn't stand by and do nothing, in case the sheriff really didn't know that Gerald was lying to him. But I'd wait before going to him, I decided. I'd get more information about Gerald, and when—and if—I discovered something important, I'd approach the sheriff. I just had to figure out how to get the info.

I wouldn't find it sitting here in the sewing studio, I decided, though it was quite peaceful in here with the whir of the machine and the delicious smells of baking cookies wafting in through the pocket doors. I gathered my things and left.

"I'm heading out to get donations," I said to Sarah as she pulled chocolate chip cookies from the oven. They smelled so good my knees weakened.

"How's it going?" she asked.

"Great. Everybody wants to donate. It's pretty easy," I said. "Makes me wonder why Iris hadn't approached any of the merchants."

"It does seem odd," Sarah agreed.

"Need anything while I'm out?"

Sarah thought for a few seconds. "Not right now. Maybe you could make a delivery for me later?"

"Sure," I said, and left the bakery.

Another perfect day in Hideaway Grove presented itself as I headed down Main Street. The sun was warm and bright, doors stood open welcoming shoppers, and visitors and locals strolled along the sidewalks.

Outside Barry's Pet Emporium an older couple paused to let their dog drink from the water bowl beside the door. The little beagle had on an orange collar with a matching bow that made me think of Cheddar, the cat that caused more traffic near misses than Miss Merriweather. I hoped Cheddar wouldn't stop for a drink on such a busy street, and instead would go to Earlene's house; she along with lots of folks in town kept water bowls out for our four-legged citizens.

"Abbey? Oh, Abbey?"

Anna called my name as I passed her thrift shop. I turned back and saw her hurrying after me. I figured she wanted to ask when I planned to pick up the iron and ironing board I'd purchased—I'd already taken the sewing machine to the sewing studio—but she jumped right in with something else.

"I think I've made a terrible mistake," Anna

said, twisting her fingers together. "Those photos you showed me . . ."

For a few seconds I felt as distressed as Anna looked. If she'd been wrong identifying Iris's mystery man as Gerald Avery, it meant I'd been wrong adding him to my suspect list.

Good thing I hadn't immediately gone to Zack with the news.

"You're not sure now that you recognized him?" I asked.

"No. No, it's not that. It was him. I'm sure." Anna drew in a heavy breath and leaned closer, lowering her voice. "It's just that . . . well . . . it's just that I think I shouldn't have told you I recognized him."

Anna was growing more upset by the second and I didn't have a real handle on exactly why. I summoned my patience and forced myself to wait.

"If word gets out it will bring up Iris's death and all that silly talk about her being murdered," Anna said. "Everybody will start talking about it again. Everybody will say it could ruin the festival. And everybody will blame *me*."

"Oh . . ." I mumbled.

"I can't be the target of all that gossip and ugly talk. I just can't put myself in that position."

I couldn't blame her. It had, after all, driven Earlene out of Hideaway Grove.

"I mean, I don't want to be a bad person," Anna went on. "I don't want to withhold some important information from the sheriff. But all that talk about Iris being murdered is just craziness. Iris was having a romantic fling with that man. That's all. There was nothing sinister about it. Don't you think?"

I saw no reason to tell Anna that I'd discovered Gerald Avery had lied to the sheriff about being in Hideaway Grove, and all that talk about Iris being murdered was true, not just some craziness. But I agreed with her—bringing up Iris's death again wasn't a good idea.

"Did you tell anyone you recognized the man in the photo?" I asked.

She shook her head quickly. "No. After I thought about it, I realized what it could lead to."

"Then there's nothing to worry about," I said, in my best reassuring voice. "I'm not going to mention it to anyone."

"You're not?" she asked, sounding hopeful and relieved.

"I don't think it would serve any useful purpose."

She nodded, then frowned again. "What about the sheriff? Should I tell him?"

I didn't feel right discouraging her from coming forward with vital information, but she didn't wait for my response.

"He's awfully busy with other things," Anna said. "Important things."

I didn't say anything.

"Very important things," Anna declared, warming to her reasoning. "He should be spending his time investigating all this mischief in town. That's what he should be doing."

A few more seconds passed while Anna seemed to stew over her decision.

"Of course, if Sheriff Grumman asks, I'll tell him. I won't lie." Anna drew a cleansing breath. "Well, that settles that."

Anna went back into her store.

I headed down Main Street stopping at merchants I hadn't already hit, asking for donations for the festival raffle, explaining that I was taking over from Iris. Everybody was friendly, anxious to donate, excited about the festival. Life in a small town.

I worked my way through the businesses, all the way to the corner of Owl Avenue. Across the street sat Miss Merriweather's lovely old Victorian home. I'd seen her name on the master list of previous years' donors, but at the moment I hesitated to approach the house.

Joyce's car sat at the curb. I remembered it from when Caitlin and I had been there to drop off pet supplies. Something about Joyce always hit me wrong. I wasn't sure what it was. Some sort of off-putting aura seemed to surround her. Under other circumstances, I'd think maybe it was just me. But most everyone else in town seemed to feel the same. Plus, she was on my list of murder suspects.

I wasn't all that anxious to encounter Joyce today, but I needed to get the donations finished. I decided that once inside, I'd focus my attention on Miss Merriweather, ignore Joyce, and get out quickly.

My plan fell apart as soon as I crossed the street and walked up the driveway. The door of the detached garage stood open. Miss Merriweather's car was gone.

"Darn . . ." I muttered.

No way was I going to ask Joyce about the donation. I'd come back another time.

But as I turned to go, the front door opened. Miss Merriweather stepped out onto the porch.

"Hello, dear," she called.

She had on a pale yellow dress, flats, and her white hair was caught up in a neat bun, the quintessential image of everybody's favorite grandma.

I couldn't resist smiling as I climbed onto the porch and gestured to the garage.

"I thought you were gone," I said.

"Oh, no. No, no. Joyce took my car for service. She's such a dear. She makes sure it's in good shape. She even takes it to put gas in it for me. Those pumps are so complicated."

I heaved a mental sigh of relief, thankful Joyce's thoughtfulness kept Miss Merriweather off the streets of Hideaway Grove, at least occasionally.

"Come in, dear. Come in." Miss Merriweather went into the house and waved me inside with her.

"Do you think Joyce will be back soon?" I asked, wondering how quickly I could get this visit over with, if necessary.

"She just left. She's hoping to have lunch with a friend."

Joyce had a friend? I was surprised.

"That sweet woman from the café." Miss Merriweather tapped her finger against her chin, thinking. "Earlene. Yes, Earlene."

Now I was even more surprised. Joyce didn't know Earlene had left town? Some bit of gossip hadn't made the rounds?

"I'm in charge of getting donations for the festival raffle this year," I said.

"How lovely. Such a worthwhile cause."

"I'm taking over from Iris, so I'm running a bit behind."

"She was so excited about heading up that committee," Miss Merriweather said. "She spoke of it often."

"She did?" I couldn't keep the doubt out of my voice but Miss Merriweather didn't seem to notice.

"Come take a look."

She headed off through the house. I expected her to lead the way to the room that held her little sweeties, her birds, but instead she took me to the library.

Peace and tranquility washed over me, as it had the last time I was here. Light shone through the line of stained-glass windows. Once more, I thought of my parents and wondered where—literally—in the world they were.

"Iris and I had such lovely talks in here," Miss Merriweather said, gesturing to the two green leather wingback chairs. "She loved books, as a librarian would, of course. All sorts of books—fiction, nonfiction. And writers, of course. Encyclopedic knowledge, really."

"She must have been in heaven here," I said, looking around at the towering shelves of books.

"My grandfather was a voracious reader. He never got rid of any book. Everything he ever purchased and read is here. Iris was fascinated." Miss Merriweather smiled at the memory. "Once when I brought us tea, I walked in and found her all the way up at the top."

I noticed a ladder on tracks, used to access the top shelves.

"I was stunned," she declared. "I told Iris those were the very oldest books up there, out of date, and of no real interest now. But she insisted I was wrong. All books had great value. Oh, how she loved them."

The excitement I heard in her voice made me a little sad.

"You must miss Iris," I said.

"I do. We had nice talks. She was so interested in my family, our history, the origins of Hideaway Grove."

"Did she talk about *her* family?"

It was an honest question, I'd thought. But as soon as it came out of my mouth I realized this was an opportunity to possibly learn something about Iris that might help find her killer.

"No, not really," she said.

"Did she talk about her life back in Richland?"

"Not that I recall. I think Iris was perfectly happy here, meeting new friends, learning a new language, bringing new programs to the library."

"I understand she had a new man in her life," I said.

"Did she?"

"Someone saw them together in the alley behind Sarah's Sweets and Sassy Fashions," I said.

Miss Merriweather smiled. "How nice for them."

It seemed that she had no info to contribute to my hunt for Iris's killer. Then something else occurred to me. Zack and I had shared our concern that Miss Merriweather may have hit Iris in the alley unintentionally and without realizing it.

"Do you know the alley? Have you driven through there?" I asked.

"Oh, yes. Certainly. Traffic is so heavy on Main Street. I often dart through the alley to take a shortcut."

This wasn't what I'd hoped to hear. A wave of dread passed through me.

Miss Merriweather hadn't contributed anything to my hunt for Iris's killer.

Maybe that was because I was looking at her killer.

CHAPTER 23

One of the new residents of Hideaway Grove who'd been added to my master list of donors was Mitch. I knew he intended to have a vendor booth at the festival, so I figured asking him for a donation would be a slam dunk. Besides, after the upset I'd just experienced visiting Miss Merriweather, I was anxious to talk to somebody I didn't think was a murderer.

I found his home easily enough on Hawk Avenue, a typical cottage painted pale green surrounded by a picket fence and lots of flowers and shrubs. The only difference between his house and most of the others in Hideaway Grove was the garage. It had been converted to his workshop, I saw as I walked up the driveway. The roll-up door was open. Inside were stacks of wood, workbenches, tools, machines, and a number of projects which seemed to be in progress.

Mitch switched off the table saw as I approached.

He had on a white T-shirt, jeans, and work boots. Bits of sawdust and wood chips clung to him along with a fine mist of perspiration.

"I'm sorry to interrupt your work," I said, stepping inside. "I'm here on official town business."

He pulled off his safety glasses and tossed them onto the table saw.

"No worries. My schedule is flexible," he said, and grinned.

I thought about Mitch's previous life. He'd been consumed with his job, his career. I'd been the same way—driven to be the best, pushing to accomplish more, stand out, be a star performer. Now he spent his days creating beautiful things, not worrying about his next employee review, or an awful supervisor, or whether his coworkers would have his back.

"So this is where the magic happens?" I asked, gazing around his shop.

The place was carefully organized, I saw. It smelled pleasantly of sawdust, paint, and varnish.

He gave me a modest shrug and pointed. "That chest is going to New York. The rocker beside it will head to New Orleans when I get it finished."

"These pieces are awesome," I said, and they really were. The details he'd carved into the wood were intricate, exquisite, displaying a level of craftsmanship that could only be found in high-end custom work.

"You get orders from all over the country?" I asked.

"International, too. It's enough to keep me busy, and a little more."

"And you still have time to make these?"

I pointed to a line of miniature doghouses sitting on a shelf. He'd told me he was making them to sell at the festival. I saw right away they were the perfect size to accommodate the china dog figurines Caitlin painted—I saw that because several of her dogs were lined up with them.

"The dogs and the houses look really cute together," I said.

He nodded without saying anything.

"I guess you haven't gotten around to sending Caitlin's figurines to—what was it, your grandmothers?" I asked.

He blushed. "Busted."

As an excuse to visit Caitlin at the pet store, I guessed buying her dog figurines was a good as any and, really, kind of sweet.

"Take a look at your design board," Mitch said, seemingly anxious to change the subject.

He gestured to four pieces of wood that would comprise the frame. The wood was bare and he'd mitered the corners. It looked as if the frame would be about six feet wide and four feet high, enough to take up most of the designated wall space in the sewing studio. Perfect.

It didn't escape me that he'd put aside what were surely high-paying jobs to make the frame for my sewing studio.

"Thank you," I said. "You jumped on this really quick. I appreciate it."

"Easy job. Glad I could help," he said. "The corkboard backing was just delivered so it's almost ready to go."

"We're finishing up the covering for the frame," I said.

He paused, and I couldn't help but imagine he was thinking about Caitlin since he knew we were working on it together.

"What's this official town business you're tending to?" Mitch asked, as if he wanted again to change the subject.

"Donations for the festival raffle. I'm taking over for Iris." I must have spoken those sentences dozens of times by now.

"I'm in," he said.

"The Town of Hideaway Grove thanks you very much." I pulled the documents out of the envelope and handed them to him. "Call me and I'll pick them up, or drop them off at the bakery."

"I'll drop them off," he said. "I'll be over that way helping set up the vendor booths on the village green."

Constructing the display board for my design wall, purchasing a vendor booth, making a donation for the raffle, and helping with setup—all of which he'd cheerfully taken on. Mitch was a nice guy, no doubt about it.

"Let me know when you want your display board installed," Mitch said.

"Will do," I said as I headed down the driveway. "And thanks again!"

He waved and disappeared back into his shop.

Mitch really was a nice guy. The thought ran through my head again as I walked toward Main Street. Was Scott, Caitlin's fiancé, as nice?

I guess I'd find out if Caitlin ever brought him around.

When I reached Main Street I slipped into Anna's thrift shop. She was busy with customers so

I waved and grabbed the iron and ironing board I'd purchased from behind the checkout counter

There's no easy way to carry an ironing board. It's awkward, a little too long and a little too heavy to breeze along comfortably. Thankfully I got out of the store without knocking anything over.

Outside, I heard quick footsteps behind me and looked back to see Zack approaching. He had on civilian clothes, jeans and a navy-blue polo shirt. He smelled really good. I wondered why he was out and where he was going. He took the ironing board out of my hands, making it look a lot lighter.

"Don't tell me Anna donated this thing for the raffle," Zack said as we headed down Main Street.

"It's for the sewing studio. And, yes, she made a donation. They're going quite well."

"So why the frown?"

Zack was a trained observer—which was sort of annoying at the moment. I hadn't realized I was frowning.

"I visited with Miss Merriweather today." I gave him a knowing glance which he picked up on right away.

He switched into deputy-sheriff mode immediately.

"You talked to her about the dent in her car?" He huffed. "Abbey, I've asked you over and over not to get involved."

"And I've wondered over and over why, exactly, you think I should do what you tell me to do." It came out sounding kind of stinky, more than I meant for it to. I stopped and faced him. "Look, I'm just a little annoyed right now."

"What happened?"

He had a way of speaking, a tone in his voice,

that made me want to melt into a puddle and tell him absolutely everything I'd ever done, thought, or tried in my life—especially the bad stuff.

"Miss Merriweather, for one thing," I said. "She told me she frequently darted through the alley where Iris was killed."

Zack frowned. "Did she mention seeing Iris there?"

"No. But that doesn't mean she didn't hit her accidentally and keep going." I shook my head. "Plus, I feel really sorry for her. You should have heard the way she talked about Iris, all the visits they had, how much the two of them loved books, how they sat in her grandfather's library and chatted. And now all she has is occasional visits from someone like me, asking for a donation, and that niece of hers."

He nodded slowly, taking in what I'd said. "What's the other thing? You said Miss Merriweather was one thing troubling you. What else?"

"I stopped by Mitch's place to ask about a donation. He agreed, of course. He's such a nice guy," I said. "And I can't for the life of me understand what's going on between Caitlin and Scott, and him."

"Stay out of it." There was nothing comforting in his voice now.

"I know I should—and I'm trying to," I told him. "But thinking of the three of them got me to thinking about those arguments people in town saw between Iris and Joyce. What if there was a love triangle going on between the two of them and Gerald Avery? Has there ever been a bigger motive for murder than—"

"How did you learn his name?" he demanded.

Oops. I hadn't meant to let that slip.

"Who told you?" he asked.

I sure wasn't going to give up Anna.

"Look," he said. "If somebody at the sheriff's office is giving out confidential information that could—"

"It wasn't hard to figure out," I insisted. "I just looked it up on the internet."

That didn't seem to make him any happier.

"Abbey, you have to stay away from—"

"—the investigation. The sheriff is handling it. I know," I said.

He fumed for a few seconds, seeming to think I would come forth with more information. I didn't.

"You have to admit jealousy is a tried-and-true motive for murder," I said. "Right?"

"Maybe." He shook his head. "But between Joyce and Iris? The two of them are as different as day and night."

I couldn't disagree.

"Has the sheriff learned anything new about Iris's death?" I asked, then added, "Something you can repeat?"

Zack paused for a few seconds, mentally debating what to say, apparently. Finally, he moved closer and lowered his voice.

"Something wasn't right about Iris."

"What do you mean?"

He shifted uncomfortably. "I don't know. The more the sheriff finds out about her, the stranger she seems."

"Why?" I asked again.

"Everybody thought she was dedicated to her job, making great strides toward fitting into town and improving things at the library," he said. "But would anybody really be that dedicated, try that hard?"

The image of Mitch flashed into my head. He was trying hard to fit in, to be a part of Hideaway Grove, contribute to the town. I hadn't thought anything was odd about it. Apparently, Zack knew that something the sheriff had uncovered about Iris was different.

"I don't know," Zack mumbled. "It just makes me think she was involved in something."

"Well," I pointed out. "Somebody *did* murder her."

"And we still don't know why."

"I guess if we could figure out the motive . . ." I left the words hanging, hoping he knew more and would jump in with it. He didn't.

We walked to the bakery. Several customers were at the display case. Sarah and Jodi waved—Jodi gave me a questioning eyebrow bob upon seeing Zack—and we went into the sewing studio.

"Thanks for the help," I said as I motioned to where I'd like the ironing board placed.

He leaned it against the wall. We stared at each other for another awkward moment. I wondered again where he was going. The Night Owl for a beer with a friend? Or on a date?

Thinking he was seeing someone gave me an icky feeling. I forced my thoughts in another direction.

"Any word on my car?" I asked.

Zack didn't look awkward. He looked annoyed.

"Anxious to leave here?" he asked. "There's nothing about our little town you like, nothing that might make you want to stay?"

From the intensity of his gaze and the wave of

heat he suddenly gave off, I doubted he was asking
for my opinion of Hideaway Grove's civic and
tourist attractions. But what was it? Something personal? I wasn't sure. I was too caught up in the moment to answer.

After a few seconds, Zack stepped back.

"Think about it," he said, and left.

Cool air swirled around me in his wake, breaking the spell he'd somehow cast over me. The feelings he'd evoked warmed my insides. I hadn't felt
that way since . . . well, maybe never.

I gave myself a mental shake and forced myself
to straighten up my sewing area, although it was
perfectly fine. I wasn't sure what Zack had meant—
which was yet another *maybe* I'd been dealing with
for too long.

Maybe losing my job in L.A. wasn't my fault.
Maybe I'd get it back. Maybe I'd have to find another job. Maybe Miss Merriweather had hit Iris by
accident. Maybe on purpose. Maybe Earlene was
involved. Maybe Joyce, maybe Valerie, or Connie,
or Gerald.

Maybe, maybe, maybe. I had too many unknowns.
But one of those things, just one, was something I
could deal with.

I left the sewing studio. The customers had gone.
Sarah was at the work island icing a two-tiered birthday cake.

"Could I borrow your car?" I asked.

She looked up, surprised. Jodi turned to me,
too.

"Is something wrong?" Sarah asked.

"I'd like to go for a drive, get a change of scen-
ery," I said, trying to sound casual, and most of all,

innocent. "Maybe visit some thrift stores and find more pillowcases."

"Well, sure. When do you need it?"

"Tomorrow," I said.

Tomorrow I was going to find some evidence in Iris's murder. And I knew just where to look.

CHAPTER 24

No need punching Richland into the GPS app on my phone, I decided the next morning as I backed Sarah's Chevy out of her garage. The town where Iris used to live and work—and Gerald still lived and worked—was a straight shot north on the 101 freeway, about two hours away.

Being behind the wheel again felt strange. I paused at the end of the driveway and took a few seconds to adjust the mirrors, check out the pre-programed radio stations, then headed down Hummingbird Lane. Sarah hadn't asked anything more about my impromptu trip when she'd handed over the keys this morning, just told me to drive safe and have fun, something I couldn't recall my mom ever saying.

At the corner I lingered for an extra few seconds watching for traffic, then turned right onto Main Street. I drew a deep breath and told myself I could do this. I could make this trip and discover something that would lead to Iris's murderer. Nothing would go wrong—and then I spotted Zack.

He stood on the corner of Owl Avenue, in uniform. He glanced my way, did a double take.

I cringed. He'd seen me, recognized me. Of all the luck.

I wasn't under strict orders from the sheriff not to leave Hideaway Grove, but I hadn't wanted my trip to become common knowledge—especially to Zack.

I sped up slightly and looked in my rearview mirror. Zack stood on the corner watching, frowning. I sped up a bit more.

Would Zack radio the sheriff's office and report I was leaving town? Would the sheriff dispatch a patrol car to stop me?

A little wave of panic swept through me. My thoughts raced. More than likely, Zack would assume I was heading south, back to Los Angeles. He had no reason to think I was going in the opposite direction. Or did he? He knew I'd discovered Gerald Avery's identity and his place of work. Would Zack figure out where I was going?

Maybe. Maybe not.

My plan had been to stop at the convenience store and fill up on my way out of town, but when I approached the freeway entrance ramp I gunned it and kept going. My gaze bounced from the freeway in front of me to the freeway behind me. My palms started to sweat. My heart raced.

I wasn't cut out for a life on the run.

After about fifteen minutes with no sign of the police I figured I was in the clear, and relaxed. I

turned up the volume on the radio and listened to
Sarah's eighties station, and let the miles roll by.
And, wow, did they.

The town of Richland was just under two hours
north of Hideaway Grove. I hadn't thought much
about the distance until now that I was driving it.
About two hours each way, plus maybe a bathroom
break and a stop at a drive-thru took a big chunk
of time.

How often had Gerald made the drive? Anna
had mentioned seeing him several times in the
alley with Iris. How had he covered all those hours
away from home or away from his job? How many
fake doctor and dentist appointments could he
reasonably claim? What sort of excuse would his
wife continue to believe?

All that to see Iris? In the alley? To explain—
supposedly—how to fix something that needed repairing in her studio apartment?

It seemed more likely that Iris and Gerald were
lovers. So why had they met near the alley, blocks
away from Iris's apartment on Dove Drive?

Did anything about Iris's death make sense?

Zack had said there was something odd about
her. I couldn't disagree. But what was it? And had
it led to her murder?

I hoped Gerald would tell me when I got there.

The Home Depot where Gerald worked was lo-
cated on the edge of Richland, their huge sign easily seen from the freeway. I took the off-ramp and
headed in that direction. This area of town was rel-
atively new, it seemed. There were several small

shopping centers crowded with chain stores and fast-food restaurants.

The area at the front of the Home Depot displayed a line of barbeque grills, dozens of lawn chairs, several storage sheds, and racks of hanging baskets of blooming plants, everything a homeowner would need to fix up their place for the summer. I parked and went inside. Customers pushed carts loaded with mostly things I didn't recognize.

The store was huge. I could have wandered through the massive aisles for days and not found Gerald, so I went to the customer service desk near the entrance and told the clerk a huge lie— that I'd spoken with Gerald previously about a discount on an order of plants and needed to follow up with him. She looked as if she didn't care one way or the other and paged him to lawns and gardens. I followed the smell of fertilizer and spotted him near a table of bedding plants.

Gerald looked like his photo I'd seen on the store's website—thinning hair, drooping jowls, downturned lips. Add to that a thickening middle on the downhill slide toward fifty.

He wasn't what I'd call a handsome guy, and with a mid-level management job, plus a wife and kids, I really didn't understand the romantic draw Iris felt for him. But who was I to judge?

"Hi, Gerald. I'm Abbey," I said, as if he should recognize me.

He glanced around, confused. I looked around as if I, too, was trying to spot a woman wanting a discount on plants.

Finally, he gave up and said, "What can I help you with?"

The long drive had given me time to come up with what I should say to Gerald to get him to talk about Iris. I'd run several scenarios through my head and ultimately decided to wing it when I met him.

"I'm from Hideaway Grove," I said. "I'm a friend of Iris's."

He stiffened slightly. "Oh?"

"She passed away."

Gerald didn't respond. Obviously, he already knew.

"I wanted to let you know about her memorial service," I said, which was a lie. No service was planned for Iris that I knew of. "She'd mentioned you two knew each other."

He'd looked cautious. Now he looked suspicious.

"She told you about . . . us?"

"She did."

"You and Iris were . . . friends? Coworkers?" he asked.

Seemed Gerald needed more convincing, so I trotted out the line I'd repeated dozens of times in the past few days while asking for donations to the festival raffle.

"Actually, I've taken over for Iris," I said.

Gerald's face drained of color. He glanced around, fidgeted, and gulped hard. I guess Iris had explained to him about being stuck with heading up the donation committee.

"I was hoping you could fill me in on some information about Iris and her time here for the memorial service," I said. "How long had you two—"

"Call me here in a few days," he said, his voice

low and rushed. "We'll talk then about the ... *memorial service.*"

He spun around and hurried away.

"But—"

He disappeared down the plumbing supply aisle. I could have gone after him but I didn't think it would do any good. He could hide from me forever in this giant store, and even if I found him it seemed unlikely he'd tell me anything.

Obviously, my interrogation skills needed work. I'd gotten no information from him at all, only an empty promise that he would talk to me later, which I didn't think for a second he would actually do.

I'd come all this way for nothing, it seemed.

Disheartened, I left the store and sat in my car. Maybe I could hang out in the parking lot, wait for him to leave work for the day, and follow him home. And then what? Confront him at his house? With his wife and kids there? I didn't see this as a productive option.

It seemed there was nothing left to do but head home. Still, I wasn't ready to face that long drive again. I pulled out my phone and googled thrift shops in the area. There were four of them, only two miles away. Maybe I could find some pillowcases. At least the day wouldn't be a total bust.

My GPS took me to Richland Avenue, the street that must have been the main drag through town back in the day. Storefronts crowded the street, most of them empty and slightly run-down. Where Hideaway Grove had embraced their shops and made the area a mecca for tourists and artists, Richland had abandoned their old-school center of town.

I parked at the curb and fed the meter. Only a

few pedestrians were out; trash blew around in the breeze. I was headed for the closest thrift shop when a building across the street and down the block drew my attention—the library. Why hadn't I thought about going there?

My investigative skills definitely needed work.

This had to be the library where Iris had worked. My spirits lifted. Gerald hadn't given me any info. Surely someone in the library could.

The aura of peace and tranquility swept over me when I went inside, as entering a library always did. A number of people roamed the stacks, several sat at tables diligently working on something; all the computers were in use. Everyone was quiet.

Two women were at the desk moving stacks of books around. Both looked competent and capable, dressed conservatively in twin sets and pants, with sensible hair. I approached and waited a few seconds until they looked up at me.

"Hello," I said, remembering to keep my voice low. "I didn't know if you'd heard, but Iris Duncan passed away."

In unison, their expressions soured.

"You came all the way from Portland to tell us that?" one of them asked.

"Portland? No, Hideaway Grove."

They looked at each other, their expressions souring further.

"Well, that explains it," one of them said.

A young woman joined them with a stack of books, set them down, and started shuffling things around.

"Explains what?" I asked.

"Never mind," one of the women said. "Was there something you wanted?"

"I thought you'd like to know about Iris's memorial service," I said, trotting out the same lie I'd told Gerald.

"I hardly think anyone here would—" She stopped, noticing the younger woman. "That's fine, Brandi. You can go now."

She glanced at all of us, then left.

The librarian lifted her chin and pursed her lips. "Thank you for letting us know." A dismissal, plain and simple.

I stood there for a few seconds, waiting. Neither of them spoke, just continued their cold, detached stares. I walked away.

I doubted I'd ever have investigative skills good enough to pry info out of those two.

But I'd learned two things—the librarians thought Iris had moved to Portland, and they didn't seem as excited about Iris's job performance as the folks in Hideaway Grove had been. None of that information jumped out at me as a break-in-the-case clue to finding her murderer.

At least I could still find some pillowcases at the thrift stores, I thought as I left the library.

As I approached the thrift store I spotted Brandi ahead of me, standing outside a comic book store. She'd been waiting for me, I realized.

"Is it true?" Tears stood in her eyes. "Iris is . . . dead?"

I figured her for early twenties, with dark hair, wearing a sweater and jeans. After the reception I'd received from the librarians I was surprised to see her upset.

"You hadn't heard?" I asked.

She uttered a disgusted grunt. "This place. We've got a newspaper. Who reads a newspaper anymore?"

"It's true, I'm afraid." I didn't think it was necessary to go into the gruesome details of Iris's death. "Car accident."

Brandi sniffed and blinked back her tears. "Iris was such a nice lady. I liked her a lot."

"I got the idea the others didn't." I nodded toward the library.

"I don't know why. Iris was always friendly. She helped everybody. But they didn't like her. They were always whispering about her, watching her, like she wasn't good enough to go into some parts of the library."

"You must have missed her when she moved," I said.

"I helped her pack and put her things in storage. She had so much nice stuff." Brandi frowned. "Iris said she was moving to Portland, but you said you were from Hideaway Grove? I don't understand."

I didn't understand, either.

"I guess Iris was glad to leave, after the way she was treated here," Brandi said. "Did people like her better there?"

I wanted to say yes to make her feel better, but I hesitated. I didn't know how the librarians in Hideaway Grove felt about her. Someone had mentioned they were a bit put out because she'd made so many changes and instituted new programs that made them look bad, but I didn't know if that was true.

"Iris was very well thought of in Hideaway Grove," I said. "Was there anyone else in town she was close to?"

Brandi thought for a moment. "Not that I know of. She hadn't lived here long."

"A boyfriend, maybe?"

"I don't think so."

I wouldn't need great skills to interrogate Brandi; she seemed happy to tell me everything she knew. But I couldn't think of anything else to ask her.

She pulled her phone from her pocket and looked at the time.

"I'd better go. Thanks for coming, for letting me know about Iris," Brandi said. "I miss her."

We shared a sad smile and she left.

I made quick work of going through the thrift stores and buying pillowcases. I also picked up another sewing machine and several other things. My head was so full of everything I'd heard today, I had trouble focusing on my shopping.

I headed home with thoughts buzzing in my head. When I reached the Hideaway Grove off-ramp, I swung into the convenience store and filled up with gas. Inside, I looked for Joyce and was glad she wasn't working today. Nearby was the tire store Caitlin's fiancé's family owned. I considered stopping by and introducing myself, but I was tired from the drive and had a little headache.

The sun was setting when I swung into Sarah's driveway. Shadows stretched across the backyard as I pulled into the garage. I opened the trunk, grabbed everything I'd purchased today. Juggling the bags of pillowcases and the sewing machine, I closed the garage door and turned to go into the house, then jumped back.

Zack sat on the steps.

CHAPTER 25

"You scared me," I said, catching my breath.

"I was kind of scared, too," Zack said, rising from the steps, "thinking about where you were all day and what you were doing."

"You thought I went back to L.A.?"

"You went to see Gerald Avery."

My cheeks flushed, knowing I'd been found out. I wondered how he knew. I'd checked the freeway for patrol cars. Surely, a helicopter hadn't been dispatched.

"It wasn't hard to figure out," he said. "Was it worth the trip?"

I'd had a long day. My head hurt. I was tired and hungry. He'd ambushed me getting out of the car. I'd been forced into this unpleasant day partly because Zack had refused to tell me much of anything the sheriff had uncovered, so I wasn't inclined to be forthcoming at the moment.

"You can't share any information because it's an

ongoing investigation," I said. "And I can't share anything because—"

"—you're being stubborn."

"I'm not being stubborn," I insisted, although actually I was. I stewed for a moment. "Look, we both have information about Iris's death. One of us needs to show some faith and share that info."

He looked at me. I looked back. A minute dragged by. He kept staring, waiting. So did I.

"When I said one of us needs to share information," I said, "I meant *you*."

His lip curled up. He fought it, but finally a dimple appeared as a smile broke over his face.

"Okay," he said, surrendering. "Let's talk."

Zack took the sewing machine and my shopping bags from me and placed them on the steps, then sat down. He scooted over a bit and patted the spot beside him. I sat down.

Heat radiated from him. He smelled really good.

"Sheriff Grumman learned about Gerald Avery from Iris's phone contacts," Zack said. "Sheriff also found a couple of people in Richland, casual friends she'd called a few times. Sylvia—Sylvia Peyton—at our library was in Iris's contacts. Other than that, there was only the usual stuff—doctor, dentist, insurance. And that was it."

"No family?"

"Nope."

"Strange," I said. "I talked to Gerald, briefly. He didn't seem upset when I told him Iris was dead, so I figured he already knew. He definitely didn't want to talk about it. He said I should call him later, but there was something odd about our conversation."

"Odd how?"

"He sure didn't act like a man whose lover had recently died," I said. "I stopped by the library where Iris worked. The ladies there definitely did not like her. But get this—she'd told them she was moving to Portland."

Zack considered this info for a few seconds. "She had quite a bit of money in the bank. Cash deposits. From Gerald?"

"Maybe he was helping her out financially. I mean, he must have been crazy about her to make that long drive to see her."

"I don't know," he said, as if he doubted my theory. "I'm not convinced theirs was a romantic relationship."

"You think he was involved in her death? You think he killed her?"

"I think it's a definite possibility."

I thought so, too.

"Iris hadn't worked in Richland long before she moved here," I said, remembering what Brandi had told me. "She moved around a lot. I wonder why."

We were quiet for a minute, both of us thinking.

"Seems there are a lot of unknowns about Iris," Zack said.

"But none of them point to her killer."

We sat for a few more minutes, then by unspoken agreement got up. Zack picked up my shopping bags and the sewing machine. I got the back door key from under the yellow flower pot—he rolled his eyes but didn't say anything—and we went inside.

A light burned over the stove in the kitchen. Zack put my things on the counter. From down the hall I heard the faint murmur of the television in Sarah's bedroom.

Zack walked back to the door. I followed. On the porch he turned back.

"From now on, don't go out of town—" He stopped, as if thinking better of it, and started again. "From now on, I'd appreciate it if you'd let me know when you're leaving town—especially if you're going to talk to a possible murder suspect."

"Fair enough," I said, and couldn't help smiling.

"I couldn't stand it if something happened to you." He leaned closer.

His breath was hot against my lips. My heart rate picked up.

Light flooded the kitchen behind me. Zack stepped back.

"Abbey, you're home. I didn't hear you come in," Sarah said. "Hi, Zack. I brought home some chocolate chip cookies. Would you like some?"

"No, thanks." He gave me a look of profound longing, and left.

I slumped against the door.

"We're done," I announced.

"Awesome," Caitlin declared.

We stepped back from the frame for the design wall that Mitch had dropped off at the sewing studio yesterday while I was in Richland, and admired our work. The diamond-shaped fabric remnants we'd sewn together, enhanced by spongy batting, were now hot-glued in place. All we needed now was for Mitch to mount it on the wall, along with the cork backing he'd also left here.

"I hope Mitch can come by soon," Caitlin said,

looking around the room. "We're getting short on time."

The pillowcase party was tonight and the sewing studio needed work—general cleaning and arranging the sewing machines and other things that would accommodate everyone comfortably. I'd been relieved when Caitlin showed up early this morning to help.

"First, I need your opinion on something." I got the pattern for the aprons I wanted to make for Sarah and Jodi, and showed it to her. "Remember this?"

While Caitlin studied the pattern I unrolled a bolt of the green gingham fabric across the table I'd been using to cut the pillowcase dresses.

"I remember," she said. "Cute idea. I love it."

I showed her the spools of embroidery thread Connie had helped me pick out.

"What do you think?" I asked.

"Perfect," she declared. "Abbey, you really have an eye for color. You're more creative than you realize."

"I think my creativity got buried while I was slogging through all those business classes in college," I said.

Caitlin drew a quick breath and whirled toward the pocket doors. Mitch stood there with his toolbox.

"I figured you two would be working on this." His words were meant for both of us, but he looked only at Caitlin.

"Good timing," I said, since Caitlin seemed to have lost her breath.

At that moment, Connie ambled into the sewing studio. She held up a shopping bag. "Your totes came in."

"Just put them down anywhere," I said.

Connie turned a critical eye toward the gingham fabric laid out on the table. "Let me give you a hand with this," she offered.

I set to work pinning the apron pattern on the fabric, under her watchful eye, then cut it out. Across the room Mitch and Caitlin worked together installing the design feature on the wall. They chatted, consulted each other, and several times I heard Caitlin giggle. Last night with Zack in Sarah's kitchen popped into my head.

"I'll get you started on the design," Connie said, taking the fabric to the embroidery machine.

She set it up, walked me through it again as she'd done in her store, and the machine started stitching, my little owl materializing right before my eyes. It really was cute. I felt a jolt of pride I didn't remember ever experiencing at my job in L.A.

"Think you can manage?" Connie asked.

I nodded.

"Okay. See you tonight."

She left and, a little nervous, I kept working.

Mitch seemed to take an inordinate amount of time to finish the job of attaching the design board to the wall, consulting Caitlin continually while I worked on sewing the aprons. He stayed and moved the tables around for tonight's pillowcase party. We lined them up facing each other so everyone could chat while we worked. Mitch climbed under the tables and double-checked that everything was plugged into the power strips and was working.

There was something reassuring about seeing a man do physical labor.

"Give me your bill," I said as he closed his tool-box.

"End of the month." Mitch lingered for a moment, then left.

Caitlin seemed to deflate.

"I know you don't want to hear this," I said, "but you two make a great couple."

"Us?" Caitlin countered. "What about you and Zack? He was in here first thing yesterday, asking Sarah where you were going. He came to the shop and asked me if I knew. Then he hung out around Hummingbird Lane watching for you to come back."

"He did?" I guess that explained why he was at the house when I got home last night.

Maybe it also explained why he almost kissed me.

I didn't want to think about it.

"Are you sharing a vendor booth with Mitch at the festival?" I asked, anxious to change the subject.

"No, I'm not. I can't. There's Scott and my dad, and . . ." She shook her head. "I just can't."

"I saw the miniature doghouses Mitch is making. They look perfect with your dog figurines. I know they'd sell well," I said.

"That's not the point," she insisted. "It's not simply a matter of sharing a booth with Mitch. It's what it might lead to—and I don't know what that would mean. My whole life could be turned upside down."

My job back in Los Angeles flashed in my head. I hadn't heard from Madison about the possibility of my getting reinstated, and I'd thought about calling her for an update. I hadn't. Did I really want to know what their answer was? Would my whole life be turned upside down?

"I know," I said softly, because I understood perfectly well what she was going through.

"I've got to go," she said, and looked pretty miserable when she left.

Maybe I'd pushed her too far. Maybe I should mind my own business and stay out of it. Somehow, I couldn't.

The sewing studio was in good shape for tonight's pillowcase party. I'd cleaned and tested the machines I'd purchased from the thrift shops, and put in new needles. I wound about a dozen bobbins with a variety of colored threads; I remembered from my classes at the rec center that nobody liked winding the bobbin. I rounded up scissors from Sarah's house that had accumulated over the years, set up the ironing board, and made sure the iron was in working order.

Pinning some of the dresses I'd made to the design wall was a challenge—I wish Caitlin had stayed to help—but I finally got them looking pretty good. I grouped fabric remnants, lace, and bias tape together as examples of possible designs.

My last chore was general cleanup. I swept the floor, gathered the trash, and went into the bakery. Sarah and Jodi were both at the work island, dozens of fresh-baked cookies spread out in front of them.

"Smells great," I said as I crossed the kitchen.

"Your cookies for the party tonight," Sarah told me. I'd ordered them a few days ago and paid her for them—I certainly didn't expect her to donate them—though she did give me a break on the price.

I opened the bins beside the back door and pulled out the trash bags. Several cardboard boxes were stacked nearby.

"I'll help you with those," Jodi offered.

She grabbed the boxes as I pushed the door open. Something streaked through the alley. I yelped and jumped back. Startled, Jodi did the same.

"What's wrong?" Sarah asked, and hurried over.

"Don't tell me somebody else got killed back there!" Jodi wailed.

"No, no, it's just—" I stepped into the alley and spotted an orange ball of fluff disappearing across Hummingbird Lane. "It's just Cheddar."

Jodi and Sarah followed me outside.

"Oh, that cat," Jodi declared. "She's always back here."

"I've seen her before." Another image—a memory—of her came to me. "The day Iris was hit, Cheddar ran through the alley. I saw her. Just a quick flash. I'd forgotten, with everything else that had happened."

"Well, I'm not surprised," Jodi said. "That cat is all over town."

"And everybody worries about her," Sarah said.

Something else came to me. A cat calendar set to the wrong date. A water bowl beside a back door that had to be kept full.

"Earlene?" I asked.

"Oh, my goodness," Jodi declared. "Earlene was so worried about that cat. She was so afraid she'd dart out into the street and get hit. She kept an eye out for her all the time."

That was the reason Earlene was cutting through the alley the day Iris was hit, I realized. She'd followed Cheddar. She hadn't been involved in Iris's death at all.

What a relief. At last I could mark a name off my suspect list.

I hope that meant I was on a roll.

CHAPTER 26

❧

"This is so nice," Anna declared. "You've done a beautiful job."

I couldn't keep the proud smile off my face as I walked into the sewing studio surrounded by the women who'd shown up for my pillowcase party. An appreciative murmur went through the group.

"Caitlin designed the covering for the frame of the design wall," I said, pointing. "I would have been lost without her."

Another round of oohs and aahs followed.

Caitlin had come over a few minutes ago and had given her nod of approval to everything I'd placed on the design wall. She loved the coordinating samples of remnants, lace, and other notions I'd put together.

Phoebe had slipped away from her job at the drugstore early to join us and brought her mom's sewing machine, along with a friend. Lily worked at Flight of Flowers, the florist down the street. She sported a blond ponytail and a fearful smile.

"My sewing skills aren't the best," she said.

"Then you'll fit right in," I said, and everybody laughed. "Except for Connie, of course. Our expert."

"Just years of not having a life," Connie declared, setting up the sewing machine she'd brought with her.

I'd figured Connie would be here and I thought Valerie at the bookstore might come, too, since she'd been supportive about advertising the party in her shop window. Apparently, the sisters still weren't getting along, so Valerie had stayed away.

Melinda, the waitress at the Parliament Café, was here, too, which surprised me. Sylvia Peyton, one of the Hideaway Grove librarians, showed up also. I'd never met her, so it was nice to have a new face in the mix.

"Abbey, it was so generous of you to put this together," Melinda said.

Mentally, I cringed a bit. I hadn't been completely generous about setting up the pillowcase party. I'd done it in the hope I could discover clues to Iris's death with some of the townsfolk corralled in one place, not distracted by interruptions.

"Especially the cookies," Anna declared, and everyone laughed.

Sarah's treats were a big hit. She'd arranged them on trays and placed them on a table just inside the sewing studio before going home for the night. I'd bought bottles of water and napkins.

"Let's get started," I suggested.

I'd arranged the room with sewing machines on the tables, and used another table for cutting the dresses. I'd set up the ironing board nearby. Another table was covered with the green gingham fabric for the aprons I was working on for Sarah and Jodi.

I took a few minutes to explain how the dresses were constructed and everybody agreed they really were simple to make, even Phoebe and Lily.

"What's this?" Melinda asked, pointing to the gingham fabric.

"I'm making aprons for Sarah and Jodi," I said, and showed them the one I'd almost finished.

"Look at that adorable owl," Anna said. "And I love the saying you've embroidered on it."

"Check this out." I held up one of the tote bags I'd been working on. It was a neutral cotton canvas with an open top that featured my little owl and the phrase "Look Whoo's Reading."

"You *have* to sell those at the festival," Sylvia said.

"I'm considering renting a booth," I said. "If I can get enough totes made in time."

"You will," Connie predicted. "Or just take orders at the festival."

Lily volunteered to cut the pillowcases. Anna fired up the iron to press the folds in the bias tape and smooth wrinkles out of the pillowcases. Everyone else settled behind a sewing machine. I helped Lily with cutting the pillowcases to size, and making the armholes, while I tended to the embroidery machine stitching the tote bags.

"I thought we'd take turns sewing and cutting so everyone would get a chance to make a dress," I suggested.

Everyone agreed.

Conversation flowed well, despite the whir of the sewing machines. It helped that I'd positioned everything close together.

"They're setting up the vendor booths on the

village green for the festival," Anna commented.

"This could be one of our best festivals yet," Connie said. "Especially now that all that talk about Iris's death has stopped."

"Did the sheriff ever find out who hit Iris in the alley?" Melinda asked.

Everyone exchanged looks but no one responded.

"Not that I heard," Connie finally said.

"I can't imagine who would want to harm Iris," Lily said, carefully cutting out an armhole.

I'd thought of several people, but I didn't say anything.

"You know, I think there's something . . . well, something kind of sad about Iris," Lily said.

The sewing machines stopped. Anna set down the iron. Everyone looked at Lily.

"My dad owns the building where Iris lived in that studio apartment," Lily said, pointing in that direction with the scissors. "The unit is furnished, but we had to empty it of all of Iris's personal belongings. And, well, there weren't any."

"What do you mean?" Anna asked.

"No photos, no keepsakes, nothing like that," Lily said. "Nothing that made it look like a home, just a place to live."

I thought about what Brandi at the Richland library had told me about Iris putting her things in storage with the intention of fetching them after she was settled. Iris had lived in Hideaway Grove for months, but she hadn't gotten them?

"All she had in her apartment were things related to her job at the library," Lily said. "Travel brochures for Italy, and those language instruction books for the classes at the library. Iris gave all her time and attention to her job, but she was so excited about Italy. She died before she got to go. I think it's sad."

"I think it's strange," Anna insisted.

I did, too.

"It seemed Iris spent all her time working for the community," Lily said.

I wasn't so sure about that, given how she'd ignored the donations for the festival raffle.

"That was it?" Melinda asked. "You didn't find anything else at her apartment?"

"Well," Lily said, "there was money."

"Money?" Melinda echoed.

Lily carefully snipped another pillowcase dress armhole, then said, "Cash. Lots of it."

"How much?" Anna spoke first, but we all had the same question on the tip of our tongue.

"Almost three thousand dollars," Lily said. "My dad gave it to the sheriff."

"That's a lot of money," Phoebe declared.

"There were travel brochures and magazines open to articles about Italy all over the apartment," Lily said. "I think Iris was saving it to go there."

"With who?" Anna asked.

Anna's gaze locked with mine and a meaningful look passed between us. We were thinking the same thing—Gerald Avery, Iris's mystery man and supposed lover. Was he going to abandon his wife and children, leave his job? Was Iris going to turn her back on Hideaway Grove? Were the two of them going to run away to Italy together?

"That's strange," Sylvia said. "All the time Iris and I worked together at the library she never once mentioned actually going to Italy."

"Why wouldn't she have mentioned it?" Caitlin asked. "That does seem strange."

"There are all sort of strange things happening in town," Melinda declared. "Why just yesterday, Joyce came into the café asking about Earlene—again. I don't know how many times she's been in for the same reason."

"She's been in the florist asking if we'd seen her, too," Lily said.

"And the drugstore," Phoebe added.

"What's up with Earlene, anyway?" Connie asked. "Has anyone heard from her?"

No one responded. I guess I wasn't the only one Earlene was no longer communicating with.

"Joyce was asking about Earlene? That is strange. I've never known that woman to be concerned about anyone," Anna declared. "Not even her aunt. The way she ignores Miss Merriweather, some-times—it's strange, and it's shameful. Joyce can be so erratic at times—a real hothead."

"I think you can blame that ironclad will set up by the Merriweather family," Connie said. "I heard there were so many codicils and requirements—a legal tangle that might never get sorted out. And all of it designed to keep Joyce and her mother, God rest her soul, from inheriting a dime or laying claim to as much as a cup and saucer of the Merriweather estate."

"And Mr. Schwartz, he's been the family attorney for years," Sylvia said. "He's not about to let anything happen that might jeopardize Miss Merriweather's interests. He's a terrific lawyer."

"In a way you can understand Joyce's anger and hostility," Lily said.

"Did you see the argument she got into with Valerie? Right in front of the bookstore. For a minute, I thought they might actually come to blows." Phoebe cringed. "Sorry, Connie. I shouldn't have mentioned Valerie."

"We'll get over it . . . eventually," Connie said, waving away Phoebe's concern. "That's the way it is with sisters."

I hoped that was true.

"How are the raffle donations going?" Melinda asked.

"What's this?" Sylvia asked. "You're handling the donations?"

"I'm taking over for Iris." I repeated that phrase again, as I had so many times lately.

Sylvia frowned, jarring a memory. Gerald Avery and my conversation with him presented itself in my thoughts. He'd had an odd reaction to that statement as well.

"Everybody is participating, thankfully, since it's last minute," I said.

"I'm surprised Iris wasn't on top of the donations," Caitlin said. "It seems so unlike her."

"Interesting," Sylvia mused, her frown deepening. "She took time off from the library to contact businesses about donations."

Anna and I exchanged another look, both of us, I suspected, mentally speculating that Iris had, instead, used the time to meet with Gerald.

"How are things at the library?" Connie asked. "You're shorthanded now with Iris gone."

"Things are much quieter." Sylvia's cheeks flushed, realizing her comment hadn't been flattering to Iris. She forced a smile and rushed ahead. "Iris was like a tornado, always stirring things up—in a good way, of course. She had the library's best interest at heart."

"You're continuing those new programs she started?" Connie asked.

I guessed she was hoping that wouldn't happen, thereby restoring business to Valerie's bookstore and helping Connie and her sister heal the rift Iris had caused with her events at the library.

"We'll keep the language lessons, since it wouldn't be right to cancel them when the class is so interested," Sylvia said. "You know, Iris was thrilled with those lessons. She attended, just like everyone else. She even spoke Italian to our patrons sometimes. I'd thought she was just trying to drum up attendance for the classes but now . . . well, I wonder if she really was planning to vacation there."

Or move there?

The idea took me by surprise. Of course, the three thousand dollars found in Iris's apartment, and what Zack had described as a nice nest egg in her bank account, wouldn't be enough to actually make a major move and get established. Iris would have needed more money if she was going to make that dream come true. Was she, perhaps, relying on Gerald to help fund the move? Or did she have another plan?

Had Iris shared those plans with her friends at the library? I wondered. She'd spent the majority of her time there, as we all did when we had a job, so maybe she'd mentioned something. Maybe something that had nothing to do with Italy. Maybe something that would explain why she'd been run down in the alley and killed.

I needed to talk to Sylvia privately—not here where our conversation would be judged and likely repeated all over town. I had to get her alone where she'd feel free to tell me everything she knew about Iris. How could I—

"Oh!" The idea hit me so hard I jumped.

Everybody turned to me. I felt my cheeks flush, my brain scrambling to come up with something that would cover my outburst.

"I just had the craziest idea," I announced. "Wouldn't it be fun if we could all go to Milan and check out the fashions!"

Chatter, giggles, and excitement rose from the group.

"The food there would be so delicious," Melinda said.

"And think about the wine!" Anna declared.

Everybody spoke up, adding to the conversation, laughing.

I didn't intend to go to Milan, of course. I was going to the library and I was going to corner Sylvia and find out what else she knew about Iris, and I had the perfect excuse to do it—the library books in the tote bag Earlene had picked up at Iris's accident scene and been too afraid to turn in to the sheriff. She'd asked me to take them back to the library. I'd forgotten all about them. Only—

Where had I put that tote bag?

CHAPTER 27

The hooks beside the back door—*that's* where I put that tote bag.

"Of course," I muttered aloud.

I was in the sewing studio straightening up after the pillowcase party ended, and I'd been wracking my brain trying to remember where I'd put Iris's tote bag that Earlene had given me. Finally, it came to me.

A perfect way to end the day, I decided.

The pillowcase party had been a huge success. We'd worked our way through a stack of pillowcases—it was slow going, with everybody learning—and turned them into adorable dresses. Everybody was thrilled to pin their finished garment on the design board. We'd decided to meet again in a few days.

I'd thanked everyone and sent them on their way, with the intention of tidying up the sewing studio myself. They'd insisted they couldn't leave me with the cleanup. I was okay with it; I couldn't ask them for anything more after they'd generously donated their time sewing the dresses.

Now I was especially glad I hadn't.

The bakery was closed, Sarah and Jodi were long gone, and only a single light burned over the display cases. I hurried to the row of hooks beside the back door, and sure enough, buried under sweaters, jackets, umbrellas, and aprons was Iris's tote bag. Inside were two library books—my excuse to corner Sylvia for more info on Iris—that I would return first thing tomorrow.

I wondered if there would be a fine for the books being overdue, and pulled them out of the tote bag. I did a double take.

One was *Casino Royale*, the first novel by Ian Fleming that featured James Bond. The other was *We Seven*, an account of the early days of the American space program. These hardly seemed like the kind of books Iris would have checked out of the library for pleasure reading.

In fact, they didn't even seem like library books. From the look of the covers, I could tell they were really old, but they were in pristine condition.

I laid both books on the kitchen work island and flipped them open. *Casino Royale* had been autographed by Ian Fleming; it was a first edition. *We Seven* was published in 1962 and had been signed by all of the Mercury Seven astronauts.

Wow.

I went into the sewing studio, opened my laptop, googled *Casino Royale*, and gasped when it showed up on a rare book site—valued at nineteen thousand dollars. I checked *We Seven*. It was valued at twelve thousand.

My eyes popped open wider and my jaw sagged.

Books could go for that much money? Even rare books? I had no idea.

How had Iris been able to check these out of the library? Why would the library even have something so valuable?

I looked closer at the books. Library books this old would have had that little pocket glued to the back inside cover that held the date-stamped checkout card. Neither book had it.

Then it hit me—Iris didn't take them out of the library. These books belonged to her. But could she really have purchased them, at those prices? She had a nice nest egg in the bank, plus some cash in her apartment, but these books seemed out of her reach. So that could mean—

I stopped myself, refusing for a moment to believe where my thoughts had gone. Yet nothing else made sense.

Had Iris stolen the books? From the Owl's Nest bookstore? It was understandable that a librarian would love rare books. But enough to steal them?

Could she have done that? Iris? Hideaway Grove's calm, conservative, community-minded librarian?

Well, actually, Iris wasn't as wonderful as everyone thought. There was another side to her—involved with a married man, deliberately making the other librarians look bad with her new programs, refusing to change even though her actions seriously hurt Valerie's bookstore. She'd done all those things. I wondered what else she was capable of.

One way to find out.

I dithered for a moment trying to decide if it would be better to walk around Hideaway Grove with over thirty thousand dollars' worth of rare books in a tote bag, or leave them here unattended. I decided to take them with me.

Sarah had left me the key to the front door when she'd left, so I locked up and headed down Main Street. A few people were out, some likely going to dinner, others walking their dogs.

Thoughts whirled through my head, followed by a jolt of fear. Was I on my way to confront Iris's murderer?

Iris had been a thorn in Valerie's side since she'd arrived in Hideaway Grove. She'd damaged Valerie's business with her library programs, refused to stop, and had ruined her relationship with her sister. Did Valerie discover that Iris had stolen books from her store—rare, expensive books? Had she spotted Iris in the alley, been suddenly overcome by anger, and struck her with her car?

I was about to find out.

Valerie stood behind the door of the Owl's Nest bookstore, key in hand, when I walked up. She shook her head, indicating she was closing.

"It's important," I shouted through the glass.

She huffed, then let me in.

I didn't waste any time. I pulled the two books out of the tote.

"These belong to you," I said. "First editions signed by the authors."

She glanced at them, then rolled her eyes. "If I owned books that valuable, I wouldn't be scrambling to make payroll every week."

"They aren't yours?" I asked, stunned.

"I wish," she said.

"I think they belong to you," I insisted, watching

closely for her reaction. "Iris stole them from your store."

Her gaze sharpened as if she realized what I was implying.

"And you think—what? That I retaliated against Iris by running her down with my car in the alley?" she demanded.

"Did you?"

"No!" Valerie's burst of anger vanished. Tears pooled in her eyes. "As if Iris hasn't caused me enough problems already, now I'm accused of killing her. When that rumor circulates through town, I might as well close the store and move away."

I thought of Earlene and knew she was right.

"I had nothing to do with Iris's death," Valerie declared, her voice quivering.

I believed her—and I felt bad for upsetting her.

"If these books aren't yours, who do they belong to?" I asked.

"How would I possibly know?"

I left the Owl's Nest and stood on Main Street. I'd been so sure the books were stolen from there. Where else could they have come from? I wondered once more if Iris could have owned the books. But if so, why would she have had them with her as she cut through the alley to meet her lover Gerald Avery?

Another idea came to me, and this one was even more troubling. Miss Merriweather. Had Iris taken the books from her grandfather's library, right from under her nose, pretending to be there for a friendly visit?

Miss Merriweather would be so hurt if that were true. My heart ached a little at the thought. She'd treasured her time with Iris, enjoyed her company so much. I didn't want to take those memories away from her.

But if Iris had actually stolen the books from her, Miss Merriweather should have them back. It occurred to me there was a way I could get around hurting her—at least until I found out if my suspicions were true. And if they were, what would it mean?

Another thought popped into my head, leaving me feeling a bit queasy. Did Miss Merriweather know Iris was stealing from her? Had she driven her car through the alley and struck Iris—on purpose?

For a few seconds I considered going to Zack with my suspicion. If I did, he'd be obligated to follow up, make it official. I didn't want to do that to Miss Merriweather. Not yet. Not until I knew, at least, whether the books had come from her grandfather's library. Then, maybe, all my worry would be for nothing. It was possible Miss Merriweather had loaned the books to Iris.

I walked toward Hummingbird Lane so deep in thought I jumped when my phone buzzed. Madison's name appeared on the ID screen.

"You're *in*, girl," Madison shouted when I answered.

In the background I heard the driving beat of a live band and raised voices, and figured Madison was at a club or maybe a concert.

"You're *in* and she's *out*," Madison gleefully reported. "That awful supervisor you had. She's gone. Escorted out of the building. Everybody's celebrating."

Stunned, I paused on the sidewalk. "They fired her? She's really gone?"

"Yep. Upper management finally got something right. Can you believe it?"

No, I couldn't.

"That means you're getting your job back," Madison said.

"I am?" I had trouble believing that, too.

"Why wouldn't you? You'll see. You'll be getting a call from HR any time, begging you to come back," Madison predicted. Voices around her got louder. "Call me when you hear from them!"

Our call ended. I stood there for a few seconds staring at nothing, trying to take it in. I was going to get my old life back?

I'd have to get my car back first.

I pushed all thoughts of Los Angeles out of my head and hurried to Hummingbird Lane. Sarah was in the kitchen eating a sandwich and soup at the table, and flipping through a magazine. I asked if I could borrow her car again.

"Of course." Sarah gestured to her keys on the peg beside the back door where they always hung. "Going somewhere fun?"

I didn't want to tell her about the rare books, my suspicion, or where I was going, so I said, "No, just an errand I need to run."

"I thought maybe you and your pillowcase party friends were adjourning to the Night Owl."

That sounded like more fun than my decision to stay behind and do the cleaning after they left.

"Maybe next time," I said, and grabbed the keys.

"Drive safe," Sarah said.

Outside, I opened the garage and backed out onto Hummingbird Lane, keeping an eye out for Cheddar. At the corner I looked both ways—more concerned about spotting Zack again than checking for oncoming traffic—and turned right.

I glanced down Owl Avenue as I drove past, relieved that I didn't see Joyce's blue sedan parked in front of Miss Merriweather's house. I hoped that meant she was at work; since I didn't know where she lived, it was my only chance of seeing her.

Sure enough, Joyce's car was parked outside the convenience store near the freeway entrance. I pulled into a space near the door and went inside. The aisles were crowded with food items, snacks, and a few staples. Refrigerated cases held drinks, water, and beer. The place smelled like hot dogs, onions, and coffee, thanks to the self-service food counter in the corner.

I needed to talk to Joyce alone. I wanted to show her the two books and ask if she knew whether they belonged to the library in Miss Merriweather's house. If she confirmed my suspicion, I'd have to go to Zack, even if it threw suspicion onto Miss Merriweather.

I hesitated for a moment. I didn't want Miss Merriweather to be responsible for Iris's death, especially over valuable books. But if it wasn't her, who could it have been?

Joyce was behind the counter handling a sale. She had on dingy jeans and an orange smock with a stain on the front. Her hair was pulled back in a messy ponytail. I waited until her customer left, and approached the counter.

"Abbey!"

I cringed as Brooke suddenly appeared beside me. Her hair was carefully styled, her makeup was done, and for some reason she was wearing yoga togs.

Joyce looked at her, seemingly as annoyed with her interruption as I was.

"So, how is *everything* going?" Brooke asked, sounding perky and altogether pleased with herself.

I knew she was referring to the dreaded donation committee she'd maneuvered me into heading up.

"Great." I turned to Joyce, hoping it would discourage Brooke from lingering. "I'm taking over for Iris."

"You're *what?*" Joyce demanded.

Of all the times I'd repeated that sentence, no one had ever gotten angry before.

"I'm new in town," I explained, trying to make it sound simple and reasonable.

Joyce's frown hardened. My opportunity to talk with her about the stolen books wasn't getting off to a good start.

"So, that pillowcase party of yours was tonight, wasn't it?" Brooke asked, still sporting her fake smile. "How did it go?"

"Great," I told her.

"It's over already?"

"We got a lot done," I said. "Nothing's left but the cleanup."

"Did you need something?" Joyce asked, apparently finding Brooke as annoying as I did.

"Twenty on four," she said, and handed cash to Joyce. "Well, got to run. Bye."

Brooke left the store as Joyce punched in her gas purchase. We shared an irritated look.

The store was empty of customers and I was anxious to get this chore handled. I pulled the two books out of the tote bag I'd brought in with me.

"Do you recognize these?" I asked.

Joyce studied the books, looked at me, then at the books again.

"They're rare first editions," I explained. "I think they belong to your aunt."

The door swung open and a mom with four young kids came into the store. The children spread out, jumping up and down, pointing, asking for things.

"Iris had them," I said.

"How did you get them?" she demanded.

"Earlene picked up the tote in the alley after Iris's accident. She asked me to return the books to the library, but I'm pretty sure they belong to Miss Merriweather."

"Iris, huh?" Joyce's anger grew. "And you're taking over for her, right?"

One of the little girls let out a scream for no apparent reason. Another girl screamed, too. Their mom started fussing at them about using their indoor voices. One of the boys started crying.

"I've never seen those books before," Joyce told me.

"You're sure?"

"Sure."

I hesitated, disappointed. "Well, thanks."

I put the books back into the tote bag and left. Driving home to Aunt Sarah's, I wondered what to do next. Visit Miss Merriweather myself? Talk to Zack?

No clear path came to me as I parked the car in the garage and went inside. I heard the shower running. I hung the keys by the door and left.

It was getting dark now and few people were out. I was tempted to cut through the alley to the rear entrance of the bakery but thought about Iris and took Main Street instead.

I unlocked the front door and went inside. The scent of baked goods lingered in the air. I hit the light switch, walked into the sewing studio, and dropped my things on the cutting table, deciding where to start the cleanup. Behind me, the door burst open. Joyce walked in.

CHAPTER 28

Joyce stood at the entrance to the sewing studio, blocking it. The orange smock I'd seen her wear at the convenience store was now replaced with a dark jacket. She'd pulled the hood up, stirring a memory.

"You're taking over for Iris, are you?" she asked.

I hadn't locked the front door. It hadn't occurred to me that I should. Not here. Not in Hideaway Grove.

"Yes, I'm in charge now."

My voice was weak with—what? Fear? Yet there was no reason for concern. Joyce was just asking about the donation committee.

"You've still got them with you?" Joyce jerked her chin toward the tote bag lying on the cutting table atop yards of gingham fabric. "You know what they're worth?"

My heart rate picked up. No, Joyce wasn't here to ask about the donation committee.

The silence in the bakery roared in my ears.

Outside, through the bakery's big windows and the glimpse I got of Main Street, I saw no one walk past.

I hadn't told Sarah I was coming here.

"They're worth thousands," I managed to say, my throat tight. "About thirty thousand."

"Good haul." A smirk twisted Joyce's face. "That Iris. I have to hand it to her. She knew books."

Possibilities, scenarios, clues assembled in my mind, trying to fit together.

"That bitch." Joyce uttered the word, her anger building.

Comments I'd heard from the townsfolk blazed in my head—Joyce was a hothead, erratic, unpredictable. Violent.

I backed up a step.

She took a step forward.

I dug deep for some courage. "What do you want?"

Joyce uttered an ugly laugh. "Just like Iris, are you? Well, you can forget it. I'm not settling for scraps again."

I wished I'd called Zack.

"For the books, you mean?" I nodded toward the tote bag.

"Of course!" Joyce's anger erupted. "I saw what she was doing! I caught her red-handed! My aunt let it happen, right under her nose!"

"Iris was stealing books from Miss Merriweather's library," I realized.

"It wasn't *her* library! It belongs to the family— everything in that house, in this town, belongs to the family." She fumed for a few seconds, as if lost in a memory. "Until my grandfather changed everything. I wasn't good enough for him. I was tainted. Just because my mother didn't conduct her life the way he wanted her to. He cut her off—and me with her."

I wasn't sure exactly what was unfolding, but I could see Joyce was on the ragged edge, ready to explode. I needed to get away from her, but crossing the sewing studio to escape through the pocket doors was a gauntlet of tables, chairs, the ironing board, and storage boxes. The best I could do right now was not appear weak while I figured a way out.

"Look, Joyce, what do you want? I've got things to do," I said, and managed to sound impatient and annoyed.

"Eighty percent," she declared. "And I'm not taking a penny less this time."

This time.

Everything clicked into place.

"Iris stole rare books from Miss Merriweather's library, and sold them," I said. "You two were in it together. Partners."

My phone buzzed inside my handbag on the cutting table.

"She was no partner of mine." Joyce swore under her breath. "Partners share. She didn't share anything with me, just gave me a pittance to keep me quiet. She thought she had me. I couldn't report what she was doing without implicating myself. She thought there was nothing I could do."

"Who did she sell the books to?" I asked, but I already knew—Gerald Avery.

"She wouldn't tell me who he was—just some guy she met at one of those book conventions who

knew collectors that didn't care about prove-
nance, didn't ask questions, and paid in cash."

Iris had done this before, I realized. She'd probably stolen books from the libraries where she'd
worked and, likely, it was the reason she'd changed
jobs so often when the librarians figured out what
she was doing. It was the reason, too, why Iris had
lied about moving to Hideaway Grove, claiming
she was headed to Portland instead. She didn't want
anyone at the Richland library to call and warn our
local librarians about what she was doing.

"But I found out. I was driving down Main
Street and spotted them together near the alley,
Iris giving him books, him giving her money. I fol-
lowed him all the way back to Richland, to that
store where he works. I had a little chat with him,"
Joyce said.

When I'd spoken with Gerald at the home improvement store I'd thought his reaction had
been odd. Now I knew why. He thought I was in on
the book thefts.

"I confronted Iris when I got back, told her I
knew who her contact was." A nasty smile spread
over Joyce's face. "She'd been stringing me along,
promising to cut me in for a bigger share of the
money but never turning loose one extra cent.
Now she had to give in. I had her and she knew it.
She promised she'd take me with her the next
time they met."

Joyce seemed to be savoring the memory. I
eased away from her a bit to the end of the cutting
table.

"I didn't trust her and I was right not to," Joyce
went on. "I saw her on Main Street, that heavy tote

bag slung over her shoulder. I knew what was in it. Books. Books she's stolen and was going to sell—without me there, like she'd promised."

In the bakery, a flash of headlights reflected off the display case.

"You were driving Miss Merriweather's car," I said, remembering she'd told me Joyce often helped out by taking it for gas or repairs.

Joyce seemed to shake off the memories. "So, how about it? I'll get the books, handle the hand-off. I'll cut you in. Easy money. All you have to do is keep quiet."

I gasped softly. Joyce was asking me to join her conspiracy.

She saw my hesitation. "It's not illegal. The books in that library—everything in that house—should belong to me, too. I'm entitled to them. It's not breaking the law."

Other incidents in Hideaway Grove suddenly made sense.

"The vandalism in the alley, the break-in at Earlene's house. You tried to break into the bakery. You stalked me through town," I said. "You did all those things, looking for the tote bag with the books in it that Iris was carrying."

Joyce had seen Iris walk into the alley. It could mean only one thing.

"You followed Iris into the alley."

"To scare her. That's all."

"You wanted to get those books. You wanted to get them and sell them yourself, and keep all the money," I said.

Joyce glared at me. She didn't deny it; I didn't expect her to.

"You thought the tote bag had been left in the

alley, overlooked by the sheriff," I said. "When you didn't find it outside Sassy Fashions or in the Dumpster, you thought Earlene had it, but you didn't find it in her house after you broke in. You thought it must have been brought into the bakery."

The impact of my words hung between us for a moment.

"You hit Iris with Miss Merriweather's car." The words were so horrible I could barely speak them.

"I was only going to scare her! That's all! So she'd know I was onto her!"

A bell chimed in the distance.

"You killed her."

"All right!" Joyce's anger exploded again. "Just keep your mouth shut and I'll give you half!"

"No!" Now I was as outraged as Joyce. "I'm not going to be part of your scheme. You killed Iris."

"She had it coming!" Joyce shrieked. "I'm glad I did it!"

Joyce rushed toward me, startling me with her speed. I shuffled backward. She grabbed Gretchen's scissors off the cutting table, raised them high over her head. I rounded the table. She followed, slicing the scissors through the air, the blades barely missing my shoulder.

I looked around, desperate for a weapon of my own, or at least a way to defend myself. I pulled a chair away from the table and thrust it at Joyce. She sidestepped it, then grabbed it, and with strength I hadn't imagined, pulled it out of my hands. My foot caught on something. I fell to the floor. Joyce loomed above me, raising the scissors over her head.

Commotion at the pocket doors barely registered as I kicked Joyce, catching her on the knee. She screamed. More screams filled the room.

Joyce jabbed the scissors toward my stomach. I kicked again, hard, and this time knocked the scissors from her hand. She dropped to her knees and lunged for them.

Voices, shouts sounded behind me and suddenly all the women from the pillowcase party appeared. Caitlin, Anna, and Phoebe grabbed the yards of gingham fabric from the cutting table, threw it over Joyce, then wound it around her, locking her arms down. Sylvia ripped open a package of bias tape. Lily grabbed it. She and Melinda tied it around Joyce's ankles.

I scrambled to my feet, shaking.

Joyce, trussed up on the floor, squirmed and cursed.

"I called the sheriff," Connie shouted, waving her phone.

"We felt guilty, leaving you to clean up alone," Caitlin said, hurrying to my side. "We went to the Night Owl. We called, wanting you to join us."

"You didn't answer. So we came back," Melinda added.

"I'm glad you did," I managed to say.

"She killed Iris," Anna said, stunned, pointing at Joyce. "We heard her. She killed her."

"And she tried to kill *you*," Phoebe declared.

"She would have if all of you hadn't . . . hadn't—" Emotions rose, cutting off my words.

"What the hell?" Sheriff Grumman appeared at the pocket doors, glaring at Joyce wrapped in gingham fabric and bias tape, all of us standing over her.

Everybody started talking at once, shouting, and pointing at Joyce.

Zack elbowed past the sheriff. He saw me and rushed over.

I burst out crying. He locked me in his arms and held me tight.

CHAPTER 29

The banner HIDEAWAY GROVE—FOUND! stretched across the village green heralding the entrance to the arts and crafts festival. Vendor booths housed in small white tents lined the perimeter, along with food stands. A jazz quartet took their turn in the bandstand. A kids' section featured face painting, a petting zoo, and cookie decorating. Stilt walkers and jugglers performed while shoppers roamed the grounds and meandered through the portion of Main Street that had been closed to traffic.

"Looks like our best festival in years," Caitlin said. "Everybody loves your bags."

We were standing in the vendor booth I'd rented. For the past few days, since Joyce's arrest, I'd spent hours embroidering tote bags with my cute little owl and "Look Whoo's Reading" slogan. I'd expanded it to "Look Whoo's Shopping" and "Look Whoo's Antiquing." I'd sold dozens already.

"They love your little guys, too," I pointed out.

Alongside my tote bags sat a display of Caitlin's beautifully painted dog figurines. I'd convinced her to let me have them on consignment and she'd reluctantly agreed. Sales were brisk. So were sales of the miniature doghouses Mitch had built. By some strange coincidence he and I had ended up with booths side by side—I'm guessing it had something to do with Mitch's assistance setting up for the festival. Caitlin and Mitch had been talking. No sign of her fiancé, Scott.

Amid the crowd of shoppers, Connie and Anna threaded their way to the booth.

"I had to slip away from the store and see how your totes were selling." Connie turned a critical eye onto my embroidery and nodded her approval. "Nice work. Very nice."

"Do you mind handing these out?" Anna gave me a stack of flyers advertising her thrift store. I'd offered to display things for everyone who'd participated in my pillowcase party—and saved me from Joyce. She was in jail, and I was happy to let the Sheriff's Department deal with her from now on.

"Business is booming on Main Street," Connie said.

"Sarah and Jodi were at the bakery before dawn," I said. "They're expecting a big day."

"Thank goodness the festival is going well," Connie said. "I was so worried this would be a complete disaster after that incident with Iris, and then Joyce."

Hideaway Grove had buzzed with talk following Joyce's arrest but it had faded quickly. Everybody seemed anxious to put the disturbing news behind them and focus on the festival.

"I can hardly believe Iris was actually stealing rare books from sweet Miss Merriweather, and selling them," Anna said. "She had a good job at the library. Why would she have done that?"

I'd wondered the same. But now, looking back, I'd come to believe that Iris had bigger plans than living in Hideaway Grove and working at the library. She'd been adamant about featuring events about Italy at the library and pursuing her Italian lessons. Her studio apartment had nothing personal in it. She was amassing cash. A long stay in Italy seemed to be her goal, maybe even a permanent move there.

"I guess Earlene was right about Iris all along," Connie said. "She really was murdered."

"I feel bad that nobody believed her," Anna said. "I wish there was some way to let her know, some way for the whole town to apologize to her."

"Maybe we'll have a party for her when she gets back," Connie suggested.

"She's not coming back," Caitlin said. "Lily told me Earlene had contacted a real estate agent in town and is going to sell her house. She loves living near her sister."

Good news, I thought. Earlene deserved to be happy, after the ordeal she'd been through.

My phone vibrated in my pocket. No name appeared on the ID screen but I recognized the number—my old employer back in Los Angeles. Startled, I could only stare at it. Madison had said someone from HR or management would call, asking me to come back to work. Was this it? Was this the call?

"Excuse me, ladies. Step aside."

Zack pushed his way to my booth. He wore his uniform and a frown.

"I need you to come with me." He motioned for me to follow.

Caitlin, Connie, and Anna exchanged troubled glances. My heart rate picked up.

"What's wrong?" I asked.

"Just come along," Zack insisted.

"I'll call Sarah and let her know," Connie whispered.

"Watch the booth, will you?" I said to Caitlin.

She nodded, but immediately rushed to Mitch at the booth next door.

I had no idea what was happening. Things had seemed to be going well between Zack and me since the tension of Iris's investigation had been resolved. He'd even admitted that I was right, as was Earlene, that Iris had been murdered; Sheriff Grumman had made no such admission.

"What's going on?" I asked, thankful Zack hadn't put handcuffs on me or grabbed my elbow to guide me through the crowd.

"You'll see." He sounded stern, but I saw his lip curl up on one side and that dimple pop out as we headed down Main Street.

"What are you up to?" I asked.

He was quiet until we reached the next corner, then stopped. With a grand wave he gestured down the street.

"Your car."

"My—"

Down the block, at the curb in front of Sarah's Sweets, sat a flatbed tow truck with my car on it.

"My car!"

I ran down the street, my mouth open, eyes wide, and stopped beside it. I couldn't remember ever being so thrilled.

Sarah and Jodi came out of the bakery.

"Looks like you really surprised her," Sarah said to Zack.

A full smile bloomed on his face—two dimples.

Sarah and Jodi beamed with delight, wearing the aprons I'd made for them. Delicious scents poured out of the bakery. Next door was Sassy Fashions. Across the street was the pet supply store. Nearby was the florist, the bookstore, the fabric store, the thrift store.

So many of the places that had come to play a part in my life here in Hideaway Grove.

Geraldine came out of her store to see what was going on. Anna and Connie hurried toward us. Lily waved from the florist. Phoebe held open the door to the drugstore, watching us.

So many of the people who'd played a part in my life here in Hideaway Grove.

"So, you've got your car back," Zack said.

My phone in my pocket buzzed again. I ignored it.

"Where do you want to go?" he asked.

"Nowhere."

Dear Reader,

A chance meeting with a dear friend reignited my love of sewing. Many years ago I took great joy in making clothes for my young daughter. Though my sewing skills weren't great, I managed to make a few things for myself. So when my friend casually mentioned she was making pillowcase dresses for girls in Africa, I jumped at the chance to start sewing again, this time for a good cause.

My friend and I routinely got together for "fashion shows" to share the dresses we'd made. We went to thrift shops and sewing centers to find pillowcases and notions. Friends and family got involved to support our efforts. It quickly became a rewarding, joyful community effort.

I've been making pillowcase dresses for about six years and have donated over one thousand dresses. They're very easy to make, and allow me to be creative in a way other than writing. I donate my dresses to Little Dresses for Africa, who distributes them. And, of course, this is what inspired me to write the Sewing Studio mystery series.

Happy reading and sewing!
Dorothy

INSTRUCTIONS FOR SEWING A PILLOWCASE DRESS

Constructing a pillowcase dress requires only a pillowcase, notions, a sewing machine, and basic sewing skills.

You'll need:
a gently used pillowcase
double-fold bias tape
elastic
thread, straight pins, and measuring tape

Cut off the sewn end of the pillowcase. This will determine the length of the dress.

Fold the pillowcase in half and cut armholes. Cut through all thickness. Cut 4 inches down and 2 inches in.

Fold down the top about $\frac{3}{8}$-inch. Stitch to make a casing. Slide 6 inches of $\frac{1}{4}$-inch elastic through the casing to cause it to gather. Stitch the ends. Repeat on the back.

Cut two 38-inch lengths of double-fold bias tape for the armholes. Fold each in half and stitch along armholes leaving extra at the top to tie the dress at the shoulder.

Add lace, rickrack, or other trims to embellish your design (optional).

TIPS FOR SEWING PILLOWCASE DRESSES

A good place to find gently used pillowcases is a thrift store; shop on discount days for a lower price. Check out yard and estate sales. Put out the word to friends and family that you're looking for donations.

Watch for sales at fabric stores for trims and notions. Hobby Lobby frequently offers 50 percent off all sewing notions. Joann Fabric has weekly coupons. Keep an eye out for clearance items.

A cotton or cotton blend pillowcase works best.

Extra-wide double-fold bias tape is easiest to work with.

After setting up a small sewing studio in quaint Hideaway Grove, Abbey Chandler is focused on finding crafty, creative ideas to build up her clientele. But murder can be bad for business . . .

Some of the independent shops in this sleepy town are barely hanging on financially—and that includes Sarah's Sweets, Abbey's aunt's bakery. The shop's advantage—aside from the deliciousness of its products—is the fact that it's the only bakery in the area. But it looks like that's about to change. The second wife of a wealthy businessman wants her own bakery—and money is no object.

When murder unravels the plans for the competing shop, Aunt Sarah is an immediate suspect—and Hideaway Grove's merchants are on pins and needles about a big upcoming women's conference, fearing the organization will cancel their booking because of the crime. Abbey's doing her best to stay optimistic and stitch some custom tote bags for the attendees, but she's also concerned with patching up Aunt Sarah's good reputation. And when it comes to sorting through the possible motives of the victim's family members and associates, she's got a few tricks up her sleeve . . .

Please turn the page for an exciting sneak peek of Dorothy Howell's next Sewing Studio mystery HANGING BY A THREAD coming soon wherever print and e-books are sold!

CHAPTER 1

"So how does it feel to be a movie director, Abbey? You must be so excited!"

Anna's voice intruded, yanking me out of my worrisome thoughts. Mentally, I cringed. I'd been asked that question, or a similar version, too many times already.

"Are you the director, Abbey?" Connie asked before I could say anything. "I thought you were the producer."

I was neither—and both, plus the cameraman, sound guy, location scout, lighting expert, as well as the wardrobe, hair, and makeup crew, and anything else that needed to be handled. Little of which I knew much about. I'd been promised an experienced film crew, but so far I was running a one-person show.

I'd been *volunteered* for a number of projects since I'd arrived in Hideaway Grove, and this was the latest. I was okay getting involved with the town while I got my own business up and running—which, like the film project, was proving harder than I'd thought.

"Director, producer, whatever," Anna said, and waved a spool of green thread around. "That movie you're making for the town's website will showcase everything Hideaway Grove has to offer and get more tourists in here. It's just what the town needs."

Hideaway Grove, with its specialty shops, antique stores, and art galleries, depended on tourists, visitors, and conferences to stay afloat.

"Amen to that," Connie declared as she ran another perfectly straight seam through the sewing machine.

We were in the sewing studio I'd put together in the big storage room in my Aunt Sarah's bakery working on pillowcase dresses, a charity project I headed up. Like Connie's fabric store and Anna's thrift shop, Sarah's Sweets had been a mainstay in Hideaway Grove for decades.

Connie and Anna, who were in their forties, along with Sylvia, one of our librarians, were seated at the sewing machines I'd set up on banquet tables. We sewed dresses out of gently used pillowcases that we donated to the church. Several times a year, volunteers traveled to Africa and distributed them to girls in remote villages.

I should have been sitting and sewing like the others, but I kept pacing the room, keeping an eye on my embroidery machine set up on another table and peering through the open pocket doors into the adjoining bakery. Jodi, who worked part-time, chatted with the customers in line at the display case. My aunt Sarah stood at the big work island in the kitchen, tapping on her phone and frowning. Until lately, I'd rarely seen her frown. Now, I rarely saw her smile.

"And you're making the whole movie using your phone?" Sylvia asked, pausing with scissors and bias tape in her hands.

I turned back to the women seated at the sewing machines. I'd set up the studio with the tables facing each other so we could chat while we sewed. A design board showcased examples of pillowcase dresses and ideas for fabrics and trims. I'd recently added a rolling rack where several dresses hung—another project I'd *volunteered* to take on.

"Video, sound, editing, everything," I said. "Just using my phone."

"You must have done that all the time when you worked for that big company in Los Angeles," she said.

I'd retreated to Hideaway Grove after I'd lost my job at a marketing firm in L.A. and my life had imploded, glad to return to the town where I'd spent wonderful childhood summers with Aunt Sarah. With no kids of her own, Aunt Sarah had thrown herself into making our summers together a delightful adventure while my university-professor parents searched for ancient artifacts in remote locations around the world. They hadn't wanted me with them, nor had I wanted to be there.

"Is something wrong, Abbey?" Sylvia asked, concern in her voice.

I realized then that, like my aunt, I was frowning.

"I'm a little worried about Aunt Sarah," I admitted.

The whir of the sewing machines stopped. All three women looked up at me, waiting.

"She hasn't said anything," I told them. "But I think she's concerned about the new bakery that's opening."

"I knew it!" Anna smacked her palm on the table.

"Sarah has the only bakery in town, the only one we need," Connie said. "And now here comes that Blaine Hutchinson—"

"That gold digger," Anna declared.

"We're all small business owners, barely hanging on financially," Connie said. "More competition could kill us."

Anna huffed. "I don't know what Vaughn Harding was thinking, agreeing to lease that space to Blaine."

"He didn't dare refuse," Connie said.

"It's a prime location, right there at the hotel, the government and conference centers, among all the best restaurants and shops, and the village green," Anna said. "It's the first area of town all the tourists go to."

I'd thought those same things, even though Aunt Sarah hadn't commented on it. I hadn't expected her to. She'd run her bakery alone right from the start. She'd handled her finances, maintained the building, and managed every aspect of her bakery without input from another soul. She'd never asked for a thing from anyone. When I'd arrived back in town she'd welcomed me into her home, allowed me to set up my sewing studio in her bakery storage room, and had refused my offer of rent. Still, I left cash for her on the kitchen table every week.

"A bakery, of all things," Connie said. "Why would that Blaine Hutchinson open a bakery?"

"Oh, and the racket," Sylvia complained. Her job at the library gave her a front row seat to everything happening on that end of town. "I've never heard so much construction noise—and it never ends. Almost everybody who comes into the library remarks on it."

"I heard that Blaine hasn't been satisfied with the work," Connie reported. "She insists they keep doing things over."

Voices in the bakery drew my attention. Lily, another volunteer I was expecting today, called a greeting to Aunt Sarah and Jodi as she rushed into the sewing studio.

"Am I too late?" she asked, looking a bit frazzled.

Lily was about my age—twenty-four. Where I had dark hair and was a little taller than average, she was a petite blonde. She'd been one of my first volunteers. She worked at Flights of Flowers florist just two blocks down Main Street, next door to Blaine's new bakery.

"Sorry," Connie said and switched off her sewing machine. "I've got to get back to the store. It's almost closing time."

"It's that late?" Anna glanced at her watch. "I'd better go, too."

"Oh, shoot!" Lily declared. "I couldn't get away from the florist. There was another . . . incident next door."

"We were just talking about her," Anna said and rose from her chair. "What happened now?"

Talk had circulated around town for weeks about what a disruptive neighbor Blaine was, getting into squabbles over most everything with Rochelle, the owner of the flower shop.

"Parking," Lily said. "Blaine keeps taking up two spaces in the lot behind the shops."

Blaine drove a big Cadillac. She'd insisted on a custom paint job—gold—which had done nothing to diminish her gold-digger image around town.

Sylvia put aside the dress she was working on. "I'd better go, too. I know Sarah is going to lock up for the night soon."

"I'll let you know when we're meeting again," I told Lily.

Getting the ladies back into the sewing studio was always on an as-needed basis. When I'd put together enough pillowcases and notions to start on another batch of dresses, I texted my usual volunteers with a time and date to meet. I always put a sign in the bakery window, inviting anyone interested to join in. I'd never been disappointed with the turnout.

"Are you sure we can't help you clean up?" Connie asked.

Every time we met, the ladies offered to help me tidy up the sewing studio but I always refused. They'd given their time to sew dresses. I wouldn't ask them to do more.

"Thanks, but I've got it," I said.

We left the sewing studio. In the bakery, the delicious smells wafted over me, bringing on the rush of childhood memories that was always welcome.

The bakery was painted mint green, with accents of pale pink and yellow. Several small, white tables and yellow, padded chairs sat by the front windows. A shelf held display cakes for special occasions, all beautifully handcrafted. A refrigerated case contained orders for pickup, and another fea-

tured cakes ready to be personalized for walk-in
customers. The glass display case at the front of
the bakery greeted customers with a mouthwater-
ing array of cookies, cupcakes, and brownies. Gift
items were offered for sale—cookbooks, mugs,
birthday candles, plates and napkins, as well as cake
stands, cookie cutters, and measuring spoons.

Aunt Sarah stood at the work island in the
kitchen, swirling pink icing onto cupcakes. Jodi
waited on two customers at the display case.
Business as usual.

But I couldn't help wondering how long it
would last. Surely, the new bakery would impact
Aunt Sarah's business. And then what? Would she
be able to hang on, financially? Would she be able
to afford Jodi, even though she worked only part-
time? Where would Jodi work if Aunt Sarah had to
let her go? Could Aunt Sarah—healthy, fit and
trim, but almost sixty years old—manage the day-
to-day on her own? Or, worse, what would happen
to Aunt Sarah if her bakery went under? Was she
financially ready for retirement?

When the last customer left the store, Anna
stepped up to the display case.

"Everything looks delicious," she said. "It's so
hard to decide."

"You can't beat our sugar cookies," Jodi said.

Jodi, thirtyish, had dark hair that set off her
blue eyes, and a curvy figure. She and Aunt Sarah
made a great team. They shared an intense degree
of care for their handcrafted baked goods and created an inviting neighborhood environment the
tourists and locals flocked to.

"I'll take one," Anna said.

Jodi frowned. "One?"

"One dozen!" she said and they both laughed.

The bell over the door chimed as Sylvia opened it to leave. Outside, the sun was going down, but the streetlamps hadn't come on yet. Traffic was light. A couple strolled past.

"Thanks for coming today," I called.

Sylvia and Connie waved as they left the bakery.

"I know you're about to close. Is it too late to get a cupcake?" Lily peered over the display case into the kitchen where Aunt Sarah was at the work island. "I can't resist pink icing."

"I know what you mean," Jodi declared. "I can't resist a pink cupcake or a man with big, wide shoulders."

Lily giggled. "I'll take two."

"Men or cupcakes?"

The bell over the door chimed again and a woman hurried inside. I expected her to head straight to the display case but she didn't.

"I'm so glad I caught you," she said to me in a low voice.

It took me a second to realize who she was. I'd seen Imogene around Hideaway Grove and knew she owned a business, but I couldn't remember what it was, at the moment. She was in her sixties, with white hair and rosy cheeks; in a red dress and mop cap she could easily pass for Mrs. Claus.

"Could we chat a bit?" Imogene glanced at Jodi and Lily at the display case and Aunt Sarah in the kitchen and lowered her voice further. "In your sewing studio?"

I gestured for her to go ahead of me and followed her inside. I'd often given impromptu tours of the sewing studio, though there wasn't that much to see at the moment. I had a plan to improve the space, as soon as I could afford it.

Imogene walked to the farthest corner of the room and fidgeted a bit, showing no interest in my design board, my rack of completed pillowcase dresses, or anything else in the studio. I started feeling a little uncomfortable.

"This is somewhat . . . somewhat difficult for me." Imogene whispered. "I need help and I thought of you. I heard about that . . . that situation you were in with Miss Merriweather."

Miss Merriweather was the sweet, kind, elderly granddaughter of the town's founder. The memory of what had happened still left me feeling uneasy.

Imogene seemed sweet and kind, too. I drew a breath and braced myself.

"What sort of help do you need?" I asked.

She glanced around, then at me again. "I'm afraid that something, well, something untoward is going on at my shop."

Untoward. I wasn't sure what that meant, exactly, or how I could help her.

"Now, I know this might sound silly," Imogene said. "I'm sure you'll think that nobody, except for maybe a small child, would steal from a toy store."

I remembered then that Imogene owned Dottie's Toys, an adorable shop on Main Street near the government center and the village green.

"A shoplifter?" I asked.

Anyone who owned a retail business had to deal with that from time to time. Aunt Sarah had lost some of her gift merchandise to sticky fingered customers.

Imogene shook her head. "Oh, no. It's more

than that. Much more. You see, for quite a while now I've been putting aside vintage toys that I've found at antique stores, estate sales, yard sales, swap meets, that sort of thing. You know, for the craft fair at the women's conference."

Hideaway Grove's next big event was the regional meeting of the Women's Alliance for Progress, a three-day conference that was coming up soon and was expected to be a much-needed boost to the town's economy.

"The theme of their conference is *How Far We've Come*," Imogene said. "The organization started back in the fifties, you know."

The conference committee had insisted that everything about their event should have a retro look and feel to it. Aunt Sarah and Jodi had been working on special desserts from that era; they were having more luck than I was with the conference prep.

Imogene glanced around making sure, once more, that we were alone. "Some of the toys I set aside are gone. Missing. Stolen, I'm afraid."

"Stolen out of your store?"

"The stockroom. I haven't put them out on display because I'm not ready to sell them, though I certainly could use the income," Imogene said. "I'd planned to showcase them at the conference craft fair and, hopefully, sell them to the attendees. The toys are very desirable. You know, childhood memories. The women who'll be attending are somewhat well-to-do, I understand, and I'd hoped I'd get a good price for them."

"You're sure they're stolen? Maybe one of your employees sold them by mistake?"

"Impossible. I put them in a special place in my

stockroom and specifically told everyone not to
touch them. I even put up a sign. Many of the toys
are in their original packaging. Handling them
too much could decrease their value significantly."

I thought for a moment. "How do you think
your customers are getting into your stockroom to
steal them?"

Imogene's already rosy cheeks reddened further. "It couldn't be a customer. I'm afraid . . . I'm
afraid it's one of my staff. One of the girls who
works for me."

That bit of info put a different spin on Imogene's problem. Bad enough to have expensive
merchandise stolen, but to have it taken by someone she'd hired and trusted was worse.

"How can I help?" I asked.

"I want you to catch the culprit and get my toys
back." She paused as if more deeply pained than
before. "I know who's taking them. I think I know.
I'm pretty sure."

"Have you confronted her?"

"Oh, no. I couldn't possibly do that. She's the
nicest girl. Just the nicest girl ever."

"Then go to the sheriff. He would—"

"No, no, no." Imogene shook her head frantically.

"Why not?"

"You see, I suspect it's Holly who's taking the
toys," she said, as if that explained everything.

I just looked at her, waiting. When she didn't go
on, I said, "And?"

"Holly is Sheriff Grumman's niece."